George Gissing

Thyrza - a Tale

Vol. 1

George Gissing

Thyrza - a Tale
Vol. 1

ISBN/EAN: 9783337089023

Printed in Europe, USA, Canada, Australia, Japan

Cover: Foto ©Andreas Hilbeck / pixelio.de

More available books at **www.hansebooks.com**

THYRZA

A TALE

BY

GEORGE GISSING

AUTHOR OF 'DEMOS'
ETC.

ἄμμες δὲ βροτοὶ οἵδε· βροτοὺς βροτοὶ ἀείδωμες.

IN THREE VOLUMES

VOL. I.

LONDON
SMITH, ELDER, & CO., 15 WATERLOO PLACE
1887

CONTENTS

OF

THE FIRST VOLUME.

THYRZA.

CHAPTER I.

AMONG THE HILLS.

THERE were three at the breakfast-table : Mr. New-thorpe, his daughter Annabel, and their visitor, Anna-bel's cousin, Miss Paula Tyrrell. It was a small, low, soberly-furnished room, the walls covered with carelessly hung etchings and water-colours, and with photographs which were doubtless mementoes of travel ; dwarf book-cases held overflowings from the library, volumes in disorder, clearly more for use than ornament. The casements were open to let in the air of a July morn-ing ; between the thickets of the garden the eye caught glimpses of sun-smitten lake and sheer hillside. For the house stood on the shore of Ullswater.

Of the three breakfasting, Miss Tyrrell was cer-tainly the one whose presence would least allow itself to be overlooked. Her appetite was hearty, but it scarcely interfered with the free flow of her airy talk, which was independent of remark or reply from her

companions. Though it was not apparent in her demeanour, this young lady was suffering under a calamity;
her second 'season' had been ruined at its very culmin-
ation by a ludicrous *contretemps* in the shape of an
attack of measles. Just when she flattered herself that
she had never looked so lovely, an instrument of destiny embraced her in the shape of an affectionate child,
and lo! she was a fright. Her constitution had soon
thrown off the evil thing, but Mrs. Tyrrell decreed her
banishment for a time to the remote dwelling of her
literary uncle. Once more Paula was lovely, and yet
one could scarcely say that the worst was over, seeing
that she was constrained to pass summer days within
view of Helvellyn when she might have been in Picca-
dilly.

Mr. Newthorpe seldom interrupted his niece's
monologue, but his eye often rested upon her, seemingly in good-natured speculation, and he bent his head
acquiescingly when she put in a quick 'Don't you think
so?' after a running series of comments on some matter
which smacked exceedingly of the town. He was not
more than five-and-forty, yet had thin grizzled hair,
and a sallow face with lines of trouble deeply scored
upon it; his costume was very careless, indeed all but
slovenly, and his attitude in the chair showed, if not
weakness of body, at all events physical indolence.

Some word that fell from Paula prompted him to
ask:

'I wonder where Egremont is?'

Annabel, who had been sunk in thought, looked up with a smile. She was about to say something, but her cousin replied rapidly:

'Oh, Mr. Egremont's in London—at least he was a month ago.'

'Not much of a guarantee that he is there now,' Mr. Newthorpe rejoined.

'I'll drop him a line and see,' said Paula. 'I meant to do so yesterday, but forgot. I'll write and tell him to send me a full account of himself. Isn't it too bad that people don't write to me! Everybody forgets you when you're out of town in the season. Now you'll see I shan't have a single letter again this morning; it is the cruelest thing!'

'But you had a letter yesterday, Paula,' Annabel remarked.

'A letter? Oh, from mamma; that doesn't count. A letter isn't a letter unless you feel anxious to see what's in it. I know exactly all that mamma will say from beginning to end before I open the envelope. Not a scrap of news, and with her opportunities, too! But I can count on Mr. Egremont for at least four sides— well, three.'

'But surely he is not a source of news?' said her uncle with surprise.

'Why not? He can be very jolly when he likes and I know he'll write a nice letter if I ask him to. You can't think how much he's improved just lately He was down at the Ditchleys' when we were there in

February; he and I had ever such a time one day when the others were out hunting. Mamma won't let me hunt; isn't it too bad of her? He didn't speak a single serious word all the morning, and just think how dry he used to be! Of course he can be dry enough still when he gets with people like Mrs. Adams and Clara Carr, but I hope to break him of the habit entirely.'

She glanced at Annabel, and laughed merrily before raising her cup to her lips. Mr. Newthorpe just cast a rapid eye over his daughter's face; Annabel wore a look of quiet amusement.

'Has he been here since then?' Paula inquired, tapping a second egg. 'We lost sight of him for two or three months, and of course he always makes a mystery of his wanderings.'

'We saw him last in October,' her uncle answered, 'when he had just returned from America.'

'He said he was going to Australia next. By-the-by, what's his address? Something, Russell Street. Don't you know?'

'No idea,' he replied, smiling.

'Never mind. I'll send the letter to Mrs. Ormonde; she always knows where he is, and I believe she's the only one that does.'

When the meal came to an end, Mr. Newthorpe went, as usual, to his study. Miss Tyrrell, also as usual, prepared for three hours of letter-writing. Annabel, after a brief consultation with Mrs. Martin,

the housekeeper, would ordinarily have sat down to
study in the morning room. She laid open a book on
the table, but then lingered between that and the
windows. At length she took a volume of a lighter
kind—in both senses—and, finding her garden hat in
the hall, went forth.

She was something less than twenty, and bore herself with grace which was perchance a little too sober
for her years; her head was wont to droop thoughtfully,
and her step measured itself to the grave music of a
mind which knew the influence of mountain solitude.
But her health was complete; she could row for long
stretches, and on occasion fatigued her father in rambles
over moor and fell. Face and figure were matched in
mature beauty; she had dark hair, braided above the
forehead on each side, and large dark eyes which regarded you with a pure intelligence, disconcerting if
your word uttered less than sincerity.

She was sixteen when her mother died. Less than
three months after that event Mr. Newthorpe left
London for this country house, which neither he nor his
daughter had since quitted. He had views of his own
on the subject of London life as it affects young ladies.
By nature a student, he had wedded a woman who
became something not far removed from a fashionable
beauty; it was a passionate attachment—on both sides
at first—and to the end he loved his wife with the love
which can deny nothing. The consequence was that
the years of his prime were wasted—nay, not so, for

love is never waste; but the intellectual promise of his youth found no fulfilment. Another year and Annabel would have entered the social mill; she had beauty enough to achieve distinction, and the means of the family were ample to enshrine her. But she never 'came out.' No one would at first believe that Mr. Newthorpe's retreat was final, no one save a close friend or two who understood what his life had been, and how he dreaded for his daughter the temptations which had warped her mother's womanhood. 'In any case,' wrote Mrs. Tyrrell, his sister-in-law, when a year and a half had gone by, 'you will of course let me have Annabel shortly. I pray you to remember that she is turned seventeen. You surely won't deprive her of every pleasure and every advantage?' And the recluse made answer: 'If bolts and shackles were needful, I would use them mercilessly rather than allow my girl to enter your Middlesex pandemonium. Happily, the fetters of her reason suffice. She is growing into a woman, and by the blessing of the gods her soul shall be blown through and through with the free air of heaven, whilst yet the elements in her are blending to their final shape.' An impracticable parent, this. Mrs. Tyrrell raised her eyebrows, and shook her head, and talked sadly of 'poor Annabel,' who was buried alive.

She walked down to a familiar spot by the lake, where a rustic bench was set under shadowing leafage; in front two skiffs were moored on the strand. The

sky was billowy with slow-travelling shapes of white-
ness ; a warm wind broke murmuring wavelets along
the pebbly margin. The opposite slopes glassed themselves in the deep dark water—Swarth Fell, Hallin
Fell, Place Fell, one after the other ; above the
southern bend of the lake rose noble summits, softly
touched with mist which the sun was fast dispelling.
The sweetness of summer was in the air ; so quiet was
it that every wing-rustle in the brake, every whisper of
leaf to leaf, made a distinct small voice ; a sheep-dog
barking over at Howtown seemed close at hand. Annabel loved to abandon herself to this mystery of calm ;
it was often a doubt with her whether time spent in
such seeming idleness was not in truth more gainful
than that wherein she bent over her books.

This morning she had certainly no inclination to
read, yet her face was not expressive of the calm reflection which was her habit. She opened the book
upon her lap and glanced down a page or two, but
without interest. At length external things were
wholly lost to her, and she gazed across the water with
continuance of solemn vision. Her face was almost
austere in this mood which had come upon her.

Someone was descending the path which led from
the high road ; it was a step too heavy for Paula's, too
rapid to be Mr. Newthorpe's. Annabel turned her head,
and saw a young man, perhaps of seven-and-twenty,
dressed in a light walking-suit, with a small wallet
hanging from his shoulder and a stick in his hand.

At sight of her he took off his cap and approached her bare-headed.

'I saw from a quarter of a mile away,' he said, 'that someone was sitting here, and came down on the chance that it might be you.'

She rose with a very slight show of surprise, and returned his greeting with calm friendliness.

'We were speaking of you at breakfast. My cousin couldn't tell us for certain whether you were in England, though she knew you were in London a month ago.'

'Miss Tyrrell is with you?' he asked, as if it were very unexpected.

'But didn't you know? She has been ill, and they sent her to us to recruit.'

'Ah! I have been in Jersey for a month; I have heard nothing.'

'You were able to tear yourself from London in mid-season?'

'But when was I a devotee of the Season, Miss Newthorpe?'

'We hear you progress in civilisation.'

'Well, I hope so. I've had a month of steady reading, and feel better for it. I took a big chest of books to Jersey. But I hope Miss Tyrrell is better?'

'Quite herself again. Shall we walk up to the house?'

'I have broken in upon your reading.'

She exhibited the volume; it was Ruskin's 'Sesame and Lilies.'

' Ah ! you got it.   And like it ? '

' On the whole.'

' That is disappointing.'

Annabel was silent, then spoke of another matter as they walked up from the lake.

This Mr. Egremont had not the look of a man who finds his joy in the life of Society.   His clean-shaven face was rather bony, and its lines expressed independence of character; his forehead was broad, his eyes glanced quickly and searchingly, or widened themselves in an absent gazing which revealed the imaginative temperament.   His habitual cast of countenance was meditative, with a tendency to sadness.   In talk he readily became vivacious; his short sentences, delivered with a very clear and conciliating enunciation, seemed to indicate energy.   It was a peculiarity that he very rarely smiled, or perhaps I should say that he had the faculty of smiling only with his eyes; at such moments his look was very winning, very frank in its appeal to sympathy, and compelled one to like him. Yet at another time his aspect could be shrewdly critical; it was so when Annabel fell short of enthusiasm in speaking of the book he had recommended to her when at Ullswater last.   Probably he was not without his share of scepticism.   For all that, it was the visage of an idealist.

Annabel led him into the house and to the study door, at which she knocked ; then she stood aside for him to enter before her.   Mr. Newthorpe was writing ;

he looked up absently, but light gathered in his eyes as he recognised the visitor.

'So here you are! We talked of you this morning. How have you come?'

'On foot from Pooley Bridge.'

They clasped hands, then Egremont looked behind him, but Annabel had closed the door and was gone.

She went up to the room in which Paula sat scribbling letters.

'Ten minutes more!' exclaimed that young lady. 'I'm just finishing a note to mamma—so dutiful!'

'Have you written to Mr. Egremont?'

Paula nodded and laughed.

'He is downstairs.'

Paula started, looking incredulous.

'Really, Bell?'

'He has just walked over from Pooley Bridge.'

'O Bell, do tell me! Have those horrid measles left any trace? I really can't discover any, but of course one hasn't good eyes for one's own little speckles. Well, at all events, everybody hasn't forgotten me. But do look at me, Bell.'

Her cousin regarded her with conscientious gravity.

'I see no trace whatever. Indeed, I should say you are looking better than you ever did.'

'Now that's awfully kind of you! And you don't pay compliments, either. Shall I go down? Did you tell him where I was?'

Had Annabel been disposed to dainty feminine

malice, here was an opportunity indeed. But she looked at Paula with simple curiosity, seeming for a moment to lose herself. The other had to repeat her question.

'I mentioned that you were in the house,' she replied. 'He is talking with father.'

Paula moved to the door, but suddenly paused and turned.

'Now I wonder what thought you have in your serious head?' she said, merrily. 'It's only my fun, you know.'

Annabel nodded, smiling.

'But it is only my fun! Say you believe me. I shall be cross with you if you put on that look.'

'Of course, I know you are full of fun.'

'Of folly, you would like to say, wouldn't you now? But it's my nature, Bell; I couldn't be wise like you, if I tried ever so. Now let's go down arm-in-arm, and help me to be very proper. I mustn't scandalise uncle.'

They went into the morning room. Annabel stood at the window; her companion flitted about, catching glimpses of herself in reflecting surfaces. In five minutes the study door opened, and men's voices drew near.

Egremont met Miss Tyrrell with the manner of an old acquaintance, but unsmiling.

'I am fortunate enough to see you well again without having known of your illness,' he said.

'You didn't know that I was ill?'

Paula looked at him dubiously. He explained, and in doing so quite dispelled the girl's illusion that he was come on her account. When she remained silent, he said:

'You must pity the poor people in London.'

'Certainly I do. I'm learning to keep my temper and to talk wisely. I know nobody in London who could teach me to do either the one or the other.'

'Well, I suppose you'll go out till luncheon-time,' said Mr. Newthorpe. 'Egremont wants to have a pull. You'll excuse an old man.'

They left the house, and for an hour drank the breath of the hillsides. Paula was at first almost taciturn, very unlike herself; she dabbled her fingers over the boat-side, and any light remark that she made was addressed to her cousin. Annabel exerted herself to converse, chiefly telling of the excursions that had been made with Paula during the past week.

'What have you been doing in Jersey?' Paula asked of Egremont presently. Her tone was indifferent, a little condescending.

'Reading.'

'Novels?'

'No.'

'And where are you going next?'

'I shall live in London. My travels are over, I think.'

'We have heard that too often,' said Annabel.

'Did you ever calculate how many miles you have travelled since you left Oxford?'

'I have been a restless fellow,' he admitted, regarding her with quiet scrutiny, 'but I dare say some profit has come of my wanderings. However, it's time to set to work.'

'Work!' asked Paula in surprise. 'What sort of work?'

'Local preacher's.'

Paula moved her lips discontentedly.

'That is your way of telling me to mind my own business. Don't you find the sun dreadfully hot, Annabel? Do please row into a shady place, Mr. Egremont.'

His way of handling the oars showed that he was no stranger to exercise of this kind; his frame, though a trifle meagre, was well set. By degrees, a preoccupation which had been manifest in him gave way under the influence of the sky, and when it was time to approach the landing-place he had fallen into a mood of cheerful talk, light with Paula, with Annabel more earnest. His eyes often passed from one to the other of the faces opposite him, with unmarked observation : frequently he fixed his gaze on the remoter hills in brief musing.

Mr. Newthorpe had come down to the water to meet them; he had a newspaper in his hand.

'Your friend Dalmaine is eloquent on education,' he said, with a humorous twitching of the eyebrows.

'Yes, he knows his House,' Egremont replied. 'You observe the construction of his speech. After well-sounding periods on the elevation of the working-classes, he casually throws out the hints that employers of labour will do wisely to increase the intelligence of their hands, in view of foreign competition. Of course that is the root of the matter, but Dalmaine knows better than to begin with crude truths.'

In the meanwhile the boat was drawn up and the chain locked. The girls walked on in advance; Egremont continued to speak of Mr. Dalmaine, a rising politician, whose acquaintance he had made on the voyage home from New York.

'One of the few sincere things I ever heard from his lips was a remark he made on trade-unions. "Let them combine by all means," he said; "it's a fair fight." There you have the man; it seems to him mere common sense to regard his factory hands as his enemies. A fair fight! What a politico-economical idea of fairness!'

He spoke with extreme scorn, his eyes flashing and his nostrils trembling. Mr. Newthorpe kept a quiet smile, sympathetic yet critical.

Annabel sought her father for a word apart before lunch.

'How long will Mr. Egremont stay?' she asked, apparently speaking in her quality of house-mistress.

'A day or two,' was the reply. 'We'll drive over

to Pooley Bridge for his bag this afternoon; he left it at the hotel.'

'What has he on his mind?' she continued, smiling.

'Some idealistic project. He has only given me a hint. I dare say we shall hear all about it to-night.'

CHAPTER II.

THE IDEALIST.

WHEN Egremont began his acquaintance with the Newthorpes he was an Oxford undergraduate. A close friendship had sprung up between him and a young man named Ormonde, and at the latter's home he met Mr. Newthorpe, who, from the first, regarded him with interest. A year after Mrs. Newthorpe's death, Egremont was invited to visit the house at Ullswater ; since then he had twice spent a week there. This personal intercourse was slight to have resulted in so much intimacy, but he had kept up a frequent correspondence with Mr. Newthorpe from various parts of the world, and common friends aided the stability of the relation.

He was the only son of a man who had made a fortune by the manufacture of oil-cloth. His father began life as a house-painter, then became an oil merchant in a small way, and at length married a tradesman's daughter, who brought him a moderate capital just when he needed it for an enterprise promising greatly. In a short time he had established the firm of Egremont & Pollard, with extensive works in Lambeth. His wife died before him ; his son received a liberal education, and in early manhood found himself, as far as he knew, without a living relative, but with ample means of independence. Young Walter Egremont retained an interest in the business, but had no intention of devoting himself to a commercial life. At the University he had made alliances with men of standing, in the academical sense, and likewise with some whose place in the world relieved them from the necessity of establishing a claim to intellect. In 'this way society was opened to him, and his personal qualities won for him a great measure of regard from those whom he most desired to please.

Somebody had called him 'the Idealist,' and the name adhered to him. At two-and-twenty he published a volume of poems, obviously derived from study of Shelley, but marked with a certain freshness of impersonal aspiration which was pleasant enough: they had the note of sincerity rather than the true poetical promise. The book had no successor; having found this utterance for his fervour, Egremont began a series of ramblings over sea, in search, he said, of himself. The object seemed to evade him; he returned to England from time to time, always in appearance more restless, but always overflowing with ideas, for which he had the readiest store of enthusiastic words. He was able to talk of himself without conveying the least impression of egotism to those who were in sympathy with his intellectual point of view: he was accused of conceit only by a few who were jealous of him or were too

conventional to appreciate his character. With women
he was a favourite, and their society was his greatest
pleasure; yet, in spite of his fervid temperament—in
appearance fervid, at all events—he never seemed to fall
in love. There were who said that the self he went so
far to discover would prove to have a female form.
Perhaps there was truth in this; perhaps he sought,
whether consciously or no, the ideal woman. None of
those with whom he companioned had a charge of light
wooing to bring against him, though one or two would
not have held it a misfortune if they had tempted him to
forget his speculations and declare that he had reached his
goal. But his striving always seemed to be for something remote from the world about him. His capacity
for warm feeling, itself undeniable, was never dissociated
from that impersonal zeal which was the characteristic
of his expressions in verse. In fact, he had written no
love-poem.

Annabel and her father observed a change in him
since his last visit. This was the first time that he
had come without an express invitation, and they
gathered from his speech that he had at length found
some definite object for his energies. His friends had
for a long time been asking what he meant to do with
his life. It did not appear that he purposed literary
effort, though it seemed the natural outlet for his eager
thought, and of the career of politics he at all times
spoke with contempt. Was he one of the men, never
so common as nowadays, who spend their existence in

canvassing the possibilities that lie before them and delay action till they find that the will is paralysed ? One did not readily set Egremont in that class, principally, no doubt, because he was so free from the offensive forms of self-consciousness which are wont to stamp such men. The pity of it, too, if talents like his were suffered to rust unused; the very genuineness of his idealism made one believe in him and look with confidence to his future. Mr. Newthorpe sometimes said that he wished some catastrophe would leave the young man penniless, and so supply the immediate motive for exertion ; yet he could not bring himself to accept the view of the case which his experience pressed upon him : he had special reasons for desiring that common sense should for once fail in its prophecies.

Having dined, all went forth to enjoy the evening upon the lawn. The men smoked; Annabel had her little table with tea and coffee ; Paula had brought out a magazine, and affected to read. Annabel noticed, however, that a page was very seldom turned.

' Have you seen Mrs. Ormonde lately ? ' Mr. Newthorpe asked of Egremont.

' I spent a day at Eastbourne before going to Jersey.'

' She has promised to come to us in the autumn,' said Annabel. ' But she seems to have such a difficulty in leaving her Home. Had she many children about her when you were there ? '

' Ten or twelve.'

' Do they all come from London ? ' asked Annabel.

'Yes. She has relations with sundry hospitals and the like. By-the-by, she told me one remarkable story. A short time ago, out of eight children that were in the house, only one could read, a little girl of ten, and this one regularly received letters from home. Now there came for her what seemed to be a small story-paper, or something of the kind, in a wrapper. Mrs. Ormonde gave it her without asking any questions, and in the course of the morning, happening to see her reading it, she went to look what the paper was. It proved to be a weekly advocate of Atheism, and on the front page stood a vile woodcut offered as a burlesque illustration of some Biblical incident! She was amazed, and not a little angry. "Father always brings it home and gives it me to read," said the child. "It makes me laugh!"'

'Probably she knew nothing of the real meaning of it all,' said Mr. Newthorpe.

'On the contrary, she understood the tendency of the paper surprisingly well; her father had explained everything to the family. Well, you know that Mrs. Ormonde is no dogmatist; she had reason in her anger. There was the only child out of eight who could read, having her advantage abused by a father who had no sense of beauty or fitness.'

'One of the interesting results of popular education,' remarked Mr. Newthorpe philosophically. 'It is inevitable.'

'What did Mrs. Ormonde do?' Annabel asked.

' It was a difficult point. No good would have been done by endeavouring to set the child against her father; she would be home again in a fortnight. So Mrs. Ormonde simply asked if she might have the paper when it was done with, and, having got possession, threw it into the fire with vast satisfaction. Happily it didn't come again.'

' What a gross being that father must be !' Annabel exclaimed.

' Gross enough,' Egremont replied, ' yet I shouldn't wonder if he had brains above the average in his class. A mere brute wouldn't do a thing of that kind ; ten to one he honestly believed that he was benefiting the girl, educating her out of superstition. By sending the paper to the Home, he probably wished to show that he had the courage of his opinions ; he may have hoped that Mrs. Ormonde would give him an opportunity of proving his enlightenment in an argumentative letter. A woman less wise would have amply gratified him.'

' A century of it to come, Egremont !' repeated Mr. Newthorpe, watching the smoke from his cigar. ' Progress is a costly article.'

' But why should the poor people be left to such ugly-minded teachers, father ? ' Annabel exclaimed. ' Surely those influences may be opposed !'

' I doubt whether they can be,' said her father. ' The one insuperable difficulty lies in the fact that we have no power greater than commercial enterprise. Nowadays nothing will succeed save on the com-

mercial basis; from church to public-house the principle applies. There is no way of spreading popular
literature save on terms of supply and demand. Take
the Education Act; it was devised and carried simply
for the reason indicated by Egremont's friend Dalmaine; a more intelligent type of workmen is demanded that our manufacturers may keep pace with
those of other countries. Not a jot more teaching will
be given than is held just commercially profitable.
Well, there is a demand for comic illustrations of the
Bible, and the demand is met; the paper exists because
it pays. An organ of culture for the people who enjoy
burlesquing the Bible couldn't possibly be made to pay.'

'But is there no one who would undertake such
work without hope of recompense in money? We are
not all mere tradespeople.'

As soon as she had uttered the words, she flushed
painfully. She had spoken without thought of Egremont's parentage, and in the instant of recollection she
exaggerated the offensiveness of her remark. She could
not look at Egremont, but knew well that his eyes were
fixed upon her. In truth he was smiling, quite un-
scathed.

'I have an idea for a beginning of such work, Miss
Newthorpe,' he said, in a voice rather lower than
hitherto. 'I came here because I wanted to talk it over.'

Annabel met his look for a moment, expressing all
the friendly interest which she felt. Mr. Newthorpe,
who had been pacing on the grass, came to a seat. He

placed himself next to Paula. She glanced at him, and he said kindly :

‘ You are quite sure you don’t feel cold ? ’

‘ I dare say I’d better go in,’ she replied, checking a little sigh as she closed her magazine.

‘ No, no, don’t go, Paula ! ’ urged her cousin, rising. ‘ You shall have a shawl, dear ; I’ll get it.’

‘ It is very warm,’ put in Egremont. ‘ There surely can’t be any danger in sitting till it grows dark.’

This little fuss about her soothed Paula for a while.

‘ O, I don’t want to go,’ she said. ‘ I feel I’m getting very serious and wise, listening to such talk. Now we shall hear, I suppose, what you mean by your “ local preacher ” ? ’

Annabel brought a shawl and placed it carefully about the girl’s shoulders. Then she said to her father :

‘ Let me sit next to Paula, please.’

The change of seats was effected. Annabel secretly took one of her cousin’s hands and held it. Paula seemed to regard a distant object in the garden.

There was silence for a few moments. The evening was profoundly calm. A spirit of solemn loveliness brooded upon the hills, glorious with sunset. The gnats hummed, rising and falling in myriad crowds about the motionless leaves. A spring which fell from a rock at the foot of the garden babbled poetry of the twilight.

‘ I hope it is something very practicable,’ Annabel resumed, looking with expectancy at Egremont.

'I will have your opinion on that. I believe it to be practical enough; at all events, it is a scheme of very modest dimensions. That story of the child and her paper fixed certain thoughts that had been floating about in my mind. You know that I have long enough tried to find work, but I have been misled by the common tendency of the time. Those who want to be of social usefulness for the most part attack the lowest stratum. It seems like going to the heart of the problem, of course, and any one who has means finds there the hope of readiest result—material result. But I think that the really practical task is the most neglected, just because it does not appear so pressing. With the mud at the bottom of society we can practically do nothing; only the vastest changes to be wrought by time will cleanse that foulness, by destroying the monstrous wrong which produces it. What I should like to attempt would be the spiritual education of the upper artisan and mechanic class. At present they are all but wholly in the hands of men who can do them nothing but harm—journalists, socialists, vulgar propagators of what is called free-thought. These all work against culture, yet here is the field really waiting for the right tillage. I often have in mind one or two of the men at our factory in Lambeth. They are well-conducted and intelligent fellows, but, save for a vague curiosity, I should say they live without conscious aim beyond that of keeping their families in comfort. They have no religion, a matter of course; they talk incessantly of politics, knowing nothing better. But they are very far above the gross multitude. I believe such men as these have a great part to play in social development, that in fact *they* may become the great social reformers, working on those above them—the froth of society— no less than on those below.'

He had laid down his half-finished cigar, and, having begun in a scrupulously moderate tone, insensibly warmed to the idealist fervour. His face became more mobile, his eyes gave forth all their light, his voice was musically modulated as he proceeded in his demonstration. He addressed himself to Annabel, perhaps unconscious of doing so exclusively.

Mr. Newthorpe muttered something of assent. Paula was listening intently, but as one who hears of strange, far-off things, very difficult of realisation.

'Now suppose one took a handful of such typical men,' Egremont went on, 'and tried to inspire them with a moral ideal. At present they have nothing of the kind, but they own the instincts of decency, and that is much. I would make use of the tendency to association, which is so strong among them. They have numberless benefit clubs; they stand together resolutely to help each other in time of need and to exact terms from their employers—the fair fight, as the worthy Member for Vauxhall calls it. Well, why shouldn't they band for moral and intellectual purposes? I would have a sort of freemasonry, which had nothing to do with eating and drinking or with the dispensing of charity; it should be wholly concerned with spiritual advancement. These men cannot become rich, and so are free from one kind of danger; they are not likely to fall into privation; they have a certain amount of leisure. If one could only stir a few of them to enthusiasm for an ideal of life! Suppose one could teach them to feel the purpose of such a book as " Sesame and Lilies," which you only moderately care for, Miss Newthorpe——'

'Not so!' Annabel broke in, involuntarily. 'I think it very beautiful and very noble.'

'What book is that?' asked Paula with curiosity.

'I'll give it to you to read, Paula,' her cousin replied.

Egremont continued:

'The work of people who labour in the abominable quarters of the town would be absurdly insignificant in comparison with what these men might do. The vulgar influence of half-taught revolutionists, social and religious, might be counteracted; an incalculable change for good might be made on the borders of the social inferno, and would spread. But it can only be done by personal influence. The man must have an ideal himself before he can create it in others. I don't know that I am strong enough for such an undertaking, but I feel the desire to try, and I mean to try! What do you think of it?'

'*Macte virtute!*' murmured Mr. Newthorpe. 'I believe you will do something, at all events.'

'Thinking it so clearly must be half doing it,' said Annabel.

Egremont replied to her with a clear regard.

'But the details,' Mr. Newthorpe remarked. 'Are you going to make Lambeth your field?'

'Yes, Lambeth. I have a natural connection with the place, and my name may be of some service to me there; I don't think it is of evil odour with the workmen. My project is to begin with lectures. Reserve your judgment; I have no intention of standing forth as an apostle; all I mean to do at first is to offer a free course of lectures on a period of English literature. I shall not throw open my doors to all and sundry, but specially invite a certain small number of men, whom I shall be at some pains to choose. We have at the works a foreman named Bower; I have known him, in a way, for years, and I believe he is an intelligent man. Him I shall make use of, telling him nothing of my wider aims, but simply getting him to discover for me the dozen or so of men who would be likely to care for my lectures. By-the-by, the man of whom I was speaking, the father of Mrs. Ormonde's patient, lives in Lambeth; I shall certainly make an effort to draw him into the net?'

'I shall be curious to hear more of him,' said Mr. Newthorpe. 'And you use English literature to tune the minds of your hearers?'

'That is my thought. I have spent my month in Jersey in preparing a couple of introductory lectures.

It seems to me that if I can get them to understand
what is meant by love of literature pure and simple,
without a thought of political or social purpose—especially without a thought of cash profit, which is so
disastrously blended with what little knowledge they
acquire—I shall be on the way to founding my club of
social reformers. I shall be most careful not to alarm
them with hints that I mean more than I say. Here
are certain interesting English books; let us see what
they are about, who wrote them, and why they are
deemed excellent. That is our position. These men
must get on a friendly footing with me. Little by little
I shall talk with them more familiarly, try to understand each one. Success depends upon my personal
influence. I may find that it is inadequate, yet I have
hope. Naturally, I have points of contact with the
working class which are lacking to most educated
men; a little chance, and I should myself have been a
mechanic or something of the kind. This may make
itself felt; I believe it will.'

Night was falling. The last hue of sunset had died
from the swarth hills, and in the east were pale points
of starlight.

'I think you and I must go in, Paula,' said Annabel, when there had been silence for a little.

Paula rose without speaking, but as she was about to
enter the house she turned back and said to Egremont:

'I get tired so soon, being so much in the open air.
I'd better say good-night.'

Her uncle, when he held her hand, stroked it affectionately. He often laughed at the child's manifold follies, but her prettiness and the *naïveté* which sweetened her inbred artificiality had won his liking. Much as it would have astonished Paula had she known it, his feeling was for the most part one of pity.

'I suppose you'll go out again,' Paula said to her cousin as they entered the drawing-room.

'No. I shall read a little and then go to bed.' She added with a laugh, 'They will sit late in the study, no doubt, with their cigars and steaming glasses.'

Paula moved restlessly about the room for a few minutes, then from the door she gave a 'good-night,' and disappeared without further ceremony.

The two men came in very shortly. Egremont entered the drawing-room alone, and began to turn over books on the table. Then Annabel rose.

'It promises for another fine day to-morrow,' she said. 'I must get father away for a ramble. Do you think he looks well?'

'Better than he did last autumn, I think.'

'I must go and say good-night to him. Will you come to the study?'

He followed in silence, and Annabel took her leave of both.

The morning broke clear; it was decided to spend the greater part of the day on the hills. Paula rode, the others drove to a point whence their ramble was to begin. Annabel enjoyed walking: very soon her being seemed to set itself to more spirited music, the veil of reflection fell from her face, and she began to talk lightheartedly.

Paula behaved with singularity. At breakfast she had been very silent, a most unusual thing, and during the day she kept an air of reserve, a sort of dignity which was amusing. Mr. Newthorpe walked beside her pony, and adapted himself to her favourite conversation, which was always of the town and Society.

Once Annabel came up with a spray of mountain saxifrage.

'Isn't it lovely, Paula?' she said. 'Do look at the petals.'

'Very nice,' was the reply, 'but it's too small to be of any use.'

There was no more talk of Egremont's projects. Books and friends and the delights of the upland scenery gave matter enough for conversation. Not long after noon the sky began to cloud, and almost as soon as the party reached home again there was beginning of rain. They spent the evening in the drawing-room. Paula was persuaded to sing, which she did prettily, though still without her native vivacity. Again she retired early.

After breakfast on the morrow it still rained, though not without promise of clearing.

'You'll excuse me till lunch,' Paula said to Annabel and Egremont, when they rose from the table. 'I have a great deal of correspondence to see to.'

'Correspondence' was a new word. Usually she said, 'I have an awful heap of letters to write.' Her dignity of the former day was still preserved.

Having dismissed her household duties, Annabel went to the morning room and sat down to her books. She was reading Virgil. For a quarter of an hour it cost her a repetition of efforts to fix her attention, but her resolve was at length successful. Then Egremont came in.

'Do I disturb you?' he said, noticing her studious attitude.

'You can give me a little help, if you will. I can't make out that line.'

She gave him one copy and herself opened another. It led to their reading some fifty lines together.

'Oh, why have we girls to get our knowledge so late and with such labour!' Annabel exclaimed at length. 'You learn Greek and Latin when you are children; it ought to be the same with us. I am impatient; I want to read straight on.'

'You very soon will,' he replied absently. Then, having glanced at the windows, which were suddenly illumined with a broad slant of sunlight, he asked: 'Will you come out? It will be delightful after the rain.'

Annabel was humming over dactylics. She put her book aside with reluctance.

'I'll go and ask my cousin.'

Egremont averted his face. Annabel went up to

Paula's room, knocked and entered. From a bustling sound within, it appeared likely that Miss Tyrrell's business-like attitude at the table had been suddenly assumed.

'Will you come out, Paula? The rain is over and gone.'

'Not now.'

'Mr. Egremont wishes to go for a walk. Couldn't you come?'

'Please beg Mr. Egremont to excuse me. I am tired after yesterday, dear.'

When her cousin had withdrawn, Paula went to the window. In a few minutes she saw Egremont and Annabel go forth and stroll from the garden towards the lake. Then she reseated herself, and sat biting her pen.

The two walked lingeringly by the water's edge. They spoke of trifles. When they were some distance from the house, Egremont said:

'So you see I have at last found my work. If you thought of me at all, I dare say my life seemed to you a very useless one, and little likely to lead to anything.'

'No, I had not that thought, Mr. Egremont,' she answered simply. 'I felt sure that you were preparing yourself for something worthy.'

'I hope that is the meaning of these years that have gone so quickly. But it was not conscious preparation. It has often seemed to me that in travelling and gaining experience I was doing all that life demanded of me. Few men can be more disposed to idle dreaming than I am. And even now I keep asking myself whether this too is only a moment of idealism, which will go by and leave me with less practical energy than ever. Every such project undertaken and abandoned is a weight upon a man's will; if I fail in perseverance, my fate will be decided.'

'I feel assured that you will not fail. You could not speak as you did last night and yet allow yourself to falter in purpose when the task was once begun. What success may await you we cannot say; the work will certainly be very difficult. Will it not ask a lifetime?'

'No less, if it is to have any lasting result.'

'Be glad then. What happier thing can befall one than to have one's life consecrated to a worthy end?'

He walked on in silence, then regarded her.

'Such words in such a voice would make any man strong. Yet I would ask more from you. There is one thing I need, to feel full confidence in myself, and that is a woman's love. I have known for a long time whose love it was that I must try to win. Can you give me what I ask?'

The smile which touched his lips so seldom was on them now. He showed no agitation, but the light of his eyes was very vivid as they read her expression. Annabel had stayed her steps; for a moment she looked troubled. His words were not unanticipated, but the answer with which she was prepared was more difficult to utter than she had thought it would be. It was the first time that a man had spoken to her thus, and though in theory such a situation had always seemed to her very simple, she could not now preserve her calm as she wished. She felt the warmth of her blood, and could not at once command her wonted voice. But when at length she succeeded in meeting his look steadily, her thought grew clear again.

'I cannot give you that, Mr. Egremont.'

As his eyes fell, she hastened to add:

'I think of you often. I feel glad to know you, and to share in your interest. But this is no more than the friendship which many people have for you —quite different from the feeling which you say would aid you. I have never known that.'

He was gazing across the lake. The melancholy always lurking in the thoughtfulness of his face had become predominant. Yet he turned to her with the smile once more.

'Those last words must be my hope. To have your friendship is much. Perhaps some day I may win more.'

'I think,' she said, with a sincerity which proved how far she was from emotion, 'that you will meet another woman whose sympathy will be far more to you than mine.'

'Then I must have slight knowledge of myself. I have known you for seven years, and though you were a child when we first spoke to each other, I foresaw then what I tell you now. Every woman that I meet I compare with you; and if I imagine the ideal woman, she has your face and your mind. I should have spoken when I was here last autumn, but I felt that I had no right to ask you to share my life as long as it remained so valueless. You see '—he smiled—' how I have grown in my own esteem. I suppose that is always the first effect of a purpose strongly conceived. Or should it be just the opposite, and have I only given you a proof that I snatch at rewards before doing the least thing to merit them ? '

Something in these last sentences jarred upon her, and gave her courage to speak a thought which had often come to her in connection with Egremont.

' I think that a woman does not reason in that way if her deepest feelings are pledged. If I were able to go with you and share your life, I shouldn't think I was rewarding you, but that you were offering me a great happiness. It is my loss that I can only watch you from a distance.'

The words moved him. It was not with conscious insincerity that he spoke of his love and his intellectual aims as interdependent, yet he knew that Annabel revealed the truer mind.

' And my desire is for the happiness of your love ! ' he exclaimed. ' Forget that pedantry—always my fault. I cannot feel sure that my other motives will keep their force, but I know that this desire will be only stronger in me as time goes on.'

Yet when she kept silence, the habit of his thought again uttered itself.

' I shall pursue this work that I have undertaken, because, loving you, I dare not fall below the highest life of which I am capable. I know that you can see into my nature with those clear eyes of yours. I could not love you if I did not feel that you were far above me. I shall never be worthy of you, but I shall never cease in my striving to become so.'

The quickening of her blood, which at first troubled her, had long since subsided. She could now listen to him, and think of her reply almost with coldness. There was an unreality in the situation, which made her anxious to bring the dialogue to an end.

' I have all faith in you,' she said. ' I hope, I feel assured, that something will come of your work. But it will only be so if you pursue it for its own sake.'

The simple truth of this caused him to droop his eyes again with a sense of shame. He grew impatient with himself. Had he no plain, touching words in which to express his very real love—words such as every man can summon when he pleads for this greatest boon ? Yet his shame heightened the reverence in which he held her; passion of the intellect breathed in his next words.

' If you cannot love me with your heart, in your mind you can be one with me. You feel the great and the beautiful things of life. There is no littleness in your nature. In reading with you just now I saw that

your delight in poetry was as spirit-deep as my own ;
your voice had the true music, and your cheeks warmed
with sympathy. You do not deny me the right to
claim so much kinship with you. I, too, love all that
is rare and noble, however in myself I fall below such
ideals. Say that you admit me as something more
than the friend of the everyday world ! Look for once
straight into my eyes and know me !'

There was no doubtful ring in this; Annabel felt
the chords of her being smitten to music. She held
her hand to him.

' You are my very near friend, and my life is richer
for your influence.'

' I may come and see you again before very long,
when I have something to tell you ? '

' You know that our house always welcomes you.'

He released her hand, and they walked homewards.
The sky was again overcast. A fresh gust came from
the fell-side and bore with it drops of rain.

' We must hasten,' Annabel said, in a changed voice.
' Look at that magnificent cloud by the sun !'

' Isn't the rain sweet here!' she continued, anxious
to re-establish the quiet, natural tone between them.
' I like the perfume and the taste of it. I remember
how mournful the rain used to be in London streets.'

They regained the house. Annabel passed quickly
upstairs. Egremont remained standing in the porch,
looking forth upon the garden. His reverie was broken
by a voice.

'How gloomy the rain is here! One doesn't mind
it in London; there's always something to do, and
somewhere to go.'

It was Paula; Egremont could not help showing
amusement.

'Do you stay much longer?' he asked.

'I don't know.'

She spoke with indifference, keeping her eyes
averted.

'I must catch the mail at Penrith this evening,' he
said. 'I'm afraid it will be a wet drive.'

'You're going, are you? Not to Jersey again, I
hope?'

'Why not?'

'It seems to make people very dull. I shall warn
all my friends against it.'

She hummed an air and left him.

Late in the afternoon Egremont took leave of his
friends. Mr. Newthorpe went out into the rain, and
at the last moment shook hands with him heartily.
Annabel stood at the window and smiled farewell.

The wheels splashed along the road; rain fell in
torrents. Egremont presently looked back from the
carriage window. The house was already out of view,
and the summits of the circling hills were wreathed
with cloud.

CHAPTER III.

A CORNER OF LAMBETH.

A WORKING man, one Gilbert Grail, was spending an hour of his Saturday afternoon in Westminster Abbey. At five o'clock the sky still pulsed with heat; black shadows were sharp-edged upon the yellow pavement; between the bridges of Westminster and Lambeth the river was a colourless gleam. But in the sanctuary evening had fallen; above the cool twilight of the aisles floated a golden mist, and the echo of a footfall hushed itself among the tombs.

He was a man past youth but of less than middle age, with meagre limbs and shoulders a little bent. His clothing was rough but decent; his small and white hands gave evidence of occupation which was not rudely laborious. He had a large head, thickly covered with dark hair, which, with his moustache and beard, heightened the wanness of his complexion. A massive forehead, deep-set eyes, thin, straight nose, large lips constantly drawn inwards, made a physiognomy impressive rather than pleasing; the cast of

thought was upon it, of thought eager and self-tor-
menting, the mark of a spirit ever straining after
something unattainable. At moments when he found
satisfaction in reading the legend on some monument,
his eyes grew placid and his beetling brows smoothed
themselves; but the haunter within would not be
forgotten, and, as if at a sudden recollection, he dropped
his eyes in a troubled way, and moved onwards brooding. In those brief intervals of peace his countenance
expressed an absorbing reverence, a profound humility.
The same was evident in his bearing; he walked as
softly as possible and avoided treading upon a sculp-
tured name.

When he passed out into the sunny street, he stood
for an instant with a hand veiling his eyes, as if the
sudden light were too strong. Then he looked hither
and thither with absent gaze, and at length bent his
steps in the direction of Westminster Bridge. On the
south side of the river he descended the stairs on to the
Albert Embankment and walked along by St. Thomas's
Hospital.

Presently he overtook a man who was reading as
he walked, a second book being held under his arm; it
was a young workman of three- or four-and-twenty,
tall, of wiry frame, square-shouldered, upright. Grail
grasped his shoulder in a friendly way, asking:

' What now ? '

' Well, it's tempted eighteenpence out of my
pocket,' was the other's reply, as he gave the volume

to be examined. 'I've wanted a book on electricity for some time.'

He spoke with a slight north-of-England accent. His name was Luke Ackroyd; he had come to London as a lad, and was now a work-fellow of Grail's. There was rough comeliness in his face and plenty of intelligence, something at the same time not quite satisfactory if one looked for strength of character; he smiled readily and had eyes which told of quick but unsteady thought, a mouth, too, which expressed a good deal of self-will and probably a strain of sensuality. His manner was hearty, his look frank to a fault and full of sensibility.

'I found it at the shop by Westminster Bridge,' he continued. 'You ought to go and have a look there to-night. I saw one or two things pretty cheap that I thought were in your way.'

'What's the other?' Grail inquired, returning the work on electricity, which he had glanced through without show of much interest.

'O, this belongs to Jo Bunce,' Ackroyd replied laughing. 'He's just lent it me.'

It was a collection of discourses by gentlemen of the antitheistic persuasion; the titles, which were startling to the eye, sufficiently indicated the scope and quality of the matter. Grail found even less satisfaction in this than in the other volume.

'A man must have a good deal of time to spare,' he said, with a smile, 'if he spends it on stuff of that kind.'

'O, I don't know about that. You don't need it, but there's plenty of people that do.'

'And that's the kind of thing Bunce gives his children to read, eh?'

'Yes; he's bringing them up on it. He's made them learn a secularist's creed, and hears them say it every night.'

'Well, I'm old-fashioned in such matters,' said Grail, not caring to pursue the discussion. 'I'd a good deal rather hear children say the ordinary prayer.'

Ackroyd laughed.

'Have you heard any talk,' he asked presently, 'about lectures by a Mr. Egremont? He's a son of Bower's old governor.'

'No, what lectures?'

'Bower tells me he's a young fellow just come from Oxford or Cambridge, and he's going to give some free lectures here in Lambeth.'

'Political?'

'No. Something to do with literature.'

Ackroyd broke into another laugh, louder this time, and contemptuous.

'Sops to the dog that's beginning to show his teeth,' he exclaimed. 'It shows you what's coming. The capitalists are beginning to look about and ask what they can do to keep the people quiet. Lectures on literature! Fools! As if that wasn't just the way to remind us of what we've missed in the way of education. It's the best joke you could hit on. Let him lecture away, by all means. He'll do more than he thinks.'

'Where does he give them?' Grail inquired.

'He hasn't begun yet. Bower seems to be going round to get men to hear him. Do you think you'd like to go?'

'It depends what sort of a man he is.'

'A conceited young fool, I expect.'

Grail smiled.

In such conversation they passed the Archbishop's Palace, then, from the foot of Lambeth Bridge, turned into a district of small houses and multifarious workshops. Presently they entered Paradise Street.

The name is less descriptive than it might be. Poor dwellings, mean and cheerless, are interspersed with factories and one or two small shops; a public-house is prominent, and a railway-arch breaks the perspective of the thoroughfare midway. The street at that time—six years ago—began by the side of a graveyard, no longer used, and associated in the minds of those who dwelt around it with numberless burials in a dire season of cholera. The space has since been converted into a flower-garden, open to the children of the neighbourhood, and in summer time the bright flower-beds enhance the ignoble baldness of the by-way.

When they had nearly reached the railway-arch, Ackroyd stopped.

'I'm just going in to Bower's shop,' he said. 'I've got a message for poor old Boddy.'

'Boddy?'

'You know of him from the Trent girls, don't you?'

'Yes, yes,' Grail answered, nodding. He seemed about to add something, but checked himself, and with a 'good-bye' went his way.

Ackroyd turned his steps to a little shop close by. It was of the kind known as the small general; over the door stood the name of the proprietor: 'Bower,' and on the woodwork along the top of the windows was painted in characters of faded red: 'The Little Shop with the Large Heart.' Little it certainly was, and large of heart if the term could be made to signify an abundant stock; the interior was so packed with an indescribable variety of merchandise that there was scarcely space for more than two customers between door and counter. From an inner room came the sound of a violin, playing a lively air.

When the young man stepped through the doorway he was at once encompassed with the strangest blend of odours; every article in the shop—groceries of all kinds, pastry, cooked meat, bloaters, newspapers, petty haberdashery, firewood, fruit, soap—seemed to exhale its essence distressfully under the heat; impossible that anything sold here should preserve its native savour. The air swarmed with flies, spite of the dread example of thousands that lay extinct on sheets of smeared newspaper.

On the counter, among other things, was a perspiring yellow mass, retailed under the name of butter; its destiny hovered between avoirdupois and the measure of capacity. A literature of advertisements hung around; gingerbeer, blacking, blue, &c., with a certain 'Samaritan salve' proclaimed themselves in many-coloured letters. One descried, too, a scrubby but significant little card, which bore the address of a loan office.

The music issued from the parlour behind the shop; it ceased as Ackroyd approached the counter, and at the sound of his footsteps appeared Mrs. Bower. She was a stout woman of middle age, red of face, much given to laughter, wholesomely vulgar. At four o'clock every afternoon she laid aside her sober garments of the working day and came forth in an evening costume which was the admiration and the envy of Paradise Street. Popular from a certain wordy good-humour which she always had at command, she derived from this evening garb a social superiority which friends and neighbours, whether they would or no, were constrained to recognise. She was deemed a well-to-do woman, and as such—Paradise Street held it axiomatic—might reasonably adorn herself for the respect of those to whom she sold miscellaneous pennyworths. She did not depend upon the business; her husband, as we already know, was a foreman at Egremont & Pollard's oil-cloth manufactory; they were known to have money laid by. You saw in her face that life had been smooth

with her from the beginning.　She wore a purple dress
with a yellow fichu in which was fixed a large silver
brooch; on her head was a small lace cap.　Her hands
were enormous and very red.　As she came into the
shop, she mopped her forehead with a handkerchief;
perspiration streamed from every pore.

'What a man you are for keepin' yourself cool, Mr.
Hackroyd!' she exclaimed, 'it's like a breath o' fresh air
to look at you, I'm sure.　If this kind o' weather goes
on, there won't be much left o' me.　I'm a-goin' like
the butter.'

'It's warmish, that's true,' said Luke, when she had
finished her laugh.　'I heard Mr. Boddy playing in
there, and I've got a message for him.'

'Come in and sit down.　He's just practisin' a new
piece for his club to-night.'

Ackroyd advanced into the parlour.　The table was
spread for tea, and at the tray sat Mrs. Bower's daughter, Mary.　She was a girl of nineteen, sparely made
and rather plain featured, yet with a thoughtful, interesting face.　Her smile was brief, and always passed
into an expression of melancholy, which in its turn did
not last long; for the most part she seemed occupied
with thoughts which lay on the borderland between
reflection and anxiety.　Her dress was remarkably
plain, contrasting with her mother's, and her hair was
arranged in the simplest way.

In a round-backed chair at a distance from the
table sat an old man, with a wooden leg, a fiddle

on his knee. His face was parchmenty, his cheeks
sunken, his lips compressed into a long straight line;
his small grey eyes had an anxious look, yet were
ever ready to twinkle into a smile. He wore a suit
of black, preserved from sheer decay by a needle too
evidently unskilled; wrapped about a scarcely visible
collar was a broad black neckcloth of the antique
fashion; his one shoe—the wooden member needed
none—was cobbled into shapelessness. Mr. Boddy's
spirit had proved more durable than his garments;
often hard set to earn the few shillings a week
that sufficed to him, he kept up a long-standing re-
putation for joviality, and with the aid of his fiddle
made himself welcome at many a festive gathering in
Lambeth.

'Give Mr. Hackroyd a cup o' tea, Mary,' said Mrs.
Bower. 'How you poor men go about your work days
like this is more than I can understand. I haven't life
enough in me to drive away a fly as settles on my nose.
It's all very well for you to laugh, Mr. Boddy. There's
good in everything, if we only see it, and you may thank
the trouble you've had as it's kep' your flesh down.'

Ackroyd addressed the old man.

'There's a friend of mine in Newport Street would
be glad to have you do a little job for him, Mr. Boddy.
Two or three chairs, I think.'

Mr. Boddy held forth his stumpy wrinkled hand.

'Give us a friendly grip, Mr. Ackroyd! There's
never a friend in this world but the man as finds you

work ; that's the philosophy as has come o' my three-score-and-nine years. What's the name and address ? I'll be round the first thing on Monday morning.'

The information was given.

' You just make a note o' that in your head, Mary my dear,' the old man continued. ' 'Taint very likely I'll forget, but my memory do play me a trick now and then. Ask me about things as happened fifty years ago, and I'll serve you as well as the almanac. It's the same with my eyes. I used to be near-sighted, and now I'll read you the sign-board across the street easier than that big bill on the wall.'

He raised his violin, and struck out with spirit ' The March of the Men of Harlech.'

' That's the toon as always goes with me on my way to work,' he said, with a laugh. ' It keeps up my courage ; this old timber o' mine stumps time on the pavement, and I feel I'm good for something yet. If only the hand 'll keep steady ! Firm enough yet, eh, Mr. Ackroyd ? '

He swept the bow through a few ringing chords.

' Firm enough,' said Luke, ' and a fine tone, too. I suppose the older the fiddle is, the better it gets ? '

' Ah, 'taint like these fingers. Old Jo Racket played this instrument more than sixty year ago ; so far back I can answer for it. You remember Jo, Mrs. Bower, ma'am ? Yes, yes, you can just remember him ; you was a little 'un when he'd use to crawl round from the work'us of a Sunday to the " Green Man." When

he went into the 'Ouse, he give the fiddle to Mat
Trent, Lyddy and Thyrza's father, Mr. Ackroyd. Ah,
talk of a player! You should a' heard what Mat could
do with this 'ere instrument. What do *you* say, Mrs.
Bower, ma'am?'

'He was a good player, was Mr. Trent. But not
better than somebody else we know of, eh, Mr. Hackroyd?'

'Now don't you go pervertin' my judgment with
flattery, ma'am,' said the old man, looking pleased for
all that. 'Matthew Trent was Matthew Trent, an'
Lambeth 'll never know another like him. He was
made o' music! When did you hear any man with a
tenor voice like his? He made songs, too, Mr. Ackroyd,
words, music, an' all. Why Thyrza sings one of 'em
still.'

'But how does she remember it?' Ackroyd asked
with much interest. 'He died when she was a baby.'

'Yes, yes, she don't remember it of her father. It
was me as taught her it to be sure, as I did most o' the
other songs she knows.'

'But she wasn't a baby either,' put in Mrs. Bower.
'She was four years. An' Lydia was four years older.'

'Four years an' two months,' said Mr. Boddy,
nodding with a laugh. 'Let's be ac'rate, Mrs. Bower,
ma'am. Thirteen year ago next fourteenth o' Decem-
ber, Mr. Ackroyd. There's a deal happened since
then. On that day I had my shop in the Cut, and I
had two legs like other mortals. Things wasn't doing

so bad with me. Why, it's like yesterday to remember. My wife she come a-runnin' into the shop
just before dinner-time. "There's a boiler busted
at Walton's," she says, "an' they say as Mr. Trent's
killed." It was Walton's, the pump-maker's, in Ground
Street.'

'It's Simpson & Thomas's now,' remarked Mrs.
Bower. 'Why, where Jim Caudle works, you know,
Mr. Hackroyd.'

Luke nodded, knowing the circumstance. The
whole story was familiar to him, indeed, but Mr. Boddy
talked on in an old man's way, for pleasure in the
past.

'So it is, so it is. Me an' my wife took the little
'uns to the 'Orspital. He knew 'em, did poor Mat, but
he couldn't speak. What a face he had! Thyrza was
frighted and cried; Lyddy just held on hard to my
hand, but she didn't cry. I don't remember to a' seen
Lyddy cry more than two or three times in my life;
she always hid away for that, when she couldn't help
herself, bless her!'

'Lydia grows more an' more like her father,' said
Mrs. Bower.

'She does, ma'am, she does. I used to say as she
was like him, when she sat in my shop of a night
and watched the people in and out. Her eyes was so
bright looking, just like Mat's. Eh, there wasn't much
as the little 'un didn't see. One day—how my wife did
laugh!—she looks at me for a long time, an' then she

says : "How is it, Mr. Boddy," she says, "as you've got
one eyelid lower than the other ? " It's true as I have
a bit of a droop in the right eye, but it's not so much as
anyone 'ud notice it at once. I can hear her say that
as if it was in this room ! An' she stood before me, a
little thing that high. I didn't think she'd be so tall.
She growed wonderful from twelve to sixteen. It's me
has to look up to her now.'

A customer entered the shop, and Mrs. Bower went
out.

'I don't think Thyrza's as much a favourite with
anyone as her sister,' said Ackroyd, looking at Mary
Bower, who had been silent all this time.

'O, I like her very much,' was the reply. 'But
there's something—— I don't think she's as easy to
understand as Lydia. Still, I shouldn't wonder if she
pleases some people more.'

Mary dropped her eyes as she spoke and smiled
gently. Ackroyd tapped with his foot.

'That's Totty Nancarrow,' said Mrs. Bower, re-
appearing from the shop. 'What a girl that is, to be
sure ! She's for all the world like a lad put into petticoats. I should think there's a goin' to be a feast over
in Newport Street. A tin o' sardines, four bottles o'
gingerbeer, two pound o' seed-cake, an' two pots o'
raspberry ! Eh, she's a queer 'un ! I can't think where
she gets her money from either.'

'It's a pity to see Thyrza going about with her so
much,' said Mary, gravely.

'Why, I can't say as I know any real harm of her,' said her mother, ' unless it is as she's a Catholic.'

'Totty Nancarrow a Catholic!' exclaimed Ackroyd. 'Why, I never knew that.'

'Her mother was Irish, you see, an' I don't suppose as her father thought much about religion. I dessay there's some good people Catholics, but I can't say as I take much to them I know.'

Mary's face was expressing lively feeling.

'How can they be really good, mother, when their religion lets them do wrong, if only they'll go and confess it to the priest? I wouldn't trust anybody as was a Catholic! I don't think the religion ought to be allowed.'

Here was evidently a subject which had power to draw Mary from her wonted reticence. Her quiet eyes gleamed all at once with indignation.

Ackroyd laughed with good-natured ridicule.

'Nay,' he said, ' the time's gone by for that kind of thing, Miss Bower. You wouldn't have us begin religious persecution again?'

'I don't want to persecute anybody,' the girl answered; 'but I wouldn't let them be misled by a bad and false religion.'

On any other subject Mary would have expressed her opinion with diffidence; not on this.

I don't want to be rude, Miss Mary,' Luke rejoined, 'but what right have you to say that their religion's any worse or falser than your own?'

'Everybody knows that it is—that cares about religion at all,' Mary replied with coldness and, in the last words, a significant severity.

'It's the faith, Mary my dear,' interposed Mr. Boddy, 'the faith's the great thing. I don't suppose as form matters so much.'

The girl gave the old man a brief offended glance and drew into herself.

'Well,' said Mrs. Bower, 'that's one way o' lookin' at it; but I can't see neither as there's much good in believin' what isn't true.'

'That's to the point, Mrs. Bower,' said Ackroyd with a smile.

There was a footstep in the shop, firm, yet light and quick, then a girl's face showed itself at the parlour door. It was a face which atoned for lack of regular features by the bright intelligence and the warmth of heart that shone in its smile of greeting. A fair broad forehead lay above well-arched brows; the eyes below were large and shrewdly observant, with laughter and love blent in their dark depths. The cheeks were warm with health; the lips and chin were strong, yet marked with refinement; they told of independence, of fervid instincts, perhaps of a temper a little apt to be impatient. It was not an imaginative countenance, yet alive with thought and feeling, all, one felt, ready at the moment's need; the kind of face which becomes the light and joy of home, the bliss of children, the unfailing support of a man's courage. Her hair was

cut short and crisped itself above her neck ; her hat of
black straw and dark dress were those of a work-girl,
poor, yet in their lack of adornment suiting well with
the active helpful impression which her look produced.

'Here's Mary an' Mr. Hackroyd fallin' out again,
Lydia,' said Mrs. Bower.

'What about now?' Lydia asked, coming in and seating herself. Her eyes passed quickly over Ackroyd's
face and rested on that of the old man with much
kindness.

'Oh, the bold talk—about religion.'

'I think it 'ud be better if they left that alone,'
she replied, glancing at Mary.

'You're right, Miss Trent,' said Luke. 'It's about
the most unprofitable thing anyone can argue about.'

'Have you had your tea?' Mrs. Bower asked of
Lydia.

'No; but I mustn't stop to have any, thank you,
Mrs. Bower. Thyrza 'll think I'm never coming home.
I only looked in just to ask Mary to come and have
tea with us to-morrow.'

Ackroyd rose to depart.

'If I see Holmes, I'll tell him you'll look in on
Monday, Mr. Boddy.'

'Thank you, Mr. Ackroyd, thank you; no fear but
I'll be there, sir.'

He nodded a leave-taking and went.

'Some work, grandad?' Lydia asked, moving to
sit by Mr. Boddy.

'Yes, my dear; the thing as keeps the world a-goin'.
How's the little un?'

'Why, I don't think she seems very well. I didn't
want her to go to work this morning, but she couldn't
make up her mind to stay at home. The hot weather
makes her restless.'

'It's dreadful tryin'!' sighed Mrs. Bower.

'But I really mustn't stay, and that's the truth.
She rose from her chair. 'Where do you think I've
been, Mary? Mrs. Isaacs sent round this morning to
ask if I could give her a bit of help. She's going to
Margate on Monday, and there we've been all the afternoon trimming new hats for herself and the girls.
She's given me a shilling, and I'm sure it wasn't worth
half that, all I did. What a queer woman she is! She
doesn't seem able to depend upon herself for anything.
You'll come to-morrow, Mary?'

'I will if—you know what.'

'Now did you ever know such a girl!' Lydia exclaimed, looking round at the others. 'You understand what she means, Mrs. Bower?'

'I dare say I do, my dear.'

'But I can't promise, Mary. I don't like to leave
Thyrza always.'

'I don't see why she shouldn't come too,' said Mary.
Lydia shook her head.

'Well, you come at four o'clock, at all events, and
we'll see all about it. Good-bye, grandad.'

She stooped and kissed his cheek, then hurried

away, throwing back a bright look as she passed into
the shop.

Paradise Street runs at right-angles into Lambeth
Walk. As Lydia approached this point, she saw that
Ackroyd stood there, apparently waiting for her. He
was turning over the leaves of one of his books, but
kept glancing towards her as she drew near. He wished
to speak, and she stopped.

'Do you think,' he said, with diffidence, 'that your
sister would come out to-morrow after tea?'

Lydia kept her eyes down.

'I don't know, Mr. Ackroyd,' she answered. 'I'll
ask her. I don't think she's going anywhere.'

'It won't be like last Sunday?'

'She really didn't feel well. And I can't promise,
you know, Mr. Ackroyd.'

She met his eyes for an instant, then looked along
the street. There was a faint smile on her lips, with
just a suspicion of some trouble.

'But you *will* ask her?'

'Yes, I will.'

She added in a lower voice and with constraint:

'I'm afraid she won't go by herself.'

'Then, come with her. Do! Will you?'

'If she asks me to, I will.'

Lydia moved as if to leave him, but he followed.

'Miss Trent, you'll say a word for me sometimes?'

She raised her eyes again and replied quickly:

'I never say anything against you, Mr. Ackroyd.'

'Thank you. Then I'll be at the end of the Walk at six o'clock, shall I ?'

She nodded, and walked quickly on. Ackroyd turned back into Paradise Street. His cheeks were a trifle flushed, and he kept making nervous movements with his head. So busy were his thoughts that he unconsciously passed the door of the house in which he lived, and had to turn when the roar of a train passing over the archway reminded him where he was.

CHAPTER IV.

THYRZA SINGS.

LYDIA, too, betrayed some disturbance of thought as she pursued her way. Her face was graver than before: once or twice her lips moved as if she were speaking to herself.

After going a short distance along Lambeth Walk, she turned off into a street which began unpromisingly between low-built and poverty-stained houses, but soon bettered in appearance. Its name is Walnut Tree Walk. For the most part it consists of old dwellings, which probably were the houses of people above the working class in days when Lambeth's squalor was confined within narrower limits. The doors are framed with dark wood, and have hanging porches. At the end of the street is a glimpse of trees growing in Kennington Road.

To one of these houses Lydia admitted herself with a latch-key; she ascended to the top floor and entered a room in the front. It was sparely furnished, but with a certain cleanly comfort. A bed stood in one corner; in another, a small washhand-stand; between them, a low chest of drawers with a looking-glass upon it. The rest was arranged for day use; a cupboard kept out of sight household utensils and food. Being immediately under the roof, the room was much heated after long hours of sunshine. From the open window came a heavy scent of mignonette.

Thyrza had laid the table for tea, and was sitting idly. It was not easy to recognise her as Lydia's sister; if you searched her features the sisterhood was there, but the type of countenance was so subtly modified, so refined, as to become beauty of rare suggestiveness. She was of pale complexion, and had golden hair; it was plaited in one braid, which fell to her waist. Like Lydia's, her eyes were large and full of light, but their blue orbs regarded nothing near; imagination dwelt in them and seemed ever busy with things remote from the workroom and the dull street. Every line of the face was delicate, harmonious, sweet; each thought that passed through her mind reflected itself in a change of expression, produced one knew not how, one phase melting into another like shifting lights upon a stream in woodland. It was not a morbid physiognomy, yet it impressed one with a sense of vague trouble. There was none of the spontaneous pleasure in life which gave Lydia's face such wholesome brightness, no impulse of activity, no resolve; all tended to preoccupation, to emotional reverie. She had not yet completed her seventeenth year, and there was still something of childhood in her movements; her form was slight, graceful, and of lower stature than her sister's. She wore a dress of small-patterned print, with a broad collar of cheap lace.

'It was too hot to light a fire,' she said, rising as Lydia entered. 'Mrs. Jarmey says she'll give us water for the tea.'

'I hoped you'd be having yours,' Lydia replied. 'It's nearly six o'clock. I'll take the tea-pot down, dear.'

When they were seated at the table, Lydia drew from her pocket a shilling and held it up laughingly.

'That from Mrs. Isaacs?' her sister asked.

'Yes. Not bad for Saturday afternoon, is it? Now I must take my boots to be done. If it began to rain, I should be in a nice fix; I haven't a sole to walk on.'

'I just looked in at Mrs. Bower's as I passed,' she continued presently. 'Mr. Ackroyd was there. He'd come to tell grandad of some work. That was kind of him, wasn't it?'

Thyrza assented absently.

'Is Mary coming to tea to-morrow?' she asked.

'Yes. At least she said she would if I'd go to chapel with her afterwards. She won't be satisfied till she gets me there every Sunday.'

'How tiresome, Lyddy!'

'But there's somebody wants you to go out as well. You know who.'

'You mean Mr. Ackroyd?'

'Yes. He met me when I came out of Mrs. Bower's, and asked me if I thought you would.'

Thyrza was silent for a little, then she said :

' I can't go with him alone, Lyddy. I don't mind if you go too.'

' But that's just what he doesn't want,' said her sister, with a smile which was not quite natural.

Thyrza averted her eyes, and began to speak of something else. The meal was quickly over, then Lydia took up some sewing. Thyrza went to the window and stood for a while looking at the people that passed, but presently she seated herself, and fell into the brooding which her sister's entrance had interrupted. Lydia also was quieter than usual ; her eyes often wandered from her work to Thyrza. At last she leaned forward and said :

' What are you thinking of, blue-eyes ? '

Thyrza drew a deep sigh.

' I don't know, Lyddy. It's so hot, I don't feel able to do anything.'

' But you're always thinking and thinking. What is it that troubles you ? '

' I feel dull. Everything is always the same, day after day. When'll it change, Lyddy ? '

Lydia drooped her eyes.

' Why don't you like to go out with Mr. Ackroyd ? ' she asked.

' Why do you so much want me to, Lyddy ? '

' Because he thinks a great deal of you, and it would be nice if you got to like him.'

' But I shan't, ever. I know I shan't.'

'Why not, dear?'

'I don't *dislike* him, but he mustn't get to think it's anything else. I'll go out with him if you'll go as well,' she added, fixing her eyes on Lydia's.

The latter bent to pick up a reel of cotton.

'We'll see when to-morrow comes,' she said.

Silence again fell between them, whilst Lydia's fingers worked rapidly. The evening drew on. Thyrza took her chair to the window, leaned upon the sill, and looked up at the reddening sky. The windows of the other houses were all open; here and there, women talked from them with friends across the street. People were going backwards and forwards with bags and baskets, on the business of Saturday evening; in the distance sounded the noise of the market in Lambeth Walk.

Shortly after eight o'clock Lydia said:

'I'll just go round with my boots, and get something for dinner to-morrow.'

'I'll come with you,' Thyrza said. 'I can't bear to sit here any longer.'

They went forth, and were soon in the midst of the market. Lambeth Walk is a long narrow street, and at this hour was so thronged with people, that an occasional vehicle with difficulty obtained slow passage. On the outer edges of the pavement, in front of the busy shops, were rows of booths, stalls and barrows, whereon meat, vegetables, fish, and household requirements of indescribable variety, were exposed for sale;

the vendors vied with one another in uproarious
advertisement of their goods. In force of vociferation
the butchers doubtless excelled; their 'Lovely, lovely,
lovely!' and their reiterated 'Buy, buy, buy!' rang
clangorous above the hoarse roaring of costermongers,
and the din of those who clattered together pots and
pans. Here and there meat was being sold by Dutch
auction, a brisk business; umbrellas, articles of clothing,
quack medicines, were disposed of in the same way,
giving occasion for abundance of coarse humour. The
market-night is the sole out-of-door amusement regularly at hand for London working people, the only one,
in truth, for which they show any real capacity. Everywhere was laughter and interchange of good-fellowship.
Women sauntered the length of the street and back
again for the pleasure of picking out the best and
cheapest bundle of rhubarb or lettuce, the biggest and
hardest cabbage, the most appetising rasher; they
compared notes, and bantered each other on purchases.
The hot air reeked with odours. From stalls where
whelks were sold rose the pungency of vinegar:
decaying vegetables trodden under foot blended their
putridness with the musty smell of second-hand
garments; the grocers' shops were aromatic; above all
was distinguishable the acrid exhalation from the shops
where fried fish and potatoes hissed in boiling grease.
There Lambeth's supper was preparing, to be eaten on
the spot, or taken away wrapped in newspaper. Stewed
eels and baked meat pies were discoverable through the

steam of other windows, but the fried fish and potatoes appealed irresistibly to the palate through the nostrils, and stood first in popularity.

The people were of the very various classes which subdivide the great proletarian order. Children of the gutter and sexless haunters of the street corner elbowed comfortable artisans and their wives; there were bare-headed hoidens from the obscurest courts, and work-girls whose self-respect was proof against all the squalor and vileness hourly surrounding them. Of the women, whatsoever their appearance, the great majority carried babies; wives themselves scarcely past childhood balanced shawl-enveloped bantlings against heavy market baskets. Little girls of nine or ten were going from stall to stall, making purchases with the confidence and acumen of old housekeepers; slight fear that they would fail to get their money's worth. Children, too, had the business of sale upon their hands; ragged urchins went about with blocks of salt, importuning the marketers, and dishevelled girls carried bundles of assorted vegetables, crying, 'A penny all the lot! A penny the 'ole lot!'

The public-houses were full; through the gaping doors you saw a tightly packed crowd of men, women and children, drinking at the bar or waiting to have their jugs filled, tobacco smoke wreathing above their heads. With few exceptions the frequenters of the Walk turned into the publi -house as a natural incident of the evening's business. The women with the babies grew thirsty in the hot, foul air of the street, and invited each other to refreshment of varying strength, chatting the while of their most intimate affairs, the eternal 'says I, says he, says she,' of vulgar converse. They stood indifferently by the side of liquor-sodden creatures whose look was pollution. Companies of girls. neatly dressed and as far from depravity as possible. called for their glasses of small beer, and came forth again with merriment in treble key.

When the sisters had done their business at the bootmaker's and were considering what their purchase should be for Sunday's dinner, Thyrza caught sight of Totty Nancarrow entering a shop. At once she said : ' I won't be late back, Lyddy. I'm just going to walk a little way with Totty.'

Lydia's face showed annoyance.

' Where is she ? ' she asked, looking back.

' In the butcher's just there.'

' Don't go to-night, Thyrza. I'd rather you didn't.'

' I promise I won't be late. Only half an hour.'

She waved her hand and ran off, of a sudden changed to cheerfulness. Totty received her in the shop with a friendly laugh. Mrs. Bower's description of Miss Nancarrow as a lad in petticoats was not inapt, yet she was by no means heavy or awkward ; she had a lithe. shapely figure, and her features much resembled those of a fairly good-looking boy. Her attire showed little care for personal adornment, but it suited her because it suggested bodily activity ; she wore a plain, tight-

fitting grey gown, a small straw hat of the brimless
kind, and a white linen collar about her neck.　Totty
was nineteen ; no girl in Lambeth relished life with so
much determination, yet to all appearance so harmlessly.
Her independence was complete; for five years she had
been parentless and had lived alone.

Thyrza was attracted to her by this air of freedom
and joyousness which distinguished Totty.　It was a
character wholly unlike her own, and her imaginative
thought discerned in it something of an ideal ; her
own timidity and her tendency to languor found a
refreshing antidote in the other's breezy carelessness.
Impurity of mind would have repelled her, and there
was no trace of it in Totty.　Yet Lydia took very ill
this recently-grown companionship, holding her friend
Mary Bower's view of the girl's character.　Her prejudice was enhanced by the jealous care with which, from
the time of her own childhood, she had been accustomed to watch over her sister.　Already there had
been trouble between Thyrza and her on this account.
In spite of the unalterable love which united them,
their points of unlikeness not seldom brought about
debates which Lydia's quick temper sometimes aggra-
vated to a quarrel.

So Lydia finished her marketing and turned homewards with a perturbed mind.　But the other two
walked with gossip and laughter to Totty's lodgings,
which were in Newport Street, an offshoot of Paradise
Street.

'I'm going with Annie West to a friendly lead,' Totty said; 'will you come with us?'

Thyrza hesitated. The entertainment known as a 'friendly lead' is always held at a public-house, and she knew that Lydia would seriously disapprove of her going to such a place. Yet she had almost a physical need of change, of recreation. Whilst she discussed the matter anxiously with herself, they entered the house and went up to Totty's room. The house was very small, and had a close, musty smell, as if no fresh air ever got into it; Totty's chamber was a poor, bare little retreat, with low, cracked, grimy ceiling and one scrap of carpet on the floor just by the diminutive bed. On a table lay the provisions she had that afternoon brought in from Mrs. Bower's. On the mantelpiece was a small card whereon was printed an announcement of the friendly lead; at the head stood the name of a public-house, with that of its proprietor, then followed: 'A meeting will take place at the above on Saturday evening, August 2, for the benefit of Bill Mennie, the well-known barber of George Street, who has been laid up through breaking of his leg, and is quite unable to follow his employment at present. We the undersigned, knowing him to be thoroughly respected and a good supporter of these meetings, they trust you will come forward on this occasion, and give him that support he so richly deserve, this being his first appeal.—Chairman:—Count Bismark. Vice:— Dick Perkins. Assisted by'—here was a long list, mostly of nicknames—'Little Arthur, Flash Bob, Young Brummy, Lardy, Bumper, Old Tacks, Jo at Thomson's, Short-pipe Tommy, Boy Dick, Chaffy Sam Coppock,' and others equally suggestive.

Whilst Thyrza perused this, Totty was singing a merry song.

' I've had ten shillings sent me to-day,' she said.

' Who by ? '

'An old uncle of mine, 'cause it's my birthday to-morrow. He's a rum old fellow. About two years ago he came and asked me if I'd go and live with him and my aunt, and be made a lady of. Honest, he did! He keeps a shop in Tottenham Court Road. He and father 'd quarrelled, and he never came near when father died and I had to look out for myself. Now he'd like to make a lady of me. He'll wait a long time till he gets the chance ! '

' But wouldn't it be nice, Totty ? ' Thyrza asked, doubtfully.

' I'd sooner live in my own way, thank you. Fancy me havin' to sit proper at a table, afraid to eat an' drink ! Not for Totty N.! What's the use o' livin', if you don't enjoy yourself ? '

They were interrupted by a knock at the door, followed by the appearance of Annie West, a less wholesome-looking girl than Totty, but equally vivacious.

'Well, will you come to the Prince Albert, Thyrza ? ' Totty asked.

'I can't stay long,' was the answer, 'but I'll go for a little while.'

The house of entertainment was at no great distance; they passed through the bar and up into a room on the first floor, where a miscellaneous assembly was just gathering. Down the middle was a long table, with benches beside it, and a round-backed chair at each end; other seats were ranged along the walls. At the upper end of the room an arrangement of dirty red hangings, in the form of a canopy surmounted by a lion and unicorn of pasteboard, showed that festive meetings were regularly held here; round about were pictures of hunting incidents, of race-horses, of politicians and pugilists, interspersed with advertisements of beverages. A piano occupied one corner.

The chairman was already in his place; on the table before him was a soup-plate, into which each visitor threw a contribution on arriving. Seated on the benches were a number of men, women and girls, all with pewters or glasses before them, and the air was thickening with smoke of pipes. The beneficiary of the evening, a portly individual with a face of high satisfaction, sat near the chairman, and by him were two girls of decent appearance, his daughters. The president puffed at a churchwarden and exchanged genial banter with those who came up to deposit offerings. Mr. Dick Perkins, the Vice, was encouraging a spirit of conviviality at the other end. A few minutes after Thyrza and her companions had entered, a youth of the seediest appearance struck introductory chords on the piano and started off at high pressure with a selection of popular melodies. The room by degrees grew full. Then the chairman rose and with jocular remarks announced the first song.

Totty had several acquaintances present, male and female; her laughter frequently sounded above the hubbub of voices. Thyrza, who had declined to have anything to drink, shrank into as little space as possible ; she was nervous and self-reproachful, yet the singing and the uproar gave her a certain pleasure. There was nothing in the talk around her and the songs that were sung that made it a shame for her to be present. Plebeian good humour does not often degenerate into brutality at meetings of this kind until a late hour of the evening. The girls who sat with glasses of beer before them and carried on primitive flirtations with their neighbours were honest wage-earners of factory and workshop, well able to make themselves respected. If they lacked refinement, natural or acquired, it was not their fault ; toil was behind them and before, the hours of rest were few, suffering and lack of bread might at any moment come upon them. They had all thrown their hard-earned pence into the soup-plate, gladly and kindly ; now they enjoyed themselves.

The chairman excited enthusiasm by announcement of a song by Mr. Sam Coppock—known to the company as 'Chaffy Sem.' Sam was a young man who clearly had no small opinion of himself; he wore a bright blue necktie, and had a geranium flower in his button-hole; his hair was cut as short as scissors could make it, and as he stood regarding the assembly he twisted the ends of a scarcely visible moustache. When he fixed a round glass in one eye and perked his head with a burlesque of aristocratic bearing, the laughter and applause were deafening.

'He's a warm 'un, is Sem!' was the delighted comment on all hands.

The pianist made discursive prelude, then Mr. Coppock gave forth a ditty of the most sentimental character, telling of the disappearance of a young lady to whom he was devoted. The burden, in which all bore a part, ran thus:

> We trecked 'er little footprints in the snayoo,
> We trecked 'er little footprints in the snayoo,
>   I shall ne'er forget the d'y
>   When Jenny lost her w'y,
> And we trecked 'er little footprints in the snayoo!

It was known that the singer had thoughts of cultivating his talent and of appearing on the music-hall stage; it was not unlikely that he might some day become 'the great Sam.' A second song was called for and granted; a third—but Mr. Coppock intimated that it did not become him to keep other talent in the background. The chairman made a humorous speech, informing the company that their friend would stand forth again later in the evening. Mr. Dick Perkins was at present about to oblige.

The Vice was a frisky little man. He began with

what is known as 'patter,' then gave melodious account of a romantic meeting with a damsel whom he had seen only once to lose sight of for ever. And the refrain was:

> She wore a lov-e-lie bonnet
> With fruit end flowers upon it,
> End she dwelt in the henvirons of 'Ol-lo-w'y !

As yet only men had sung; solicitation had failed with such of the girls as were known to be musically given. Yet an earnest prayer from the chairman succeeded at length in overcoming the diffidence of one. She was a pale unhealthy thing, and wore an ugly-shaped hat with a gruesome green feather; she sang with her eyes down and in a voice which did not lack a certain sweetness. The ballad was of spring-time and the country and love.

> Underneath the May-tree blossoms
> Oft we've wandered, you and I,
> Listening to the mill-stream's whisper,
> Like a stream soft-gliding by.

Alas! she had a drunken mother, and spent a month or two of every year in the hospital, for her day's work overtaxed her strength. She was one of those fated toilers, to struggle on as long as anyone would employ her, then to fall among the forgotten wretched. And she sang of May-bloom and love, of love that had never come near her and that she would never know; sang, with her eyes upon the beer-stained table, in a public-house amid the backways of Lambeth.

Totty Nancarrow was whispering to Thyrza:

'Sing something, old girl! Why shouldn't you?'

Annie West was also at hand, urging the same.

'Let 'em hear some real singing, Thyrza. There's a dear!'

Thyrza was in sore trouble. Music, if it were but a street organ, always stirred her heart and made her eager for the joy of song. She had never known what it was to sing before a number of people; the prospect of applause tempted her. Yet she had scarcely the courage, and the thought of Lydia's grief and anger—for Lydia would surely hear of it—was keenly present.

'It's getting late,' she replied nervously. 'I can't stay; I can't sing to-night.'

Only one or two people in the room knew her by sight, but Totty had led to its being passed from one to another that she was a good singer. The landlord of the house happened to be in the room; he came and spoke to her.

'You don't remember me, Miss Trent, but I knew your father well enough, and I knew you when you was a little 'un. In those days I had the Green Man in the Cut; your father often enough gave us a toon on his fiddle. A rare good fiddler he was, too! Give us a song now, for old times' sake.'

Thyrza found herself preparing, in spite of herself. She trembled violently, and her heart beat with a strange pain. She heard the chairman shout her name; the sound made her face burn.

'Oh, what shall I sing?' she whispered distractedly to Totty, whilst all eyes were turned to regard her.

'Sing "A Penny for your thoughts."'

It was the one song she knew of her father's making, a half-mirthful, half-pathetic little piece in the form of a dialogue between husband and wife, a true expression of the life of working folk, which only a man who was more than half a poet could have shaped.

The seedy youth at the piano was equal to any demand for accompaniment; Totty hummed the air to him, and he had his chords ready without delay.

Thyrza raised her face and began to sing. Yes, it was different enough from anything that had come before; her pure, sweet tones touched the hearers profoundly, not a foot stirred. At the second verse she had grown in confidence, and rose more boldly to the upper notes. At the end she was singing her best, better than she had ever sung at home, better than she thought she could sing. The applause that followed was tumultuous. By this time much beer had been consumed; the audience was in a mood for enjoying good things.

'That's something like, old girl!' cried Totty, clapping her on the back. 'Have a drink out of my glass. It's only ginger beer, it can't hurt you. This is jolly! Ain't it a lark to be alive?'

The pale-faced girl who had sung of May blossoms looked across the table with eyes in which jealousy

strove against admiration.   There were remarks aside
between the men with regard to Thyrza's personal
appearance.

She must sing again.   They were not going to be
left with hungry ears after a song like that.   Thyrza
still suffered from the sense that she was doing wrong,
but the praise was so sweet to her, sweeter, she thought,
than anything she had ever known.   She longed to
repeat her triumph.

Totty named another song; the faint resistance
was overcome and again the room hushed itself, every
hearer spell-bound.   It was a voice well worthy of
cultivation, excellent in compass, with rare sweet
power.   Again the rapturous applause and again the
demand for more.   Another! she should not refuse them.
Only one more and they would be content.   And a
third time she sang, a third time was borne upwards
on clamour.

'Totty, I *must* go,' she whispered.   'What's the
time?'

'It's only just after ten,' was the reply.   'You'll
soon run home.'

'After ten?   O, I must go at once.'

She left her place, and as quickly as possible made
her way through the crowd.   Just at the door she saw
a face that she recognised, but a feeling of faintness
was creeping upon her and she could think of nothing
but the desire to breathe fresh air.   Already she was
on the stairs, but her strength suddenly failed; she felt

herself falling, felt herself strongly seized, then lost consciousness.

She came to herself in a few minutes in the bar-parlour; the landlady was attending to her, and the door had been shut against intruders. Her first recognition was of Luke Ackroyd.

'Don't say anything,' she murmured, looking at him imploringly. 'Don't tell Lyddy.'

'Not I,' replied Ackroyd. 'Just drink a drop and you'll be all right. I'll see you home. You feel better, don't you?'

Yes, she felt better, though her head ached miserably. Soon she was able to walk, and longed to hasten away. The landlady let her out by the private door, and Ackroyd went with her.

'Will you take my arm?' he said, speaking very gently and looking into her face with eloquent eyes. 'I'm rare and glad I happened to be there. I heard you singing from downstairs and I asked, Who in the world's that? I know now what Mr. Boddy means when he talks so about your voice—won't you take my arm, Miss Trent?'

'I feel quite well again, thank you,' she replied. 'I'd no business to be there, Mr. Ackroyd. Lyddy 'll be very angry; she can't help hearing.'

'No, no, she won't be angry. You tell her at once. You were with Totty Nancarrow, I suppose? O, it'll be all right. But of course it isn't the kind of place for you, Miss Trent.'

She kept silence. They were walking through a quiet street where the only light came from the gas-lamps. Ackroyd presently looked again into her face.

'Will you come out to-morrow?' he asked softly.

'Not to-morrow, Mr. Ackroyd.' She added, 'If I did I couldn't come alone. It is better to tell you at once, isn't it? I don't mind with my sister, because then we just go like friends—but I don't want to have people think anything else.'

'Then come with your sister. We *are* friends, aren't we? I can wait for something else.'

'But you mustn't, Mr. Ackroyd. It'll never come. I mean it; I shall never alter my mind. I have a reason.'

'What reason?' he asked, standing still.

She looked away.

'I mean that—that I couldn't never marry you.'

'Don't say that! Thyrza! You might as well take my life as take that hope. You don't know what I felt when I heard you singing. Have you heard any harm against me, Thyrza? I haven't always been as steady a fellow as I ought to be, but that was before I came to know you. It's no good, whatever you say, I can't give up hope. Why, a man 'ud do anything for half a kind word from you—Thyrza,' he lowered his voice, 'there isn't anyone else, is there?'

She was silent.

'You don't mean that? Good God, I don't know what'll become of me if I think of that! The only thing I care to live for is the hope of having you for my wife.'

'But you mustn't hope, Mr. Ackroyd. You'll find someone much better for you than me. But I can't stop. It's so late and my head aches so. Do let me go, please.'

He made an effort over himself. The nearest lamp showed him that she was very pale.

'Only one word, Thyrza. Is there really anyone else?'

'No; but that doesn't alter it.'

She walked quickly on. Ackroyd, with a great sigh of relief, went on by her side. They came out into Lambeth Walk where the market was as noisy as ever, the shops lit up, the stalls flaring with naphtha lamps, the odour of fried fish everywhere predominant. He led her through the crowd and a short distance into her own street. Then she gave him her hand and said: 'Good-night, Mr. Ackroyd. Thank you for bringing me back. You'll be friends with me and Lyddy?'

'You'll come out with her to-morrow?'

'I can't promise. Good-night?

CHAPTER V.

A LAND OF TWILIGHT.

It happened that Mrs. Jarmey, the landlady of the house in which the sisters lived, had business in the neighbourhood of the Prince Albert, and chanced to exchange a word with an acquaintance who had just come away after hearing Thyrza sing. Returning home, she found Lydia at the door, anxiously and impatiently waiting for Thyrza's appearance. The news, of course, was at once communicated, with moral reflections, wherein Mrs. Jarmey excelled. Not five minutes later, and whilst the two were still talking in the passage, the front door opened, and Thyrza came in. Lydia turned and went upstairs.

Thyrza, entering the room, sought her sister's face; it had an angry look. For a moment Lydia did not speak; the other, laying aside her hat, said: 'I'm sorry I'm so late, Lyddy.'

'Where have you been?' her sister asked, in a voice which strove to command itself.

Thyrza could not tell the whole truth at once, though she knew it would have to be confessed eventually; indeed, whether or no discovery came from other sources, all would eventually be told of her own free will. She might fear at the moment, but in the end kept no secret from Lydia.

'I've been about with Totty,' she said, averting her face as she drew off her cotton gloves.

'Yes, you have! You've been singing at a public-house.'

Lydia was too upset to note the paleness of Thyrza's face, which at another moment would have elicited anxious question. She was deeply hurt that Thyrza made so little account of her wishes, jealous of the influence of Totty Nancarrow, stirred with apprehensions as powerful as a mother's. On the other hand, it was Thyrza's nature to shrink into coldness before angry words. She suffered intensely when the voice which was of wont so affectionate turned to severity, but she could not excuse herself till the storm was over. And it was most often from the elder girl that the first words of reconcilement came.

'That's your Totty Nancarrow,' Lydia went on, with no check upon her tongue. 'Didn't I tell you what 'ud come of going about with her? What next, I should like to know! If you go and sing in a public-house, I don't know what you won't do. I shall never trust you out by yourself again. You shan't go out at night at all, that's about it! You're an unkind girl!'

'You've no right to speak to me like that, Lydia!' Thyrza replied, with indignation. The excitement and the fainting fit had strung her nerves painfully. And for all her repentance, the echo of applause was still very sweet in her ears; this vehement reproach caused a little injury to her pride. 'It doesn't depend on you whether I go out or not. I'm not a child, and I can take care of myself. I haven't done anything wrong.'

'You have—and you know you have! You knew perfectly well I shouldn't have let you go near such a place. You know how I've begged you not to go with Totty Nancarrow, and how you've promised me you wouldn't be led into any harm. I shall never be able to trust you again. You *are* only a child! You show it! And in future you'll do as I tell you!'

Thyrza caught up her hat.

'I certainly shan't stop here whilst you're in such a bad temper,' she said in a trembling voice. 'You'll find that isn't the way to make me do as you wish.'

She stepped to the door. Lydia, frightened, sprang forward and barred the way.

'Go and sit down, Thyrza!'

'Let me go! What right have you to stop me?'

Then both were silent. At the same moment they became aware that a common incident of Saturday night was occurring in the street below. A half-tipsy man and a nagging woman had got thus far on their way home, the wife's shrill tongue running over every scale of scurrility and striking every note of ingenious malice. The man was at length worked to a pitch of frenzy, and then—thud, thud, mingled with objurga-

tions and shrill night-piercing yells. The near windy
side of murder was familiar enough to dwellers in this
region, but that woman's bell-clapper tongue had struck
shame into Lydia. She could not speak another angry
word.

'Thyrza, take your hat off,' she said quietly, moving
away a little from the door. Her cheeks burned fiery,
and she quivered in the subsidence of her temper.

Her sister did not obey, but, unable to stand longer,
she went to a chair at a distance. The uproar in the
street continued for a quarter of an hour, then by degrees passed on, the voice of the woman shrieking foul
abuse till remoteness stifled it. Lydia forced herself
to keep silence from good or ill; it was no use speaking
the thoughts she had till morning. Thyrza sat with
her eyes fixed on vacancy; she was so miserable, her
heart had sunk so low, that tears would have come had
she not forced them back. More than once of late she
had known this mood in which life lay about her barren
and weary. She was very young to suffer that oppres-
sion of the world-worn ; it was the penalty she paid for
her birthright of heart and mind.

By midnight they were lying side by side, but no
'good-night' had passed between them. When Thyrza's
gentle breathing told that she slept, Lydia still lay with
open eyes, watching the flicker of the street lamp upon
the ceiling, hearing the sounds that came of mirth or
brutality in streets near and far. She did not suffer in the
same way as her sister ; as soon as she had gently touched

Thyrza's unconscious hand, love came upon her with its warm solace ; but her trouble was deep, and she looked into the future with many doubts.

The past she could scarcely deem other than happy, though a stranger would have thought it sad enough. Her mother she well remembered—a face pale and sweet, like Thyrza's : the eyes that have their sad beauty from foresight of death. Her father lived only a year longer, then she and the little one passed into the charge of Mr. Boddy, who was paid a certain small sum by Trent's employers, in consideration of the death by accident. Then came the commencement of Mr. Boddy's misfortunes ; his shop and house were burnt down, he lost his limb in an endeavour to save his property, he lost his wife in consequence of the shock. Dreary things for the memory, yet they did not weigh upon Lydia ; she was so happily endowed that her mind selected and dwelt on sunny hours, on kind looks and words which her strong heart cherished unassailably, on the mutual charities which sorrow had begotten, rather than on the sorrow itself. Above all, the growing love of her dear one, of her to whom she was both mother and sister, had strengthened her against every trouble. Yet of late this strongest passion of her life had become a source of grave anxieties, as often as circumstance caused her to look beyond her contentment. Thyrza was so beautiful, and, it seemed to her, so weak ; always dreaming of something beyond and above the life which was her lot, so deficient in the practical qualities which that life demanded. At moments Lydia saw her responsibility in a light which almost frightened her.

They worked at a felt-hat factory, as 'trimmers'; that is to say, they finished hats by sewing in the lining, putting on the bands and the like. In the busy season they could average together wages of about a pound a week; at dull times they earned less, and very occasionally had to support themselves for a week or two without employment. Since the age of fourteen Lydia herself had received help from no one; from sixteen she had lived in lodgings with Thyrza, independent. Poor Mr. Boddy was then no longer able to do more than supply his own needs, for things had grown worse with him from year to year. Lydia occasionally found jobs for her free hours, and she had never yet wanted. She was strong, her health had scarcely ever given her a day's uneasiness; there never came to her a fear lest bread should fail. But Thyrza could not take life as she did; it was not enough for that imaginative nature to toil drearily day after day, and year after year, just for the sake of earning a livelihood. In a month she would be seventeen: it was too true, as she had said to-night, that she was no longer a child. What might happen if the elder sister's influence came to an end? Thyrza loved her: how Lydia would have laughed at anyone who hinted that the love could ever weaken! But it was not a guard against every danger.

It was inevitable that Lydia should have hoped that her sister might marry early. And one man she knew in whom—she scarcely could have told you why—her confidence was so strong that she would freely have entrusted him with Thyrza's fate. Thyrza could not bring herself to think of him as a husband. It was with Ackroyd that Lydia's thoughts were busy as she lay wakeful. Before to-night she had not pondered so continuously on what she knew of him. For some two years he had been an acquaintance, through the Bowers, and she had felt glad when it was plain that he sought Thyrza's society. 'Yes,' she had said to herself, 'I like him, and feel that he is to be relied upon.' Stories, to be sure, had reached her ears : something of an over-fondness for conviviality ; but she had confidence. To-night she seemed called upon to review all her impressions. Why ? Nothing new had happened. She longed for sleep, but it only came when dawn was white upon the blind.

When it was time to rise, neither spoke. Lydia prepared the breakfast as usual — it seemed quite natural that she should do nearly all the work of the home—and they sat down to it cheerlessly.

Since daybreak a mist had crept over the sky ; it thinned the sunlight to a suffusion of grey and gold. In the house there was the silence of Sunday morning ; the street was still, save for the jodeling of a milkman as he wheeled his clattering cans from house to house. In that city on the far side of Thames, known to these girls with scarcely less of vagueness than to simple dwellers in country towns, the autumn-like air was foretaste of holiday; the martyrs of the Season and they who do the world's cleaner work knew that rest was near, spoke at breakfast of the shore and the mountain. Even to Lydia, weary after her short sleep and unwontedly dejected, there came a wish that it were possible to quit the streets for but one day, and sit somewhere apart under the open sky. It was not often that so fantastic a dream visited her.

In dressing, Thyrza had left her hair unbraided. Lydia always did that for her. When the table was cleared, the former took up a story-paper which she bought every week, and made a show of reading. Lydia went about her accustomed tasks. How heavy the silence was.

Presently Lydia took a brush and comb and went behind her sister's chair. She began to unloosen the rough coils in which the golden hair was pinned together. It was always a joy to her to bathe her hands in the warm soft torrent. With delicate care she combed out every intricacy and brushed the ordered tresses till the light gleamed on their smooth surface; then with skilful fingers she wove the braid, tying it with a blue ribbon so that the ends hung loose. The task completed, it was her custom to bend over the little head and snatch an inverted kiss, always a moment of laughter. This morning she omitted that; she was moving sadly away, when she noticed that the face turned a little, a very little.

' Isn't it right?' she asked, keeping her eyes down.

' I think so—it doesn't matter.'

She drew near again, as if to inspect her work. Perhaps there was a slight lack of smoothness over the temple; she touched the spot with her fingers.

' Why are you so unkind to me, Thyrza?'

The words had come involuntarily; the voice shook as they were spoken.

' I don't mean to be, Lyddy—you know I don't.'

' But you do things that you know 'll make me angry. I'm quick-tempered, and I couldn't bear to think of you going to that place; I ought to have spoken in a different way.'

' Who told you I'd been singing?'

' Mrs. Jarmey. I'm very glad she did; it doesn't seem any harm to you, Thyrza, but it does to me. Dear, have you ever sung at such places before?'

Thyrza shook her head.

' Will you promise me never to go there again?'

' I don't want to go. But I get no harm. They were very pleased with my singing. Annie West was there, and several other girls. Why do you make so much of it, Lyddy?'

' Because, dearest, there's nobody in the world as much to me as you are, and I want to keep you safer than my own life! I'm older than you, Thyrza, and if you'll only trust me and do as I wish, you'll see some day that I was right. I know you're a good girl; I don't think a wrong thought ever came into your head. It isn't that, it's because you can't go about the streets and into public-houses without hearing bad things and seeing bad people. I want to keep you away from everything that isn't homelike and quiet. I want you to love me more than anyone else!'

'I do, Lyddy! I do, dear! It's only that I——'

'What——?'

'I don't know how it is. I'm discontented. There's never any change. How can you be so happy day after day? I love to be with you, but if we could go and live somewhere else. I should like to see a new place. I've been reading there about the seaside; what it must be like! I want to know things. You don't understand me?'

'I think I do. I wish we could have a change sometimes. I felt a little the same when I heard Mrs. Isaacs and her daughter talking about Margate yesterday. But we shall be better off some day, see if we aren't! Try your best not to think about those things. Suppose you ask Mr. Grail to lend you a book to read? I met Mrs. Grail downstairs last night, and she asked if we'd go down and have tea to-day. I can't, because Mary's coming, but you might. And I'm sure he'd lend you something nice if you asked him.'

'I don't think I durst. He always sits so quiet, and he's such a queer man.'

'Yes, he is rather queer, but he speaks very kind.'

'I'll see. But you mustn't speak so cross to me if I do wrong, Lyddy. It makes me have bad thoughts.

I felt as if I should like to go away, sometime when
you didn't know. I did, really!'

Lydia gazed at her anxiously.

'I don't think you'd ever have the heart to do that,
Thyrza,' she said, in a low voice.

'No,' she shook her head, smiling. 'I couldn't do
without you. And now kiss me properly, like you
always do.'

Lydia stood behind the chair again, and the laughing caress was exchanged.

'I should stay,' Thyrza went on, 'if it was only to
have you do my hair. I do so like to feel your soft
hands!'

'Soft hands! Great coarse things! Just look!'

She took one of Thyrza's, and held it beside her
own. The difference was noticeable enough; Lydia's
was not ill-shapen, but there were marks on it of all
the rough household work which she had never permitted her sister to do. Thyrza's was delicate, supple,
beautiful in its kind as her face.

'I don't care!' she said, laughing. 'It's a good,
soft, sleepy hand.'

'Sleepy, child!'

'I mean it always makes me feel dozy when it's
doing my hair.'

There was no more cloud between them. The
morning passed on with sisterly talk. Lydia had wisely
refrained from exacting promises; she hoped to resume
the subject before long—together with another that

was in her mind. Thyrza, too, had something to speak
of, but could not bring herself to it as yet.

Though it was so hot, they had to keep a small fire
for cooking the dinner. This meal consisted of a small
piece of steak chosen from the odds and ends thrown
together on the front of a butcher's shop, and a few
potatoes. It was not always they had meat; yet they
never went hungry, and, in comparing herself with
others she knew, it sometimes made Lydia a little
unhappy to think how well she lived.

Then began the unutterable dreariness of a Sunday
afternoon. From the lower part of the house sounded
the notes of a concertina; it was Mr. Jarmey who played;
he had the habit of doing so whilst half asleep between
dinner and tea. With impartiality he passed from
strains of popular hymnody to the familiar ditties of the
music hall, lavishing on each an excess of sentiment.
He shook pathetically on top notes and languished on
final chords. A dolorous music!

The milkman came along the street. He was followed by a woman who wailed 'wa-ater-creases!' Then
the concertina once more possessed the stillness. Few
pedestrians were abroad; the greater part of the male
population of Lambeth slumbered after the baked joint
and flagon of ale. Yet here and there a man in his
shirt-sleeves leaned forth despondently from a window
or sat in view within, dozing over the Sunday paper.

A rattling of light wheels drew near, and a nasal
voice cried ''Okey-Pokey! 'Okey-'Okey-'Okey! Penny

a lump!' It was the man who sold ice-cream. He came to a stop, and half a dozen boys gathered about his truck. The delicacy was dispensed to them in little green and yellow glasses, from which they extracted it with their tongues. The vendor remained for a few minutes, then on again with his ''Okey-'Okey-'Okey!' sung through the nose.

Next came a sound of distressful voices, whining the discords of a mendicant psalm. A man, a woman, and two small children crawled along the street; their eyes surveyed the upper windows. All were ragged and filthy; the elders bore the unmistakable brand of the gin-shop, and the children were visaged like debased monkeys. Occasionally a copper fell to them, in return for which the choragus exclaimed 'Gord bless yer!'

Thyrza sat in her usual place by the window, now reading for a few minutes, now dreaming. Lydia had some stockings to be darned; she became at length so silent that her sister turned to look at her. Her head had dropped forward. She slumbered for a few minutes, then started to consciousness again, and laughed when she saw Thyrza regarding her.

'I suppose Mary 'll be here directly,' she said. 'I'd better put this work out of sight.' And as she began to spread the cloth, she asked: 'What 'll you do whilst we're at chapel, Thyrza?'

'I think I'll go and have tea with Mrs. Grail; then I'll see if I dare ask for a book.'

'You've made up your mind not to go out?'

'There was something I wanted to tell you. I met Mr. Ackroyd as I was coming home last night. I told him I couldn't come out alone, and I said I couldn't be sure whether you'd come or not.'

'But what a pity!' returned Lydia. 'You knew I was going to chapel. I'm afraid he'll wait for us.'

'Yes, but I somehow didn't like to say we wouldn't go at all. What time is he going to be there?'

'He said at six o'clock.'

'Would you mind just running out and telling him. Perhaps you'll be going past with Mary, not long after?'

'That's a nice job you give me!' remarked Lydia, with a half smile.

'But I know you don't mind it, Lyddy. It isn't the first thing you've done for me.'

It was said with so much *naïveté* that Lydia could not but laugh.

'I should like it much better if you'd go yourself,' she replied. 'But I'm afraid it's no good asking.'

'Not a bit! And, Lyddy, I told Mr. Ackroyd that it would always be the same. He understands now.'

The other made no reply.

'You won't be cross about it?'

'No, dear; there's nothing to be cross about. But I'm very sorry.'

The explanation passed in a tone of less earnestness than either would have anticipated. They did not look at each other, and they dismissed the subject as soon as

possible. Then came two rings at the house-bell, signi-
fying the arrival of their visitor.

Mary Bower and Lydia had been close friends for
four or five years, yet they had few obvious points of
similarity and their differences were marked enough.
The latter grew indeed; for Mary attached herself
more closely to religious observances, whilst Lydia continued to declare with native frankness that she could
not feel it incumbent upon her to give grave attention
to such matters. Mary grieved over this attitude in
one whose goodness of heart she could not call in
question; it troubled her as an inconsequence in nature;
she cherished a purpose of converting Lydia. Yet she
found it very difficult to draw her friend into conversation on these subjects—Lydia was apt to show restive-
ness when solemn questions were put to her; though
involuntarily, she seemed to resent them. Out of good-
nature she conceded points, such as the occasional
attendance of chapel; she would admit occasionally
that her lack of piety was a fault; but her life mani-
fested slight compunction. Mary had brought herself
to the point of hoping that some sorrow might befall
her friend—nothing of too sad a nature, but still a
grief which might turn her thoughts inward. Yet, had
anything of the kind come to pass, Mary would have
been the first to hasten with consolation.

Thyrza went downstairs, and the two gossiped as
tea was made ready. Mary had already heard of the
incident at the Prince Albert; such a piece of news

could not be long in reaching Mrs. Bower's. She wished to speak of it, yet was in uncertainty whether Lydia had already been told. The latter was the first to bring forward the subject.

'It's quite certain she oughtn't to make a friend of that girl Totty,' Mary said, with decision. 'You must insist that it is stopped, Lydia.'

'I shan't do any good that way,' replied the other, shaking her head. 'I lost my temper last night, like a silly, and of course only harm came of it.'

'But there's no need to lose your temper. You must tell her she's *not* to speak to the girl again, and there's an end of it!'

Mary's 'short way with the Dissenters' struck a note of character which was apt to show itself in smaller matters. Lydia, who was conscious of too much tendency to compromise, often admired this quality in her friend. Yet she knew that it would avail nothing in the situation she had to deal with. Her views were larger than Mary's, though she felt so much less certainty on questions of supreme moment. She shook her head again.

'Thyrza's too old for that, dear. I must lead her by kindness, or I can't lead her at all. I don't think, though, she'll ever do such a thing as that again. I know what a temptation it was; she does sing so sweetly. But she won't do it again now she knows how I think about it.'

Mary appeared doubtful. Given a suggestion of

iniquity, and it was her instinct rather to fear than
to hope. Secretly she had no real liking for Thyrza ;
something in that complex nature repelled her. As she
herself had said, ' Thyrza was not easy to understand,'
but she did understand that the girl's essential motives
were of a kind radically at enmity with her own.
Thyrza, it seemed to her, was worldly in the most hopeless way.

' You'll be sorry for it if you're not firm,' she
remarked.

Lydia made no direct reply, but after a moment's
musing, she said :

' If only she could think of Mr. Ackroyd ! '

She had not yet spoken so plainly of this to Mary ;
the latter was surprised by the despondency of her tone.

' But I thought they were often together ? '

' She's only been out with him when I went as well,
and last night she told him it was of no use.'

' Well, I can't say I'm sorry to hear that,' Mary
replied, with the air of one who spoke an unpleasant
truth.

' Why not, Mary ? '

' I think he's likely to do her every bit as much
harm as Totty Nancarrow.'

' Who *do* you mean, Mary ? ' There was a touch of
indignation in Lydia's voice. ' What harm can Mr.
Ackroyd do to Thyrza ? '

' Not the kind of harm you're thinking of, dear.
But if I had a sister, I know I shouldn't like to see

her marry Mr. Ackroyd. He's got no religion, and what's more, he's always talking against religion. Father says he made a speech last week at that horrid place in Westminster Bridge Road where the Atheists have their meetings. I don't deny there's something nice about him, but I wouldn't trust a man of that kind.'

Lydia delayed her words a little. She kept her eyes on the table; her forehead was knitted.

'I can't help what he thinks about religion,' she replied at length, with firmness. 'He's a good man, I'm quite sure of that.'

'Lydia, he can't be good if he does his best to ruin people's souls.'

'I don't know anything about that, Mary. Whatever he says, he says because he believes it and thinks it right. Why, there's Mr. Grail thinks in the same way, I believe. At all events, he never goes to church or chapel. And he's a friend of Mr. Ackroyd's.'

'But we don't know anything about Mr. Grail.'

'We don't know much, but it's quite enough to talk to him for a few minutes to know he's a man that wouldn't say or do anything wrong.'

'He must be a wonderful man, Lydia.'

These Sunday conversations were always the most fruitful of trouble. Mary was prepared by her morning and afternoon exercises to be more aggressive and uncompromising than usual. But the present difficulty appeared a graver one than any that had yet risen

between them. Lydia had never spoken in the tone
which marked her rejoinder:

'Really, Mary, it's as if you couldn't put faith in
any one! You know I don't feel the same as you do
about religion and such things, and I don't suppose I
ever shall. When I like people, I like them; I can't
ask what they believe and what they don't believe.
We'd better not talk about it any more.'

Mary's face assumed rather a hard look.

'Just as you like, dear,' she said.

There ensued an awkward silence, which Lydia at
length broke by speech on some wholly different subject.
Mary with difficulty adapted herself to the change:
tea was finished rather uncomfortably.

It was six o'clock. Lydia, hearing the hour strike,
knew that Ackroyd would be waiting at the end of
Walnut Tree Walk. She was absent minded, halting
between a desire to go at once and tell him that they
could not come, and a disinclination not perhaps very
clearly explained. The minutes went on. It seemed
to be decided for her that he should learn the truth by
their failure to join him.

Church bells began to sound. Mary rose and put
on her hat, then, taking up the devotional books she
had with her, offered her hand as if to say good-bye.

'But,' said Lydia in surprise, 'I'm going with you.'

'I didn't suppose you would, dear,' the other
returned quietly.

'But haven't you had tea with me?'

Mary had not now to learn that her friend held a promise inviolable; her surprise would have been exceeding if Lydia had allowed her to go forth alone. She smiled.

'Will there be nice singing?' Lydia asked, as she prepared herself quickly. 'I do really like the singing, at all events, Mary.'

The other shook her head, sadly.

'Foolish girl!' Lydia exclaimed. 'As if that wasn't better than nothing.'

They left the house and turned towards Kennington Road. Before Lydia had gone half a dozen steps she saw that Ackroyd was waiting at the end of the street. She felt a pang of self-reproach; it was wrong of her to have allowed him to stand in miserable uncertainty all this time; she ought to have gone out at six o'clock. In a low voice she said to her companion:

'There's Mr. Ackroyd. I want just to speak a word to him. If you'll go on when we get up, I'll soon overtake you.'

Mary acquiesced in silence. Lydia, approaching, saw disappointment on the young man's face. He raised his hat to her—an unwonted attention in these parts—and she gave him her hand.

'I'm going to chapel,' she said playfully.

He had a sudden hope.

'Then your sister 'll come out?'

'No, Mr. Ackroyd; she can't to-night. She's having tea with Mrs. Grail.'

He looked down the street. Lydia was impelled to say earnestly :

'Some time, perhaps! Thyrza is very young yet, Mr. Ackroyd. She thinks of such different things.'

'What does she think of ?' he asked, rather gloomily.

'I mean she—she must get older and know you better. Good-bye! Mary Bower is waiting for me.'

She ran on, and Ackroyd sauntered away without a glance after her.

CHAPTER VI.

DISINHERITED.

When Thyrza left the two at tea and went down-stairs, she knocked at the door of the front parlour on the ground floor. The room which she entered was but dimly lighted ; thick curtains encroached upon each side of the narrow window, which was also shadowed above by a vallance with long tassels, whilst in front of it stood a table with a great pot of flowering musk. The atmo-sphere was close; with the odour of the plant blended the musty air which comes from old and neglected furniture. Mrs. Grail, Gilbert Grail's mother, was an old lady with an unusual dislike for the upset of house-hold cleaning, and as her son's prejudice, like that of most men, tended in the same direction, this sitting-room, which they used in common, had known little disturbance since they entered it a year and a half ago. Formerly they had occupied a house in Battersea ; it was given up on the death of Gilbert's sister, and these lodgings taken in Walnut Tree Walk.

A prominent object in the room was a bookcase, some six feet high and two and a half broad, quite full of books, most of them of shabby exterior. They were Gilbert's purchases at second-hand stalls during the past fifteen years. Their variety indicated a mind of liberal intelligence. There was no hint of technical pursuits. Works of history and biography predominated, but poetry and fiction were also represented on the shelves. Odd volumes of expensive publications looked forth plaintively here and there, and many periodical issues stood unbound.

Another case, a small one with glass doors, contained literature of another order, some thirty volumes which had belonged to Gilbert's father, and were now his mother's peculiar study. They were translations of sundry works of Swedenborg, and productions put forth by the Church of the New Jerusalem. Mrs. Grail was a member of that church. She occasionally visited a meeting-place in Brixton, but for the most part was satisfied with conning the treatises of the mystic, by preference that on 'Heaven and Hell,' which she read in the first English edition, an old copy in boards, much worn.

She was a smooth-faced, gentle-mannered woman, not without dignity as she rose to receive Thyrza and guided her to a comfortable seat. Her voice was habitually subdued to the limit of audibleness; she spoke with precision, and in language very free from vulgarisms either of thought or phrase. Her taste had always been for a home-keeping life: she dreaded gossipers, and only left the house when it was absolutely

necessary, then going forth closely veiled. With the
landlady she held no more intercourse than arose from
the weekly payment of rent; the other lodgers in the
house only saw her by chance on rare occasions. Her
son left home and returned with much regularity, he
also seeming to desire privacy above all things. Mrs.
Jarmey had at first been disposed to take this reserve
somewhat ill; when she knocked at Mrs. Grail's door
on some paltry excuse for seeing the inside of the room,
and found that the old lady exchanged brief words with
her on the threshold, she wondered who these people
might be who thought themselves too good for wonted
neighbourship. In time, however, her feeling changed,
and she gave everybody to understand that her ground-
floor lodgers were of the highest respectability, inmates
such as did not fall to the lot of every landlady.

Gilbert was surprised when, of her own motion,
his mother made overtures to the sisters who lived
at the top of the house. Neither Lydia nor Thyrza
was at first disposed to respond very warmly; they
agreed that the old lady was doubtless very respectable,
but at the same time decidedly queer in her way of
speaking. But during the past few months they had
overcome this reluctance, and were now on a certain
footing of intimacy with Mrs. Grail, who made it no
secret that she took great interest in Thyrza. Thyrza
always entered the sitting-room with a feeling of awe.
The dim light, the old lady's low voice, above all the
books, in her eyes a remarkable library, impressed her

strongly. If Grail himself were present, he was in-
variably reading; Thyrza held him profoundly learned,
a judgment confirmed by his mother's way of speaking
of him. For Mrs. Grail regarded her son with distinct
reverence. He, in turn, was tenderly respectful to her.
They did not know what it was to exchange an unkind
or an impatient word.

Thyrza liked especially to have tea here on Sunday.
The appointments of the table seemed to her luxurious,
for the tea-service was uniform and of pretty, old-
fashioned pattern, and simple little dainties of a kind
new to her were generally forthcoming. Moreover, from
her entrance to her leave-taking, she was flattered by
the pleasantest attentions. The only other table at
which she sometimes sat as a guest was Mrs. Bower's;
between the shopkeeper's gross good-nature and the
well-mannered kindness of Mrs. Grail there was a broad
distinction, and Thyrza was very ready to appreciate it.
For she was sensible of refinements; numberless little
personal delicacies distinguished her from the average
girl of her class, and even from Lydia. The meals
which she and her sister took in their own room might
be ever so poor; they were always served with a modest
grace which perhaps would not have marked them if it
had depended upon Lydia alone. In this respect, as in
many others, Thyrza had repaid her sister's devotion
with subtle influences tending to a comely life.

Once, when she had gone down alone to have tea,
she said to Lydia on her return, 'Downstairs they treat

me as if I were a lady,' and it was spoken with the *naïve* satisfaction which was one of her charming moods.

Till quite lately Gilbert had scarcely conversed with her at all. When he broke his habitual silence he addressed himself to Lydia. When he did speak to the younger girl it was with studied courtesy and kindness; but he seemed unable to overcome a sort of shyness with which she had troubled him since the beginning of their acquaintance. It was noticeable in his manner this evening when he shook hands with a murmured word or two. Thyrza, however, appeared a little less timid than usual; she just met his look, and in a questioning way which he could not understand at the time. The truth was, Thyrza wondered whether he had heard of her escapade of the night before; she tried to read his expression, searching for any hint of disapproval.

The easy chair was always given to her when she entered; so seldom she sat on anything easier than the stiff cane-bottomed seats of her own room that this always seemed luxurious. By degrees she had permitted herself to lean back in it. She did so want Lyddy to know what it was like to sit in that chair; but it had never yet been possible to effect an exchange. It might have offended Mrs. Grail, a thing on no account to be risked.

'Lyddy has Mary Bower to tea,' she said on her arrival this evening. 'They're going to chapel. You don't mind me coming alone, Mrs. Grail?'

'You're never anything but welcome, my dear,' murmured the old lady, pressing the little hand in both her own.

Tea was soon ready. Mrs. Grail talked with pleasant continuousness, as usual. She had fallen upon reminiscences, and spoke of Lambeth as she had known it when a girl; it was her birthplace, and through life she had never strayed far away. She regarded the growth of population, the crowding of mean houses where open spaces used to be, the whole change of times in fact, as deplorable. One would have fancied from her descriptions that the Lambeth of sixty years ago was a delightful rustic village.

After tea Thyrza resumed the low chair and folded her hands, full of contentment. Mrs. Grail took the tea-things from the room and was absent about a quarter of an hour. Thyrza, left alone with the man who for her embodied so many mysteries, let her eyes stray over the bookshelves. She felt it very unlikely that any book there would be within the compass of her understanding; doubtless they dealt with the secrets of learning, the strange, high things for which her awed imagination had no name. Gilbert had seated himself in a shadowed corner; his face was bent downwards. Just when Thyrza was about to put some timid question with regard to the books, he looked at her and said:

'Do you ever go to Westminster Abbey?'

The intellectual hunger of his face was softened; he did not smile, but kept a mild gravity of expression which showed that he had a pleasure in the girl's proximity. When he had spoken, he stroked his forehead with the tips of his fingers, a nervous action.

'I've never been inside,' Thyrza made answer. 'What is there to see?'

'It's the place, you know, where great men have been buried for hundreds of years. I should like, if I could, to spend a little time there every day.'

'Can you see the graves?' Thyrza asked.

'Yes, many. And on the stones you read who they were that lie there. There are the graves of kings, and of men much greater than kings.'

'Greater than kings! Who were they, Mr. Grail?'

She had rested her elbow on the arm of the chair, and her fingers just touched her chin. She regarded him with a gaze of deep curiosity.

'Men who wrote books,' he answered, with a slight smile.

Thyrza dropped her eyes. In her thought of books it had never occurred to her that any special interest could attach to the people who wrote them; indeed, she had perhaps never asked herself how printed matter came into existence. Even among the crowd of average readers, we know how commonly a book will be swallowed without a glance at its title page.

Gilbert continued:

'I always come away from the Abbey with fresh courage. If I'm tired and out of spirits, I go there, and it makes me feel as if I daren't waste a minute of the time when I'm free to try and learn something.'

It was a strange impulse that made him speak in this way to an untaught child. With those who were far more likely to understand him he was the most reticent of men.

'But you know a great deal, Mr. Grail,' Thyrza said with surprise, looking again at the bookshelves.

'You mustn't think that. I had very little teaching when I was a lad, and ever since I've had very little either of time or means to teach myself. If I only knew those few books well, it would be something, but there are some of them I've never got to yet.'

'Those *few* books!' Thyrza exclaimed. 'But I never thought anybody had so many, before I came into this room.'

'I should like you to see the library at the British Museum. Every book that is published in England is sent there. There's a large room where people sit and study any book they like, all day long, and day after day. Think what a life that must be!'

'Those are rich people, I suppose,' Thyrza remarked. 'They haven't to work for their living.'

'Not rich, all of them. But they haven't to work with their hands.'

He became silent. In his last words there was a little bitterness. Thyrza glanced at him; he seemed to have forgotten her presence, and his face had the wonted look of trouble kept under.

Then Mrs. Grail returned. She sat down near
Thyrza, and, after a little more of her pleasant talk,
said, turning to her son :

'Could you find something to read us, Gilbert ? '

He thought for a moment, then reached down a
book of biographies, writing of a popular colour, not
above Thyrza's understanding. It contained a life of
Sir Thomas More, or rather a pleasant story founded
upon his life, with much about his daughter Margaret.

' Yes, that'll do nicely,' was Mrs. Grail's opinion.

He began with a word or two of explanation to
Thyrza, then entered upon the narrative. As soon as,
the proposal was made, Thyrza's face had lighted up
with pleasure ; she listened intently, leaning a little
forward in her chair, her hands folded together. Gilbert,
if he raised his eyes from the page, did not look at her.
Mrs. Grail interrupted once or twice with a question
or a comment. The reading was good ; Gilbert's voice
gave life to description and conversation, and supplied
an interest even where the writer was in danger of
growing dull.

When the end was reached, Thyrza recovered herself
with the sigh which follows strained attention. But
she was not in a mood to begin conversation again ;
her mind had got something to work upon, it would
keep her awake far into the night with a succession of
half-realised pictures. What a world was that of
which a glimpse had been given her! Here indeed
was something remote from her tedious life. Her

brain was full of vague glories, of the figures of kings and queens, of courtiers and fair ladies, of things nobly said and done, and her heart throbbed with indignation at wrongs greater than any she had ever imagined. When it had all happened she knew not; surely very long ago; but the names she knew, Chelsea, Lambeth, the Tower, these gave a curiously fantastic reality to the fairy tale. And one thing she saw with uttermost distinctness : that boat going down the stream of Thames, and the dear, dreadful head dropped into it from the arch above. She would go and stand on the bridge and think of it.

Ah, she must tell Lyddy all that! Better still, she must read it to her. She found courage to say :

'Could you spare that book, Mr. Grail? Could you lend it me for a day or two? I'd be very careful with it.'

'I shall be very glad to lend it you,' Gilbert answered. His voice changed somehow from that in which he usually spoke.

She received it from him and held it on her lap with both hands. She would not look into it till alone in her room. And, having secured it, she did not wish to stay longer.

'Going already ? ' Mrs. Grail said, seeing her rise.

'Lyddy 'll be back very soon,' was the reply. 'I think I'd better go now.'

She shook hands with both of them, and they heard her run up the thin-carpeted stairs.

Mother and son sat in silence for some minutes. Gilbert had taken another book, and seemed to be absorbed in it; Mrs. Grail had a face of meditation. Occasionally she looked upwards, as though on the track of some memory which she strove to make clear.

'Gilbert,' she began at length, suggestively.

He raised his eyes and regarded her in absent way.

'I've been trying for a long time to remember what that child's face reminded me of. Every time I see her, I make sure I've seen someone like her before, and now I think I've got it.'

Gilbert was used to a stream of amusing fancifulness in his mother; analysis and resemblances were dear to her; possibly the Biblical theories which she had imbibed were in some degree answerable for the characteristic.

'And who does she remind you of?' he asked.

'Of somebody whose name I can't think of. You remember the school in Lambeth Road where Lizzie used to go?'

She referred to a time five-and-twenty years gone by, when Gilbert's sister was a child. He nodded.

'It was Mrs. Green's school, you know, and soon after Lizzie began to go, there was an assistant teacher taken on. Now can you think what her name was? You must remember that Lizzie used to walk home along with her almost every day. Miss ——, Miss ——. Oh, dear me, what *was* that name?'

Gilbert smiled and shook his head.

' I can't help you, mother. I don't even remember any such thing.'

' What a poor memory you have in ordinary things, Gilbert ! I wonder at it, with your mind for study.'

' But what's the connection ? '

' Why, Thyrza has got her very face. It's just come to me. I'm sure that was her mother.'

' But how impossible that you should have that woman's face still in your mind !' Gilbert protested, good-humouredly.

' My dear, don't be so hasty. It's as clear to me as if Lizzie had just come in and said, " Miss Denny brought me home." Why, there *is* the name ? It fell from my tongue ! To be sure ; Miss Denny ! A pale, sad-looking little thing, she was. Often and often I've been at the window and seen her coming along the street hand in hand with your sister. Now I'll ask Thyrza if her mother's name wasn't Denny, and if she didn't teach at Mrs. Green's school. Depend upon it, I'm right, Gilbert !'

Gilbert still smiled very incredulously.

' It'll be a marvellous thing if it turns out to be true,' he said.

' Oh, but I have a wonderful memory for faces. I always used to think there was something very good and sweet in that teacher's look. I don't think I ever spoke to her, though she went backwards and forwards past our house in Brook Street for nearly two years. Then I didn't see her any more. Depend upon it,

she went away to be married. Lizzie had left a little
before that. Oh yes, it explains why I seemed to know
Thyrza the first time I saw her.'

Mrs. Grail was profoundly satisfied. Again a short
silence ensued.

'How nicely they keep themselves,' she resumed,
half to herself. 'I'm sure Lydia's one of the most
careful girls I ever knew. But Thyrza's my favourite.
How she enjoyed your reading, Gilbert!'

He nodded, but kept his attention on the book.
His mother just glanced at him, and presently continued :

'I do hope she won't be spoilt. She *is* very pretty,
isn't she? But they're not girls for going out much, I
can see. And Thyrza's always glad when I ask her to
come and have tea with us. I suppose they haven't
many friends.'

It was quite against Mrs. Grail's wont to interrupt
thus when her son had settled down to read. Gilbert
averted his eyes from the page, and, after reflecting a
little, said :

'Ackroyd knows them.'

His mother looked at him closely. He seemed to
be absorbed again.

'Does he speak to you about them, Gilbert?'

'He's mentioned them once or twice.'

'Perhaps that's why Lydia goes out to chapel,' the
old lady said, with a smile.

'No, I don't think so.'

The reply was so abrupt, so nearly impatient, that Mrs. Grail made an end of her remarks. In a little while she too began to read.

They had supper at nine ; at ten o'clock Mrs. Grail kissed her son's forehead and bade him good-night, adding, 'Don't sit long, my dear.' Every night she took leave of him with the same words, and they were not needless. Gilbert too often forgot the progress of time, and spent in study the hours which were demanded for sleep.

His daily employment was at a large candle and soap factory. By such work he had earned his living for more than twenty years. As a boy, he had begun with wages of four shillings a week, his task being to trim with a knife the rough edges of tablets of soap just stamped out. By degrees he had risen to a weekly income of forty shillings, occasionally increased by pay for overtime. Beyond this he was not likely to get. Men younger than he had passed him, attaining the position of foremen and the like ; some had earned money by inventions which they put at the service of their employers ; but Gilbert could hope for nothing more than the standing of a trustworthy mechanic who, as long as he keeps his strength, can count on daily bread. His heart was not in his work ; it would have been strange if he had thriven by an industry which was only a weariness to him.

His hours were from six in the morning to seven at night. Ah, that terrible rising at five o'clock, when it seemed at first as if he must fall back again in sheer anguish of fatigue, when his eyeballs throbbed to the light and the lids were as if weighted with iron, when the bitterness of the day before him was like poison in his heart! He could not live as his fellow-workmen did, coming home to satisfy his hunger and spend a couple of hours in recreation, then to well-earned sleep. Every minute of freedom, of time in which he was no longer a machine but a thinking and desiring man, he held precious as fine gold. How could he yield to heaviness and sleep, when books lay open before him, and Knowledge, the goddess of his worship, whispered wondrous promises? To Gilbert a printed page was as the fountain of life; he loved literature passionately, and hungered to know the history of man's mind through all the ages. This distinguished him markedly from the not uncommon working man who zealously pursues some chosen branch of study. Such men ordinarily take up subjects of practical bearing; physical science is wont to be their field; or if they study history it is from the point of view of current politics. Taste for literature pure and simple, and disinterested love of historical search, are the rarest things among the self-taught; naturally so, seeing how seldom they come of anything but academical tillage of the right soil. The average man of education is fond of literature because the environment of his growth has made such fondness a second nature. Gilbert had conceived his passion by mere grace. It

had developed in him slowly. At twenty years he was
a young fellow of seemingly rather sluggish character,
without social tendencies, without the common ambitions of his class, much given to absence of mind.
About that time he came across one of the volumes of
the elder D'Israeli, and, behold, he had found himself.
Reading of things utterly unknown to him, he was inspired with strange delights; a mysterious fascination
drew him on amid names which were only a sound; a
great desire was born in him, and its object was seen in
every volume that met his eye. Had he then been
given means and leisure, he would have become at the
least a man of noteworthy learning. No such good
fortune awaited him. Daily his thirteen hours went to
the manufacture of candles, and the evening leisure,
with one free day in the week, was all he could ever
hope for.

At five-and-twenty he had a grave illness. Insuffi-
cient rest and ceaseless trouble of spirit brought him
to death's door. For a long time it seemed as if he
must content himself with earning his bread. He had
no right to call upon others to bear the burden of his
needs. His brother, a steady hard-headed mechanic,
who was doing well in the Midlands and had just
married, spoke to him with uncompromising common
sense; if he chose to incapacitate himself, he must not
look to his relatives to support him. Silently Gilbert
acquiesced; silently he went back to the factory, and,
when he came home of nights, sat with eyes gazing

blankly before him. His mother lived with him, she and his sister; the latter went out to work. All were dependent upon the wages of the week. Nearly a year went by, during which Gilbert did not open a book. It was easier for him, he said, not to read at all than to measure his reading by the demands of his bodily weakness. He would have sold his handful of books, sold them in sheer bitterness of mind, but this his mother interfered to prevent.

But he could not live so. There was now a danger that the shadow of misery would darken into madness. Little by little he resumed his studious habits, yet with prudence. At thirty his bodily strength seemed to have consolidated itself; if he now and then exceeded the allotted hours at night, he did not feel the same evil results as formerly. His sister was a very dear companion to him; she had his own tastes in a simpler form, and woman's tact enabled her to draw him into the repose of congenial talk when she and her mother were troubled by signs of overwork in him. He purchased a book as often as he could reconcile himself to the outlay, and his knowledge grew, though he seemed to himself ever on the mere threshold of the promised land, hopeless of admission.

Then came his sister's death, and the removal from Battersea back to Lambeth. Henceforth it would be seldomer than ever that he could devote a shilling to the enrichment of his shelves. When both he and Lizzie earned wages, the future did not give much trouble, but now all providence was demanded. His brother in the Midlands made contribution towards the mother's support, but Henry had a family of his own, and it was only right that Gilbert should bear the greater charge. Gilbert was nearing five-and-thirty.

By nature he was a lonely man. Amusement such as his world offered had always been savourless to him, and he had never sought familiar fellowship beyond his home. Even there it often happened that for days he kept silence; he would eat his meal when he came from work, then take his book to a corner, and be mute, answering any needful question with a gesture or the briefest word. At such times his face had the lines of age: you would have deemed him a man weighed upon by some vast sorrow. And was he not? His life was speeding by; already the best years were gone, the years of youth and force and hope—nay, hope he could not be said to have known, unless it were for a short space when first the purpose of his being dawned upon consciousness; and the end of that had been bitter enough. The purpose he knew was frustrated. The ' Might have been,' which is ' also called No more, Too late, Farewell,' often stared him in the eyes with those unchanging orbs of ghastliness, chilling the flow of his blood and making life the cruellest of mockeries. Yet he was not driven to that kind of resentment which makes the revolutionary spirit. His personality was essentially that of a student; conservative instincts were stronger in him than the misery which accused his fortune. A touch of creative genius, and you had the man whose song would lead battle against the hoary iniquities of the world. That was denied him; he could only eat his own heart in despair, his protest against the outrage of fate a desolate silence.

A lonely man, yet a tender one. The capacity of love was not less in him than the capacity of knowledge. Yet herein too he was wronged by circumstance. In youth an extreme shyness held him from intercourse with all women save his mother and his sister; he was conscious of his lack of ease in dialogue, of an awkwardness of manner and an unattractiveness of person. On summer evenings, when other young fellows were ready enough in finding companions for their walk, Gilbert would stray alone in the quietest streets until he tired himself, then go home and brood over fruitless longings. In love, as afterwards in study, he had his ideal; sometimes he would catch a glimpse of some face in the street at night, and would walk on with the feeling that his happiness had passed him—if only he could have turned and pursued it! In all women he had supreme faith; that one woman whom his heart imagined was a pure and noble creature, with measureless aspiration, womanhood glorified in her to the type of the upward striving soul—she did not come to him; his life remained chaste and lonely.

Neither had he friends. There were at all times good fellows to be found among those with whom he worked, but again his shyness held him apart, and indeed he felt that intercourse with them would afford him but brief satisfaction. Occasionally some man more thoughtful than the rest would be drawn to him by curiosity, but, finding himself met with so much reserve, involuntary in Gilbert, would become doubtful and turn elsewhither for sympathy. Yet in this respect Grail improved as time went on; as his character ripened, he was readier to gossip now and then of common things with average associates. He knew, however, that he was not much liked, and this naturally gave a certain coldness to his behaviour. Perhaps the very first man for whom he found himself entertaining something like warmth of kindness was Luke Ackroyd. Ackroyd came to the factory shortly after Gilbert had gone to live in Walnut Tree Walk, and in the course of a few weeks the two had got into the habit of walking their common way homewards together. As might have been anticipated, it was a character very unlike his own which had at length attached Gilbert. To begin with, Ackroyd was pronounced in radicalism, was aggressive and at times somewhat noisy; then, he was far from possessing Grail's moral stability, and did not care to conceal his ways of amusing himself; lastly, his intellectual tastes were of the scientific order. Yet Gilbert from the first liked him; he felt that there was no little good in the fellow, if only it could be fostered at the expense of his weaker characteristics. Yet those very weaknesses had much to do with his amiability. This they had in common: both aspired to something

that fortune had denied them. Ackroyd had his idea
of a social revolution, and, though it seemed doubtful
whether he was exactly the man to claim a larger sphere
for the energies of his class, his thought often had
genuine nobleness, clearly recognisable by Gilbert.
Ackroyd had brain-power above the average, and it was
his right to strive for a better lot than the candle-
factory could assure him. So Grail listened with a
smile of much indulgence to the young fellow's fuming
against the order of things, and if he now and then put
in a critical remark was not sorry to have it scornfully
swept aside with a flood of vehement words. He felt,
perchance, that a share of such vigour might have made
his own existence more fruitful.

This was Gilbert Grail at the time with which we
are now concerned. His mother believed that she had
discovered in him something of a new mood of late, a
tendency to quiet cheerfulness, and she attributed it in
part to the healthfulness of intercourse with a friend;
partly she assigned to it another reason. But her
assumption did not receive much proof from Gilbert's
demeanour when left alone in the sitting-room this
Sunday night. Since Thyrza's departure, he had in
truth only made pretence of reading, and now that
his mother was gone, he let the book fall from his
hands. His countenance was fixed in a supreme sadness, his lips were tightly closed, and at times moved,
as if in the suppression of pain. Hopelessness in youth,
unless it be justified by some direst ruin of the future,

is wont to touch us either with impatience or with a comforting sense that reaction is at hand; in a man of middle age it moves us with pure pathos. The sight of Gilbert as he sat thus motionless would have brought tears to kindly eyes. The past was a burden on his memory, the future lay before him like a long road over which he must wearily toil—the goal, frustration. To-night he could not forget himself in the thoughts of other men. It was one of the dread hours, which at intervals came upon him, when the veil was lifted from the face of destiny, and he was bidden gaze himself into despair. At such times he would gladly have changed beings with the idlest and emptiest of his fellow-workmen; their life might be ignoble, but it had abundance of enjoyment. To him there came no joy, nor ever would. Only when he lay in his last sleep would it truly be said of him that he rested.

At twelve o'clock he rose; he had no longing for sleep, but in five hours the new week would have begun, and he must face it with what bodily strength he might. Before entering his bedroom, which was next to the parlour, he went to the house-door and opened it quietly. A soft rain was falling. Leaving the door ajar, he stepped out into the street and looked up to the top windows. There was no light behind the blinds. As if satisfied, he went back into the house and to his room.

The factory was at so short a distance from Walnut

Tree Walk that Gilbert was able to come home for breakfast and dinner. When he entered at mid-day on Monday, his mother pointed to a letter on the mantelpiece. He examined the address, and was at a loss to recognise the writing.

' Who's this from, I wonder?' he said, as he opened the envelope.

He found a short letter, and a printed slip which looked like a circular. The former ran thus:

'Sir,—I am about to deliver a course of evening lectures on a period of English Literature in a room which I have taken for the purpose, No. — High Street, Lambeth. I desire to have a small audience, not more than twenty, consisting of working men who belong to Lambeth. Attendance will be at my invitation. of course without any kind of charge. You have been mentioned to me as one likely to be interested in the subject I propose to deal with. I permit myself to send you a printed syllabus of the course, and to say that it will give me great pleasure if you are able to attend. I should like to arrange for two lectures weekly, each of an hour's duration; the days I leave undecided, also the hour, as I wish to adapt these to the convenience of my hearers. If you feel inclined to give thought to the matter, will you meet me at the lecture-room at eight o'clock on the evening of Sunday, August 16, when we could discuss details? The lectures themselves had better, I should think, begin with the month of September.

'Reply to this is unnecessary; I hope to have the pleasure of meeting you on the 16th.—Believe me to be, yours very truly,

'WALTER EGREMONT.'

'Ah, this is what Ackroyd was speaking of on Saturday,' Gilbert remarked, holding the letter to his mother. 'I wonder what it means.'

'Who is this Mr. Egremont?' asked Mrs. Grail.

'He belongs to the firm of Egremont & Pollard, so Ackroyd tells me. You know that big factory in Westminster Bridge Road--where they make oil·cloth.'

Gilbert was perusing the printed syllabus; it interested him, and he kept it by his plate when he sat down to dinner.

'Do you think of going?' his mother inquired.

'Well, I should like to, if the lectures are good. I suppose he's a young fellow fresh from college. He may have something to say, and he may be only conceited; there's no knowing. Still, I don't dislike the way he writes. Yes, I think I shall go and have a look at him, at all events.'

Gilbert finished his meal and walked back to the factory. Groups of men were standing about in the sunshine, waiting for the bell to ring; some talked and joked, some amused themselves with horse-play. The narrow street was redolent with oleaginous matter; the clothing of the men was penetrated with the same nauseous odour.

At a little distance from the factory, Ackroyd was

sitting on a door-step, smoking a pipe. Grail took a seat beside him and drew from his pocket the letter he had just received.

'I've got one of them, too,' Luke observed with small show of interest. There was an unaccustomed gloom on his face; he puffed at his pipe rather sullenly.

'Who has told him our names and addresses?' Gilbert asked.

'Bower, no doubt.'

'But how comes Bower to know anything about me?'

'Oh, I've mentioned you sometimes.'

'Well, do you think of going?'

'No, I shan't go. It isn't at all in my line.'

Gilbert became silent.

'Something the matter?' he asked presently, as his companion puffed on in the same gloomy way.

'A bit of a headache, that's all.'

His tone was unusual. Gilbert fixed his eyes on the pavement.

'It's easy enough to see what it means,' Ackroyd continued after a moment, referring to Egremont's invitation. 'We shall be having an election before long, and he's going to stand for Vauxhall. This is one way of making himself known.'

'If I thought that,' said the other, musingly, 'I shouldn't go near the place.'

'What else can it be?'

' I don't know anything about the man, but he may have an idea that he's doing good.'

' If so, *that's* quite enough to prevent me from going. What the devil do I want with his help? Can't I read about English literature for myself!'

' Well, I can't say that I have that feeling. A lecture may be a good deal of use, if the man knows his subject well. But,' he added, smiling, ' I suppose you object to him and his position ?'

' Of course I do. What business has the fellow to have so much time that he doesn't know what to do with it ?'

' He might use it worse, anyhow.'

' I don't know about that. I'd rather he'd get a bad name, then it 'ud be easier to abuse him, and he'd be more good in the end.'

Their eyes met. Gilbert's had a humorous expression, and Ackroyd laughed in an unmirthful way. The factory bell rang; Gilbert rose and waited for the other to accompany him. But Luke, after a struggle to his feet, said suddenly :

' Work be hanged ! I've had enough of it ; I feel Mondayish, as we used to say in Lancashire.'

' Aren't you coming, then ?'

' No, I'll go and get drunk instead.'

' Come on, old man. No good in getting drunk.'

' Maybe I won't ; but I can't go back to work to-day. So long.'

With which vernacular leave-taking, he turned and

strolled away. The bell was clanging its last strokes; Gilbert hurried to the door, and once more merged his humanity in the wage-earning machine.

Two days later, as he sat over his evening meal, Gilbert noticed that his mother had something to say. She cast frequent glances at him; her pursed lips seemed to await an opportune moment.

'Well, mother, what is it?' he said presently, with his wonted look of kindness. By living so long together and in such close intercourse the two had grown skilled in the reading of each other's faces.

'My dear,' she replied, with something of solemnity, 'I was perfectly right. Miss Denny *was* those girls' mother.'

'Nonsense!'

'But there's no doubt about it. I've asked Thyrza. She knows that was her mother's name, and she knows that her mother was a teacher.'

'In that case I've nothing more to say. You're a wonderful old lady, as I've often told you.'

'I have a good memory, Gilbert. You can't think how pleased I am that I found out that. I feel more interest in them than ever. And the child seemed so pleased too! She could scarcely believe that I'd known her mother before she was born. She wants me to tell her and her sister all I can remember. Now, isn't it nice?'

Gilbert smiled, but made no further remark. The evening silence set in.

CHAPTER VII.

THE WORK IN PROGRESS.

On the sheltered side of Eastbourne, just at the springing of the downs as you climb towards Beachy Head, is a spacious and heavy-looking stone house, with pillared porch, oriel windows on the ground floor of the front, and a square turret rising above the fine row of chestnuts which flanks the road. It was built some forty years ago, its only neighbours then being a few rustic cottages; recently there has sprung up a suburb of comely red-brick houses, linking it with the visitors' quarter of Eastbourne. The builder and first proprietor, a gentle-man whose dignity derived from Mark Lane, called the house Odessa Lodge; at his death it passed by purchase into the hands of people to whom this name seemed something more than inappropriate, and the abode was henceforth known as The Chestnuts.

One morning early in November, three months after the date of that letter which he addressed to Gilbert Grail and other working men of Lambeth, our friend Egremont arrived from town at Eastbourne station and was conveyed thence by fly to the house of which I speak. He inquired for Mrs. Ormonde. That lady was not within, but would very shortly return from her morning drive. Egremont followed the servant to the library and prepared to wait.

The room was handsomely furnished and more than passably supplied with books, which inspection showed to be not only such as one expects to find in the library of a country house, but to a great extent works of very modern issue, arguing in their possessor the catholicity of taste which our time encourages. The solid books which form the substratum of every collection were brought together by Mr. Brook Ormonde, in the first instance at his house in Devonshire Square; when failing health compelled him to leave London, the town establishment was broken up, and until his death, three years later, the family resided wholly at The Chestnuts. During those years the library grew appreciably, for the son of the house, Horace Ormonde, had just come forth from the academic curriculum with a vast appetite for literature. His mother, moreover, was of the women who read. Whilst Mr. Ormonde was taking a lingering farewell of the world and its concerns, these two active minds were busy with the fire-new thought of the scientific and humanitarian age. Walter Egremont was then a frequent visitor of the house; he and Horace talked many a summer night into dawn over the problems which nowadays succeed measles and scarlatina as a form of youthful complaint. But Horace Ormonde had even a shorter span of life

before him than his invalid father; he was drowned in
bathing, and it was Egremont who had to take the
news up to The Chestnuts. A few months later, there
was another funeral from the house. Mrs. Ormonde
remained alone.

It was in this room that Egremont had waited for
the mother's coming, that morning when he returned
companionless from the beach. He was then but two-
and-twenty; his task was as terrible as a man can be
called upon to perform. Mrs. Ormonde had the
strength to remember that; she shed no tears, uttered
no lamentations. When, after a few questions, she
was going silently from the room, Walter, his own eyes
blinded, caught her hand and pressed it passionately in
both his own. She was the woman whom he reverenced
above all others, worshipping her with that pure devotion which young men such as he are wont to feel for
some gracious lady much their elder. At that moment
he would have given his own life to the sea could he
by so doing have brought her back the son who would
never return. Such moments do not come often to the
best of us, perhaps in very truth do not repeat themselves. Egremont never entered the library without
having that impulse of uttermost unselfishness brought
back vividly to his thoughts; on that account he liked
the room, and gladly spent a quiet half-hour in it.

In a little less than that Mrs. Ormonde returned
from her breathing of the sea air. At the door she

was told of Egremont's arrival, and with a look of pleased expectancy she went at once to the library.

Egremont rose from the fireside, and advanced with the quiet confidence with which one greets only the dearest friends.

'So the sunshine has brought you,' she said, holding his hand for a moment. 'We had a terrible storm in the night, and the morning is very sweet after it. Had you arrived a very little sooner, you would have been in time to drive with me.'

She was one of those women who have no need to soften their voice when they would express kindness. Her clear and firm, yet sweet, tones uttered with perfection a nature very richly and tenderly endowed; if you had heard her speak the commonest words, herself unseen, you would have known her for what she was. During the past five years she had aged in appearance; the grief which she would not expose had drawn its lines upon her features, and something too of imperfect health was visible there. But her gaze was the same as ever, large, benevolent, intellectual. In her presence Egremont always felt a well-being, a peace of mind, which gave to his own look its pleasantest quality. Of friends she was still, and would ever be, the dearest to him. The thought of her approval was always active with him when he made plans for fruitful work; he could not have come before her with a consciousness of ignoble fault weighing upon his mind.

I have come to see you,' he replied, ' first for your own sake, then to hear news from Ullswater.'

' Let us invert those motives, Walter, and be glad to see each other. Go up into the front drawing-room, will you. I will take off my bonnet and be with you directly.'

She passed upstairs, and he followed more slowly. Behind the first landing was a small conservatory; and there, amid evergreens, sat two children whose appearance would very much have surprised a chance visitor knowing nothing of the house and its mistress. They obviously came from some very poor working-class home; their clothing was of the plainest possible, and. save that they were very clean and in perfect order. they might have been sitting on a doorstep in a London back street. Mrs. Ormonde had thrown a kind word to them in hurrying by; at the sight of Egremont they hushed their renewed talk and turned shamefaced looks to the ground. He went on to the drawing-room, where there was the same comfort and elegance as in the library. Almost immediately Mrs. Ormonde joined him.

' So you want news!' she said, with her own smile, always a little sad, always mingling tenderness with reserve on the firm lips. ' Really, I told you everything essential in my letter. Annabel is in admirable health, both of body and mind. She is deep in Virgil and Dante—what more could you wish her? Her father, I'm sorry to say, is not altogether well. Indeed,

I was guilty of doing my best to get him to London for the winter.'

'Ah! That is something of which your letter made no mention.'

'No, for I didn't succeed. At least, he shook his head very persistently.'

'I heartily wish you had succeeded. Couldn't you get help from Annabel—Miss Newthorpe?'

'Never mind; let it be Annabel between us,' said Mrs. Ormonde, seating herself near the fire. 'I tried to, but she was not fervent. All the same, it is just possible, I think, that they may come. Mr. Newthorpe needs society, however content he may believe himself. Annabel, to my surprise, does really seem independent of such aids. How wonderfully she has grown since I saw her two years ago! No, no, I don't mean physically—though that is also true—but how her mind has grown! Even her letters hadn't quite prepared me for what I found.'

Egremont was leaning on the back of a chair, his hands folded together. He kept silence, and Mrs. Ormonde, with a glance at him, added:

'But she is something less than human at present. Probably that will last for another year or so.'

'Less than human?'

'Abstract, impersonal. With the exception of her father, you were the only living person of whom she voluntarily spoke to me.'

'She spoke of me?'

'Very naturally. Your accounts of Lambeth affairs interest her deeply, though again in rather too —what shall we call it?—too theoretical a way. But that comes of her inexperience.'

'Still she at least speaks of me.'

Mrs. Ormonde could have made a discouraging rejoinder. She said nothing for a moment, her eyes fixed on the fire. Then:

'But now for your own news.'

'What I have is unsatisfactory. A week ago the class suffered a secession. You remember my description of Ackroyd?'

'Ackroyd? The young man of critical aspect.'

'The same. He has now missed two lectures, and I don't think he'll come again.'

'Have you spoken to Bower about him?'

'No. The fact is, my impressions of Bower have continued to grow unfavourable. Plainly, he cares next to nothing for the lectures. There is a curious pomposity about him, too, which grates upon me. I shouldn't have been at all sorry if he had been the seceder; he's bored terribly, I know, yet he naturally feels bound to keep his place. But I'm very sorry that Ackroyd has gone; he has brains, and I wanted to get to know him. I shall not give him up; I must persuade him to come and have a talk with me.'

'What of Mr. Grail?'

'Ah, Grail is faithful. Yes, Grail is the man of them all; that I am sure of. I am going to ask him to stay after the lecture to-morrow. I haven't spoken privately with him yet. But I think I can begin now to establish nearer relations with two or three of them. I have been lecturing for just a couple of months; they ought to know something of me by this time. On the whole, I think I am succeeding. But if there is one of them on whom I found great hopes, it is Grail. The first time I saw him, I knew what a distinction there was between him and the others. He seems to be a friend of Ackroyd's, too; I must try to get at Ackroyd by means of him.'

'Is he—Grail, I mean—a married man?'

'I really don't know. Yet I should think so. I shouldn't be surprised if he were unhappily married. Certainly there is some great trouble in his life. Sometimes he looks terribly worn, quite ill.'

'The idea of an unhappy marriage doesn't quite recommend itself to me. Probably you'll find that is not the case.'

'I hope it isn't; yet he might very well wear that look if he came from a wretched home.'

'And Mr. Bunce?' she asked, with a look of peculiar interest.

'Poor Bunce is also a good deal of a mystery to me. He too always looks more or less miserable, and I'm afraid his interest is not very absorbing. Still, he takes notes, and now and then even puts an intelligent question.'

'He has not attacked you on the subject of religion yet?'

'Oh, no! We still have that question to fight out. But of course I must know him very well before I approach it. I think he bears me goodwill; I caught him looking at me with a curious sort of cordiality the other night. Poor fellow!'

'I must have that little girl of his down again,' Mrs. Ormonde said. 'I wonder whether she still reads that insufferable publication. By-the-by, I found you had told them the story at Ullswater.'

'Yes. It came up *apropos* of my scheme.'

A gong sounded down below.

'Twelve o'clock!' remarked Mrs. Ormonde. 'My birds are going to their dinner—poor little town sparrows! We'll let them get settled, then go and have a peep at them—shall we?'

'Yes, I should like to see them—and,' he added pleasantly, 'to see the look on your face when you watch them.'

'I have much to thank them for, Walter,' she said, earnestly. 'They brighten many an hour when I should be unhappy.'

Presently Mrs. Ormonde led the way downstairs and to the rear of the house. A room formerly devoted to billiards had been converted into a homely but very bright refectory; it was hung round with cheerful pictures, and before each of the two windows stood a large aquarium, full of water-plants and fishes. At the table were seated seven little girls, of ages from eight to thirteen, all poorly clad, yet all looking remarkably joyous and eating with much evidence of appetite. At the head of the table was a woman of middle age and motherly aspect—Mrs. Mapper. She had the superintendence of the convalescents whom the lady of the house received and sent back to their homes in London better physically and morally than they had ever been in their lives before. The children did not notice that Mrs. Ormonde and her companion had entered; they were chatting gaily over their meal. Now and then one of them drew a gentle word of correction from Mrs. Mapper, but on the whole they needed no rebuke. Those who had been longest in the house speedily instructed new arrivals in the behaviour they had learned to deem becoming. A girl waited at table. On that subject Mrs. Ormonde had amusing stories to relate; how more than one servant had regretfully but firmly declined to wait upon little ragamuffins (female, too), and how one in particular had explained that she made no objection to doing it only because she regarded it as a religious penance. 'With that girl,' Mrs. Ormonde was wont to add, 'I at once shook hands, and we soon became the best of friends.'

Egremont had his pleasure in regarding her face, nobly beautiful as she moved her eyes from one to another of her poor little pensioners. She had said at first that it would be impossible ever again to live in this house, when she quitted it for a time after her husband's death. How could she pass through the barren rooms, how dwell within sight and sound of the treacherous waves which had taken her dearest ? It was a royal thought which converted the sad dwelling into a home for those whose reawakening laughter would chide despondency from beneath the roof, whose happiness would ease the heavy heart and make memory a sacred solace. She had her abounding reward, the greathearted one, and such as only the greatly loving may attain to.

They withdrew without having excited attention ; Mrs. Mapper saw them, but Mrs. Ormonde made sign to her to say nothing.

'Two are upstairs, I'm sorry to say,' she remarked as they went back to the drawing-room. 'They have obstinate colds; I keep them under the bed-clothes. The difficulty these poor things have in getting rid of a cold ! With many of them I believe such a condition is chronic ; it goes on, I suppose, until they die of it.'

They talked together till luncheon time. Egremont led the conversation back to Ullswater, where Mrs. Ormonde had just spent a fortnight.

'I think I must go and see them at Christmas,' he said, 'if they don't come south.'

The other considered.

'Don't go so soon,' she said at length. ·

'So soon ? It will be six mortal months.'

'Be advised.'

Egremont sighed and left the subject.

'Tell me what you have been doing of late,' Mrs. Ormonde resumed, 'apart from your lectures.'

'Very little of which any account can be rendered. I read a good deal, and occasionally come across an acquaintance.'

'Have you seen the Tyrrells since they returned ?'

'No. I had an invitation to dine with them the other day, but excused myself.'

'On what grounds ?'

'I mean to see less of people in general.'

Mrs. Ormonde regarded him.

'I hope,' she said, 'that you will pursue no such idea. You mean, of course, that your Lambeth work is to be absorbing. Let it be so, but don't fall into the mistake of making it your burden. You are not one of those who can work in solitude.'

'I am getting a distaste for ordinary society.'

'Then I beg of you to resist the mood. Go into society freely. You are in danger as soon as you begin to neglect it.'

'I, individually ?'

'Yes.' She smiled at the deprecating look he turned on her. 'Let me be your moral physician. Already I notice that you fall short of perfect health : the refusal of that invitation is a symptom. Pray give faith to what I say; if anyone knows you, I think it is I.'

He kept silence. Mrs. Ormonde continued :

'I hear that the Tyrrells have made the acquaintance of Mr. Dalmaine. Paula mentions him in a letter.'

'Ha! With enthusiasm probably ?'

'No. They met him somewhere in Switzerland. He gave them the benefit of his experience on the education question.'

'Of course. Well, I am prejudiced against the man, as you know.'

'He is a force. It looks as if we should hear a good deal of him in the future.'

'Doubtless. The incarnate ideal of British philistinism is sure to have a career before him.'

The lady laughed.

Early in the afternoon Egremont took leave of his friend and returned to London. It was his habit, when in England, to run down to Eastbourne in this way about once a month.

Since the death of his father, his home had been represented by a set of rooms in Great Russell Street. He chose them on account of their proximity to the British Museum; at that time he believed himself destined to produce some monumental work of erudition; the subject had not defined itself, but his thoughts were then busy with the origins of Christianity, and it seemed to him that a study of certain Oriental literatures would be fruitful of results. Characteristically, he must establish himself at the very doors of the great Library. His Oriental researches, as we know, were speedily abandoned, but the rooms in Great Russell Street still kept their tenant. They were far from an ideal abode, indifferently furnished, with draughty doors and smoky chimneys, and the rent was exorbitant; the landlady

who speedily gauged her lodger's character, had already
made a small competency out of him. Even during
long absences abroad Egremont retained the domicile ;
at each return he said to himself that he must really
find quarters at once more reputable and more homelike,
but the thought of removing his books, of dealing with
new people, deterred him from the actual step. In fact,
he was very indifferent as to where or how he lived ;
all he asked was the possibility of privacy. The ugli-
ness of his surroundings did not trouble him, for he
paid no attention to them. Some day he would have a
beautiful home, but what use in thinking of that till he
had someone to share it with him. This was a mere
pied à terre ; it housed his body and left his mind
free.

The real home which he remembered was a house
looking upon Clapham Common. His father dwelt there
for the last fifteen years of his life ; his mother died
there, very shortly after the removal from the small
house in Newington where she went to live upon her
marriage. With much tenderness Egremont thought of
the clear-headed and warm-hearted man whose life-long
toil had made such provision for the son he loved. Un-
educated, homely, narrow enough in much of his thinking, the manufacturer of oil-cloth must have had singular
possibilities in his nature to renew himself in a youth
so apt for modern culture as Walter was ; thinking back
in his maturity, the latter remembered many a noteworthy trait in his father, and wished the old man could

have lived yet a few more years to see his son's work really beginning. Such memories touched him with compassion; to the mind which has enjoyed every advantage of training, there is infinite pathos in the simplicity of a humble parent. And Egremont often felt lonely. Possibly he had relatives living, but he knew of none; in any case they could not now be of real account to him. The country of his birth was far behind him; how far, he had recognised since he began his lecturing in Lambeth. None the less, he at times knew home sickness: not seldom there seemed to be a gap between him and the people born to refinement who were his associates, his friends. That phase of feeling was rather strong in him just now; disguising itself in the form of sundry plausible motives, it had induced him to decline Mrs. Tyrrell's invitation, and was fostering his temporary distaste for the society in which he had always found much pleasure. What if in strictness he belonged to neither sphere? What if his life was to be a struggle between inherited sympathies and the affinities of his intellect? All the better, perchance, for his prospect of usefulness; he stood as a mediator between two sections of society. But for his private happiness, how?

He spent this evening very idly, sometimes pacing his large, uncomfortable room, sometimes endeavouring to read one or other of certain volumes new from the circulating library. Of late he had passed many such evenings, for it was very seldom that anyone came to see

him, and for the amusements of the town he had no
inclination. He was thinking much of Annabel. It
seemed very long since his visit to Ullswater, and, by a
curious freak of mind, he had a difficulty in recalling
the details of his talk with her that morning by the lake.
Endeavouring to repeat her words, he found that they
had become a vague, remote murmur, discouraging to
his emotion. Yet she herself was real enough before his
mind's eye, and the look he saw upon her face was calm,
untouched with shadow of regret. Yes, she was deep
in Virgil and Dante; she spoke of him with interest,
'very naturally.' His heart grew heavy as he pictured
her in the quiet room bending over her books. Worst
of all, he could not imagine her other than calm, intellectual; he could not hear her voice uttering passionate
words. A great change must come over her before
her reserved maidenliness could soften to such sweet
humility.

And he had no faith in his power so to change her.

The next day was Thursday. This and Sunday were
his lecture days; his class met at half-past eight. Precisely at that hour he reached a small doorway in High
Street, Lambeth, and ascended a flight of stairs to a
room which he had furnished as he deemed most suitable.
Several rows of school-desks faced a high desk at which
he stood to lecture. The walls were washed in dis-
temper, the boarding of the floor was uncovered, the
two windows were hidden with plain shutters. The
room had formerly been used for purposes of storage by

a glass and china merchant; below was the workshop of a saddler, which explained the pervading odour of leather. A woman of the neighbourhood had charge of the place; she had it ready and the door open half an hour before lecture time.

A little group of men stood in conversation near the fire; on Egremont's appearance they seated themselves at the desks, each producing a note-book which he laid open before him. Thus ranged they were seen to be eight in number. Out of fourteen to whom invitations were addressed, nine had presented themselves at the preliminary meeting; one, we know, had since proved unfaithful. Egremont looked round for Ackroyd on entering, but the young man was not here.

On the front bench were two men whom as yet you know only by name. Mr. Bower was clearly distinguishable by his personal importance and the ennui, not to be disguised, with which he listened to the opening sentences of the lecture. He leaned against the desk behind him, and carefully sharpened the point of his pencil. He was a large man with a spade-shaped beard; his forehead was narrow, and owed its appearance of height to incipient baldness; his eyes were small and shrewd. He habitually donned his suit of black for these meetings. At the works, where he held a foreman's position, he was in good repute; for years he had proved himself skilful, steady, abundantly respectful to his employers. In private life he enjoyed the fame of a petty capitalist; since his marriage,

thirty years ago, he and his wife had made it the end
of their existence to put by money, with the result that
his obsequiousness when at work was balanced by the
blustering independence of his leisure hours. The man
was a fair instance of the way in which prosperity
affects the average proletarian; all his better qualities
—honesty, perseverance, sobriety—took an ignoble
colour from the essential vulgarity of his nature, which
would never have so offensively declared itself if ill
fortune had kept him anxious about his daily bread.
Formerly Egremont had been impressed by his intelligent manner; closer observation had proved to him of
how little worth this intelligence was, in its subordina-
tion to a paltry character. Bower regarded himself as
the originator of this course of lectures; through all
his obsequiousness it was easy to see that he deemed
his co-operation indispensable to the success of the
project. On sundry occasions he had favoured Egremont
with commendatory remarks after the lecture was over,
and in so doing had proved how incapable he was of
really understanding what he had heard. Recently,
however, he had refrained from private discussion,
partly because he grew wearier of affecting interest,
partly on account of a hurt which his dignity experienced from Egremont's neglect. At first, as was natural,
Egremont had sometimes seemed to address words
specially to him; of late he had purposely avoided
doing so, and Bower began to feel that his services
lacked recognition.

The other, of whom there has been casual mention, was Joseph Bunce. Of spare frame and with hollow cheeks which suggested insufficiency of diet, he yet had far more of manliness in his appearance than the portly Bower. You divined in him independence enough, and of worthier origin than that which secretly inflated his neighbour. His features were at first sight by no means pleasing; their coarseness was undeniable, but familiarity revealed a sensitive significance in the irregular nose, the prominent lips, the small severed chin and long throat. Egremont had now and then caught a light in his eyes which was warranty for more than his rough tongue could shape into words. He often appeared to have a difficulty in following the lecture ; would shrug nervously, and knit his brows and mutter. Whenever he noticed that, Egremont would pause a little and repeat in simpler form what he had been saying, with the satisfactory result that Bunce showed a clearer face and jotted something on his dirty note-book with his stumpy pencil.

Gilbert Grail we know. It was impossible not to remark him as the one who followed with most consecutive understanding, even if his countenance had not declared him of higher grade than any of those among whom he sat. It had needed only the first ten minutes of the first lecture to put him at his ease with regard to Egremont's claims to stand forward as a teacher ; the preliminary meeting, indeed, had removed the suspicions suggested by Ackroyd. To him these evenings were pure enjoyment. He delighted in this subject, and had an inexpressible pleasure in listening continuously to the speech of a cultivated man. Had the note-books of the class been examined (Egremont had strongly advised their use), Gilbert's jottings would probably have alone been found of substantial value, seeing that he alone possessed the mental habit neces-sary for the practice. Bunce's would doubtless have come next, though at a long distance; a Carlylean editor might have disengaged from them many a rudely forcible scrap of comment. Bower's pages would have smelt of the day-book. It was to Grail that Egremont mentally directed the best things he had to say; not seldom he was repaid by the quick gleam of sympathy on that grave interesting face.

The remaining five hearers were average artisans of the inquiring type; they followed with perseverance, though at times one or the other would furtively regard his watch or allow his eyes to stray about the room. They had made a bargain, and were bent on honourably carrying out their share in it. But Egremont already began to doubt whether he was really fixing anything in their thoughts. How were they likely to serve him for the greater purpose whereto this instruction was only preliminary? When he looked forward to that, he had to fix his eyes on Grail and forget the others. He was beginning to regret that the choice of those to whom his invitations were sent had depended upon Bower; another man might have aided him more

effectually. Yet the fact was that Bower's selection
had been a remarkably good one. It would have been
difficult to assemble nine Lambeth workmen of higher
aggregate intellect than those who responded to the
summons; it would have been, on the other hand, the
easiest thing to find nine with not a man of them
available for anything more than futile wrangling over
politics or religion. Egremont would know this some
day; he was yet young in social reform.

And the lectures? It is not too much to say that
they were remarkably good. Egremont had capacity
for teaching; with his education, had he been without
resources, he would probably have chosen an academic
career and have done service in it. There was nothing
deep in his style of narrative and criticism, and here
depth was not wanted; sufficient that he was perspicuous
and energetic. He loved the things of which he spoke,
and he had the power of presenting to others his reason
for loving them. The first lecture had been prepared
with extreme solicitude; his knowledge of the minds he
was about to address was then little more than theoretic,
for he had always in view his own father, who was by
no means the typical working man. The experience
of delivery enabled him to avoid certain errors and
'make points' which formerly he had not had in view.
With ready perception he gauged the mental attitude
of each who sat before him, with quick sympathy he
adapted himself to their requirements. Not one in
five hundred of men inexperienced in such work could

have held the ears of the class as he did for the first
two or three evenings.   It was impossible for them to
mistake his spirit—ardent, disinterested, aspiring ; impossible not to feel something of a respondent impulse.
That familiarity should diminish the effect of his
speech was only to be anticipated.   He was preaching
a religion, but one that could find no acceptance as
such with eight out of nine who heard him.   Common
minds are not kept at high-interest mark for long together by exhibition of the merely beautiful, however
persuasively it be set forth.

He had chosen the Elizabethan period, and he led
up to it by the kind of introduction which he felt
would be necessary.   Trusting himself more after the
first fortnight, he ceased to write out his lectures
verbatim ; free utterance was an advantage to himself
and his audience.   He read at large from his authors ;
to expect the men to do this for themselves—even had
the books been within their reach—would have been
too much, and without such illustration the lectures
were vain.   This reading brought him face to face
with his main difficulty : how to create in men a sense
which they do not possess.   The working man does
not read, in the strict sense of the word ; fiction has
little interest for him, and of poetry he has no com-
prehension whatever ; your artisan of brains can study,
but he cannot read.   Egremont was under no illusion
on this point ; he knew well that the loveliest lyric
would appeal to a man like Bower no otherwise than a

paragraph from the daily newspaper. Was it impossible to bestow this sense of intellectual beauty? With what earnestness he made the endeavour! He took sweet passages of prose and verse, and read them with all the feeling and skill he could command. 'Do you yield to that?' he said within himself as he looked from face to face. 'Are your ears hopelessly sealed, your minds immutably earthen?' Grail—O yes, Grail had the right intelligence in his eyes; but Ackroyd, but Bunce? Ackroyd thought of the meaning of the words; no more. Poor Bunce had darkling throes of mind, but struggled with desperate nervousness and could not be at ease till the straightforward talk began again. And Bower?—Nay, there goes more to this matter than mere enthusiasm in a teacher. Who had instructed Gilbert Grail to discern the grace of the written word? On the other hand, it was doubtful whether Walter Egremont, left to himself in the home of his good plain father, would have felt what now he did. The soil was there, but how much do we not owe to tillage! Read what Egremont on one occasion read to these men:

'He beginneth not with obscure definitions, which must blur the margent with interpretations and load the memory with doubtfulness: but he cometh to you with words set in delightful proportion, either accompanied with or prepared for the well-enchanting skill of music; and with a tale forsooth he cometh unto you —with a tale which holdeth children from play, and old men from the chimney-corner.'

What were *that* to you, save for the light of
memory fed with incense of the poets? Save for
innumerable dear associations, only possible to the instructed, which make the finer part of your intellectual
being. Walter was attempting too much, and soon
became painfully conscious of it.

He came to the dramatists, and human interest
thenceforth helped him. He could read well, and a
scene from those giants of the prime had efficiency
even with Bower. Hope revived in the lecturer.

To-night he was less happy than usual, for what
reason he could not himself understand. His thoughts
wandered, sometimes to Eastbourne, sometimes to
Ullswater; yet he was speaking of Shakespeare. Bower
was more owl-eyed than usual; the five doubtful hearers
obviously felt the time long. Only Grail gave an unfailing ear. Egremont closed with a sense of depression.

Would Bower come and pester him with fatuous
questions and remarks? No; Bower turned away and
reached down his hat from the peg. The doubtful five
took down their hats and followed the portly man from
the room. Bunce was talking with Grail, pointing
with dirty forefinger to something in his dirty note-
book. But he too speedily moved to the hat-pegs.
Grail was also going, when Egremont said:

'Could you spare me five minutes, Mr. Grail; I
should like to speak to you.'

'Certainly, sir,' was the reply.

CHAPTER VIII.

A CLASP OF HANDS.

GRAIL approached the desk with pleasure. Egremont observed it, and met his trusty auditor with the eye-smile which made his face so agreeable.

'I am sorry to see that Mr. Ackroyd no longer sits by you,' he began. 'Has he deserted us?'

Gilbert hesitated, but spoke at length with his natural directness.

'I'm afraid so, sir.'

'He has lost his interest in the subject?'

'It's not exactly the bent of his mind. He only came at my persuasion, to begin with. He takes more to science than literature.'

'Ah, I should have thought that. But I wish he could have still spared me the two hours a week. I felt much interest in him; it's a disappointment to lose him so unexpectedly. I'm sure he has a head for our matters as we'l as for science.'

Grail was about to speak, but checked himself. An inquiring glance persuaded him to say:

'He's much taken up with politics just now. They don't leave the mind very quiet.'

'Politics ? I regret more than ever that he's gone.'

Egremont moved away from the desk at which he had been standing, and seated himself on the end of a bench which came out opposite the fire-place.

'Come and sit down for a minute, will you, Mr Grail ?' he said.

Gilbert silently took possession of the end of the next bench.

'Is there no persuading him back? Do you think he would come and have a talk with me? I do wish he would; I believe we could understand each other. You see him occasionally ?'

'Every day. We work together.'

'Would you ask him to come and have a chat with me here some evening?'

'I shall be glad to, sir.'

'Pray persuade him to. Any evening he likes. Perhaps next Sunday after the lecture would do? Tell him to bring his pipe and have a smoke with me here before the fire.'

Grail smiled, and undertook to deliver the invitation.

'But there are other things I wished to speak of to you,' Egremont continued. 'Do you think it would be any advantage if I brought books for the members of the class to take away and use at their leisure? Shakespeare, of course, you can all lay hands on, but the other Elizabethan authors are not so readily found. For

instance, there's a Marlowe on the desk; would you
care to take him away with you?'

'Thank you very much, sir,' was the reply, 'but I've
got Marlowe. I picked up a second-hand copy a year
or two ago.'

'You have him! Ah, that's good!'

Egremont was surprised, but remembered that it
would not be very courteous to express such feeling.
After surprise came new warmth of interest in the man.
He began to speak of Marlowe with delight, and in a
moment he and Grail were on a footing of intimacy.

'But there are other books perhaps you haven't come
across yet. I shall be overjoyed if you'll let me be of use
to you in that way. Have you access to any library?'

'No, I haven't. I've often felt the want of it.'

Egremont fell into musing for a moment. He
looked up with an idea in his eyes.

'Wouldn't it be an excellent thing if one could
establish a lending library in Lambeth?'

Grail might have excusably replied that it would
be a yet more excellent thing if those disposed to use
such an institution had time granted them to do so ;
but with the young man's keen look fixed upon him, he
had other thoughts.

'It would be a great thing!' he replied, with subdued feeling. He seldom allowed his stronger emotions
to find high utterance; that moderated voice was
symbol of the suppression to which his life had trained
itself.

'A free library,' Egremont went on, 'with a good reading-room. That would be a seed sown, I think.'

It was an extension of his scheme, and delighted him with its prospect of possibilities. It would be preparing the ground upon which he and his adherents might subsequently work. Could he undertake to found a library at his own expense? It was not beyond his means, at all events a beginning on a moderate scale. His eyes sparkled, as they always did when a thought burst blossom-like within him.

'Mr. Grail, I have a mind to try if I can't work on that idea.'

Gilbert was stirred. This interchange of words had strengthened his personal liking for Egremont, and his own idealism took fire from that of the other. He regarded the young man with admiration and with noble envy. To be able to devise such things and straightway say 'It shall be done!' How blest beyond all utterance was the man to whom fortune had given such power! Gilbert often dreamed of the possibilities which lay in wealth, and marvelled that there was not oftener found some possessor of riches whose soul inspired him to great deeds. Here at length one such was before him. He reverenced Egremont profoundly. It was the man's nature to worship, to bend with singleness of heart before whatsoever seemed to him high and beautiful.

He had no words ready, but simply looked into Egremont's face with a quiet smile.

'Yes,' the latter continued, 'I will think it out.
We might begin with a moderate supply of books; we
might find some building that would do at first; a real
library could be built when the people had begun to
appreciate what was offered them. Better, no doubt,
if they would tax themselves for the purpose, but they
have burdens enough.'

'They won't give a farthing towards a library,' said
Grail, 'until they know its value; and that they can't
do until they have learnt it from books.'

'True. We'll break the circle.'

He pondered again, then added cheerfully:

'I say *we*. I mean you and the others who come
to my lecture. I want, if possible, to make this class
permanent, to make it the beginning of a society for
purposes I have in my mind. I must tell you something of this, for I know you will feel with me, Mr.
Grail.'

The reply was again the look of quiet trust.
Egremont had not thought to get so far as this to-
night, but Grail's personality wrought upon him, even
as his on Grail. He felt a desire to open his mind, as
he had done that evening in the garden by Ullswater.
This man was of those whom he would benefit, but, if
he mistook not, far unlike the crowd; Grail could
understand as few of his class could be expected to.

'To form a society, a club, let us say. Not at all
like the ordinary clubs. There are plenty of places
where men can meet to talk about what ought to be

done for the working class; my idea is to bring the working class to talk of what it can do for itself. And not how it can claim its material rights, how to get better wages, shorter hours, more decent homes. With all those demands I sympathise as thoroughly as any man; but those things are coming, and it seems to me that it's time to ask what working men are going to do with such advantages what they've got them. Now, my hope is to get a few men to see—what you, I know, see clearly enough—that life, to be worthy of the name, must be first and foremost concerned with the things of the heart and mind. Yet everything in our time favours the opposite. The struggle for existence is so hard that we grow more and more material: the tendency is to regard it as the end of life to make money. If there's time to think of higher things, well and good; if not, it doesn't matter much. Well, we have to earn money; it is a necessary evil; but let us think as little about it as we may. Our social state, in short, has converted the means of life into its end.'

He paused, and Gilbert looked hearty agreement.

'That puts into a sentence,' he said, 'what I have thought through many an hour of work.'

'Well, now, we know there's no lack of schemes for reforming society. Most of them seek to change its spirit by change of institutions. But surely it is plain enough that reform of institutions can only come as the natural result of a change in men's minds. Those who preach revolution to the disinherited masses give no thought to this. It's a hard and a bad thing to live under an oppressive system; don't think that I speak lightly of the miseries which must drive many a man to frenzy, till he heeds nothing so long as the present curse is attacked. I know perfectly well that for thousands of the poorest there is no possibility of a life guided by thought and feeling of a higher kind until they are lifted out of the mire. But if one faces the question with a grave purpose of doing good that will endure, practical considerations must outweigh one's anger. There is no way of lifting those poor people out of the mire; if their children's children tread on firm ground it will be the most we can hope for. But there *is* a class of working people that can and should aim at a state of mind far above that which now contents them. It is my view that our only hope of social progress lies in the possibility of this class being stirred to effort. The tendency of their present educa- tion—a misapplication of the word—must be counter- acted. They must be taught to value supremely quite other attainments than those which help them to earn higher wages. Well, there is my thought. I wish to communicate it to men who have a care for more than food and clothing, and who will exert themselves to influence those about them.'

Grail gazed at the fire, the earnest words wrought in him.

'If that were possible!' he murmured.

'Tell me,' the other resumed, quickly; 'how many

of the serious people whom you know in Lambeth ever
go to a place of worship ? '

Gilbert turned his eyes inquiringly, suspiciously.
Was Egremont about to preach a pietistic revival?

' I have very few acquaintances,' he answered, ' but
I know that religion has no hold upon intelligent working men in London.'

' That is the admission I wanted. For good or for
evil, it has passed ; no one will ever restore it. And
yet it is a religious spirit that we must seek to revive.
Dogma will no longer help us. Pure love of moral and
intellectual beauty must take its place.'

Gilbert smiled at a thought which came to him.

' The working man's Bible,' he said, ' is his Sunday
newspaper.'

' An arrow in the white ! The newspaper is the
very voice of all that is worst in our civilisation.
If ever there is in one column a pretence of higher
teaching, it is made laughable by the base tendency of
all the rest. The newspaper has supplanted the book ;
every gross-minded scribbler who gets a square inch of
space in the morning journal has a more respectful
hearing than Shakespeare. These writers are tradesmen,
and with all their power they cry up the spirit of trade.
Till the influence of the newspaper declines—the newspaper as we now know it – our state will grow worse.'

Grail was silent. Egremont had worked himself
to a fervour which showed itself in his unsteady hands
and tremulous lips.

' I had not meant to speak of this yet,' he continued.
' I hoped to surround myself with a few friends who
would gradually get to know my views, and perhaps
think they were worth something. I have obeyed an
impulse in opening my mind to you; I feel that you
think with me. Will you join me as a friend, and work
on with me for the founding of such a society as I have
described?'

' I will, Mr. Egremont,' was the clear-voiced answer.

Walter put forth his hand, and it was grasped
firmly. In this moment he was equal to his ambition,
unwavering, exalted, the pure idealist. Grail, too,
forgot his private troubles, and tasted the strong air of
the heights which it is granted us so seldom and for
so brief a season to tread. There was almost colour
in his cheeks, and his deep-set eyes had a light as of
dawn.

' We have much yet to talk of,' said Egremont, as
he rose, ' but it gets late and I mustn't keep you longer.
Will you come here some evening when there is no
lecture and let us turn over our ideas together? I
shall begin at once to think of the library. It will
make a centre for us, won't it? And remember Ackroyd. You are intimate with him?

' We think very differently of many things,' said
Grail, ' but I like him. We work together.'

' We mustn't lose him. He has the bright look of
a man who could do much if he were really moved.
Persuade him to come and see me on Sunday night.'

They shook hands again, and Grail took his departure. Egremont still stood for a few minutes before the fire; then he extinguished the gas, locked the door behind him, and went forth into the street singing to himself.

Gilbert turned into Paradise Street, which was close at hand. He had decided to call and ask for Ackroyd on his way home. The latter had not been at work that day, and was perhaps ailing; for some time he had seemed out of sorts. Intercourse between them was not as constant as formerly. Grail explained this as due to Ackroyd's disturbed mood, another result of which was seen in his ceasing to attend the lecture; yet in Gilbert also there was something which tended to weaken the intimacy. He knew well enough what this was, and strove against it, but not with great success.

Ackroyd lived with his married sister, who let half her house to lodgers. When Gilbert knocked at the door, it was she who opened. Mrs. Poole was a buxom young woman with a complexion which suggested continual activity within range of the kitchen fire; her sleeves were always rolled up to her elbow, and at whatever moment surprised she wore an apron which seemed just washed and ironed. She knew not weariness, nor discomfort, nor discontent, and her flow of words suggested a safety valve letting off superfluous energy.

'That Mr. Grail?' she said, peering out into the

darkness. 'You've come to look after that great good-for-nothing of a brother of mine, I'll be bound! Come downstairs, and I'll tell him you're here. You may well wonder what's become of him. Ill! Not he. indeed! No more ill than I am. It's only his laziness. He wants a good shaking, that's about the truth of it, Mr. Grail.'

She led him down into the kitchen. A low clothes-horse, covered with fresh-smelling, gently-steaming linen, stood before a great glowing fire. A baby lay awake in a swinging cot just under the protruding leaf of the table, and a little girl of three was sitting in night-dress and shawl on a stool in a warm corner.

'Yes, you may well stare,' resumed Mrs. Poole, noticing Grail's glance at the children. 'A quarter past ten and neither one of 'em shut an eye yet, nor won't do till their father comes home, not if it's twelve o'clock. You dare to laugh, Miss!' she cried to the little one on the stool, with mock wrath. 'The idea of having to fetch you out o' bed just for peace and quietness. And that young man there'—she pointed to the cradle; 'there's about as much sleep in him as there is in that eight-day clock! You rascal, you!'

Like her brother, she had the northern accent still lingering in her speech; it suited with her brisk, hearty ways. Whilst speaking, she had partly moved the horse from the fire and placed a round-backed chair for the visitor in a position which would have answered tolerably had she meant to roast him.

'He's in the sulks, that's what he is,' she continued, returning to the subject of Luke. 'I suppose you know all about it, Mr. Grail?'

Gilbert seated himself, and Mrs. Poole, pretending to arrange the linen, stood just before him, with a sly smile.

'I'm not sure that I do,' he replied, avoiding her look.

She lowered her voice.

'The idea of a great lad going on like he does! Why, it's the young lady that lives in your house—Miss Trent, you know. I don't know her myself; no doubt she's wonderful pretty and all the rest of it, but I'm that sick and tired of hearing about her! My husband's out a great deal at night, of course, and Luke comes and sits here hours by the clock, just where you are, right in my way. I don't mean *you're* in my way; I'm talking of times when I'm busy. Well, there he sits; and sometimes he'll be that low it's enough to make a body strangle herself with her apron-string. Other times he'll talk, talk, talk: and it's all Thyrza Trent, Thyrza Trent, till the name makes my ears jingle. This afternoon I couldn't put up with it, so I told him he was a great big baby to go on as he does. Then we had some snappy words, and he went off to his bedroom and wouldn't have any tea. But really and truly, I don't know what 'll come to him. He says he'll take to drinking, and he does a deal too much o' that as it is. And to think of him losing days from his work! Now do just tell him not to be a fool, Mr. Grail.'

With difficulty Gilbert found an opportunity to put in a word.

'But is there something wrong between them?' he asked with a forced smile.

'Wrong? Why, doesn't he talk about it to you?'

'No. I used to hear just a word or two, but there's been no mention of her for a long time.'

'You may think yourself lucky then, that's all *I* can say. Why, she wouldn't have anything to say to him. And I don't see what he's got to complain of; he admits she told him from the first she didn't care a bit for him. As if there wasn't plenty of other lasses! Luke was always such a softy about 'em; but I never knew him have such a turn as this. I'll just go and tell him you're here.'

'Perhaps he's gone to bed.'

'Not he. He sits in the cold half the night, just to make people sorry for him. He doesn't get much pity from me, the silly fellow.'

She ran up the stairs. Grail, as soon as she was gone, fell into a reverie. It did not seem a pleasant one; his face darkened almost to sternness.

In a few minutes Mrs. Poole was heard returning; behind her came a heavier foot. Ackroyd followed his sister into the kitchen. He certainly looked far from well, but had assumed a gay air, which he exaggerated.

'Come to see if I've hanged myself, old man?

Not quite so bad as that yet. I've had the toothache and the headache and Lord knows what. Now I feel hungry; we'll have some supper together. Give me a jug, Maggie, and I'll get some beer.'

'You sit down,' she replied. 'I'll run out and fetch it.'

'Why, what's the good of a jug like that!' he roared, watching her. 'Here's Grail never sits down to less than a pot, and a gallon or so won't be a drop too much for me. Take two jugs, Maggie.'

'Don't get any beer for me, Mrs. Poole,' put in Gilbert. 'I can't stop more than five minutes, and there'll be supper waiting when I get home.'

'You do as I tell you, lass,' cried Ackroyd. 'Bring all you can carry.'

He flung himself on a chair and stretched his legs.

'Been to the lecture?' he asked, as his sister left the room.

'Yes,' Gilbert replied, his wonted quietness contrasting with the other's noise. 'Mr. Egremont's been asking me about you. He's very disappointed that you've left him.'

'Can't help it. I held out as long as I could. It isn't my line. Besides, nothing's my line just now. So you had a talk with him, eh?'

'Yes, a talk I shan't forget. There are not many men like Mr. Egremont.'

Gilbert had it on his lips to speak of the library project, but a doubt as to whether he might not be betraying confidence checked him.

'He wants you to go and see him at the lecture-room,' he continued, 'either on Sunday after the lecture, or any evening that suits you. Will you go?'

Luke shook his head.

'No. What's the good?'

'I wish you would, Ackroyd,' said Gilbert, bending forward and speaking with earnestness. 'You'd be glad of it afterwards. He said I was to ask you to go and have a smoke with him by the fire; you needn't be afraid of a sermon, you see. Besides, you know he isn't that kind of man.'

'No, I shan't go, old man,' returned the other, with resolution. 'I liked his lectures well enough, as far as they went, but they're not the kind of thing to suit me nowadays. If I go and talk to him, I'm bound to go to the lectures. What's the good? What's the good of anything?'

Gilbert became silent. The little girl on the stool, who had been moving restlessly, suddenly said:

'Uncle, take me on your lap.'

'Why, of course I will, little un!' Luke replied with a sudden affectionateness one would not have expected of him. 'Give me a kiss. Who's that sitting there, eh?'

'Dono.'

'Nonsense! Say: Mr. Grail.'

In the midst of this, Mrs. Poole reappeared with the jug foaming.

'Oh, indeed ! So *that's* where you are!' she exclaimed with her vivacious emphasis, looking at the
child. 'A nice thing for you to be nursed at this hour
o' night!—Now just one glass, Mr Grail. It's a bitter
night ; just a glass to walk on.'

Gilbert pleased her by drinking what she offered.
Ackroyd had recommenced his uproarious mirthfulness.

' I wish you could persuade your brother to go to
the lectures again, Mrs. Poole,' said Gilbert. 'He
misses a great deal.'

' And he'll miss a good deal more,' she replied, 'if
he doesn't soon come to his senses. Nay, it's no good
o' me talking ! He used to be a sensible lad—that is,
he could be if he liked.'

Gilbert gave his hand for leave-taking.

' I still hope you'll go on Sunday night,' he said,
seriously.

Ackroyd shook his head again, then tossed the
child into the air and began singing. He did not offer
to accompany Grail up to the door.

CHAPTER IX.

A GOLDEN PROSPECT.

It wanted a week to Christmas. For many days the weather had been as bad as it can be even in London. Windows glimmered at noon with the sickly ray of gas or lamp; the roads were trodden into viscid foulness; all night the droppings of a pestilent rain were doleful upon the roof, and only the change from a black to a yellow sky told that the sun was risen. No wonder Thyrza was ailing.

It was nothing serious. The inevitable cold had clung to her and become feverish; it was necessary for her to stay at home for a day or two. Lydia made her hours of work as short as possible, hastening to get back to her sister. But fortunately there was a friend always at hand; Mrs. Grail could not have been more anxious about a child of her own. Her tendance was of the kind which inspires trust; Lydia, always fretting herself into the extreme of nervousness if her dear one lost for a day the wonted health, was thankful she had not to depend on Mrs. Jarmey's offices.

Thyrza had spent a day in bed, but could now sit

by the fire; her chair came from the Grails' parlour,
and was the very one which had always seemed to her
so comfortable. Her wish that Lyddy should sit in it
had at length been gratified.

It was seven o'clock on Friday evening. The table
was drawn near to Thyrza's chair, and Thyrza was
engaged in counting out silver coins, which she took
from a capacious old purse. Lydia leaned on the table,
opposite.

' Twenty-four, twenty-five, twenty-six! I'm sure I
saw a very nice overcoat marked twenty-five shillings,
not long ago.'

Lydia mused for a moment; then she said:

' I don't like to spend it, Thyrza.'

Her sister looked up in uttermost astonishment.

' What *do* you mean, Lyddy? Don't like to spend
it? Why, what have we saved it up for, then?'

' Are you sure you feel better, dear?' the other
asked, earnestly.

' Is that what you're thinking about? I've a good
mind to go out myself and buy the coat. I would this
minute, if I thought you were going to trouble about me
in that way. Why, I'm quite well; I only pretend,
just because I like to be made much of. You'll have
to get a cold next, Lyddy, and sit here all day: and
Mrs. Grail and me 'll make you that comfortable as
never was.'

Lydia allowed herself to be reassured. She said
presently:

'But we can't buy the coat without knowing grandad's measure.'

'Oh, but you know it near enough, I think.'

'Near enough! But I want it to look nice. I wonder whether I could take a measure without him knowing it? If I could manage to get behind him and just measure across the shoulders, I think that 'ud do.'

Thyrza laughed.

'Go now. He's sure to be sitting with the Bowers. Take the tape and try.'

'No, I'll take a bit of string; then he wouldn't think anything if he saw it.'

Lydia put on her hat and jacket.

'I'll be back as soon as ever I can. Play with the money like a good baby. You're sure you're quite warm?

Thyrza was wrapped in a large shawl, which hooded over her head. Lydia had taken incredible pains to stop every possible draught at door and window. A cheerful fire threw its glow upon the invalid's face.

'I'm like a toast. Just look up at the shop next to Mrs. Isaac's, Lyddy. There was a sort of brownish coat, with laps over the pockets; it was hanging just by the door. We must get a few more shillings if it makes all the difference, mustn't we?'

'We'll see. Good-bye, Blue-eyes.'

Lydia went her way. For a wonder, there was no fog to-night, but the street lamps glistened on wet pavements, and vehicles as they rattled along sent mud-volleys to either side. In passing through Lambeth Walk, Lydia stopped at the clothing shop of which Thyrza had spoken. The particular brownish coat had seemingly been carried off by a purchaser, but she was glad to notice one or two second-hand garments of very respectable appearance which came within the sum at her command. She passed on into Paradise Street and entered Mrs. Bower's shop.

In the parlour the portly Mr. Bower stood with his back to the fire; he was speaking oracularly, and, at Lydia's entrance, looked up with some annoyance at being interrupted. Mr. Boddy sat in his accustomed corner. Mrs. Bower, arrayed in the grandeur suitable to a winter evening, was condescending to sew.

'Mary out?' Lydia asked, as she looked round.

'Yes, my dear,' replied Mrs. Bower, with a sigh of resignation. 'She's at a prayer meetin', as per us'l. That's the third night this blessed week. I 'old with goin' to chapel, but like everything else it ought to be done in moderation. Mary's gettin' beyond everything. I don't believe in makin' such a fuss o' religion; you can be religious in your mind without sayin' prayers an' singin' 'ymns all the week long. There's the Sunday for that, an' I can't see as it's pleasin' to God neither to do so much of it at other times. Now suppose I give somebody credit in the shop, on the understandin' as they come an' pay their bill once a week reg'lar; do you think I should like to have 'em lookin' in two or three times every day an' cryin' out: "Oh, Mrs. Bower, ma'am,

I don't forget as I owe you so and so much; be sure I
shall come an' pay on Saturday!'" If they did that, I
should precious soon begin to think there was something
wrong, else they'd 'old their tongues an' leave it to be
understood as they was honest. Why, an' it's every bit
the same with religion!'

Mr. Boddy listened gravely to this, and had the air
of probing the suggested analogy. He had a bad cold,
poor old man, and for the moment it made him look as
if he indulged too freely in ardent beverages; his nose
was extremely red and his eyes were very watery.

'How's the little un, my dear?' he asked, as Lydia
took a seat by him.

'Oh, she's much better, grandad. Mrs. Grail is so
kind to her, you wouldn't believe. She'll be all right
again by Monday, I think.'

'Mrs. Grail's kind to her, is she?' remarked Mr.
Bower. 'Why, you're getting great friends with the
Grails, Miss Lydia.'

'Yes, we really are.'

'And do you see much of Grail himself?'

'No, not much. We sometimes have tea with them
both.'

'Ah, you do? He's a very decent, quiet fellow, is
Grail. I dare say he tells you something about Egremont now and then?'

Mr. Bower put the question in a casual way; in
truth, it was designed to elicit information which he
much desired. He knew that for some time Grail had

been on a new footing with the lecturer, that the two often remained together after the class had dispersed; it was a privilege which he regarded disapprovingly, because it lessened his own dignity in the eyes of the other men. He wondered what the subject of these private conversations might be; there had seemed to him something of mystery in Grail's manner when he was plied with a friendly inquiry or two.

'I've heard him speak of the lectures,' said Lydia. 'He says he enjoys them very much.'

'To be sure. Yes, they're very fair lectures, very fair, in their way. I don't know as I've cared quite so much for 'em lately as I did at first. I've felt he was falling off a little. I gave him a hint a few weeks ago, just told him in a quiet way as I thought he was going too far into things that weren't very interesting, but he didn't seem quite to see it. It's always the way with young men of his kind; when you give them a bit of advice, it makes them obstinate. Well, he'll see when he begins again after Christmas. Thomas and Linwood are giving it up, and I shall be rather surprised if Johnson holds out for another course.'

'But I suppose you'll go, Mr. Bower?' said Lydia.

Bower stuck his forefingers into his waistcoat pockets, held his head as one who muses, clicked with his tongue.

'I shall see,' he replied, with a judicial air. 'I don't like to give the young feller up. You see, I may say as it was me put him on the idea. We had a lot of talk about one thing and another one day at the works, and a hint of mine set him off. I should like to make the lectures successful; I believe they're a good thing, if they are properly carried out. I'm a believer in education. It's the educated men as get on in the world. Teach a man to use his brains and he'll soon be worth double wages. But Egremont must keep up to the mark if he's to have my support. I shall have to have a word or two with him before he begins again. By-the-by, I passed him in Kennington Road just now: I wonder what he's doing about here at this time. Been to the works, perhaps.'

Whilst the portly man thus delivered himself, Lydia let her arm rest on Mr. Boddy's shoulder. It was a caress which he sometimes received from her; he looked round at her affectionately, then continued to pay attention to the weighty words which fell from Mr. Bower. Mrs. Bower, who was less impressed by her husband's utterances, bent over her sewing. In this way Lydia was able craftily to secure the measurement she needed. And having got this, she was anxious to be back with Thyrza.

'I suppose it's no use waiting for Mary,' she said, rising.

'I don't suppose she'll be back not before nine o'clock,' Mrs. Bower replied. 'Did you want her partic'lar?'

'Oh no, it'll do any time.'

'Whilst I think of it,' said Mrs. Bower, letting her

sewing fall upon her lap and settling the upper part of her stout body in an attitude of dignity; 'you and your sister 'll come an' eat your Christmas dinner with us?'

Lydia cast down her eyes.

'It's very kind of you, Mrs. Bower, but I'm sure I don't know whether Thyrza 'll be well enough. I must be very careful of her for a time.'

'Well, well, you'll see. It'll only be a quiet little fam'ly dinner this year. You'll know there's places kep' for you.'

Lydia again expressed her thanks, then took leave. As she left the shop, she heard Mr. Bower's voice again raised in impressive oratory.

On entering the house in Walnut Tree Walk, she found Mrs. Grail just descending the stairs. The old lady never spoke above her breath at such casual meetings outside her own door.

'Come in for a minute,' she whispered.

Lydia followed her into the parlour. Gilbert was settled for the evening at the table. A volume lent by Egremont lay before him, and he was making notes from it. At Lydia's entrance he rose and spoke a word, then resumed his reading.

'I've just taken Thyrza a little morsel of jelly I made this afternoon,' Mrs. Grail said, apart to the girl. 'I'm sure she looks better to-night.'

'How good you are, Mrs. Grail! Yes, she does look better, but I couldn't have believed a day or two 'ud have made her so weak. I shan't let her go out before Christmas.'

'No, I don't think you ought, my dear.'

As Mrs. Grail spoke, the knocker of the house-door sounded an unusual summons, a rat-tat, not loud indeed, but distinct from the knocks wont to be heard here.

'Mr. and Mrs. Jarmey are both out,' said Lydia. 'They're gone to the theatre. Perhaps it's for you, Mrs. Grail?'

'No, that's not at all likely.'

'I'll go.'

Lydia opened. A gentleman stood without; he inquired in a pleasant voice if Mr. Grail was at home.

'I think so,' Lydia said. 'Will you please wait a minute?'

She hurried back to the parlour.

'It's a gentleman wants to see Mr. Grail,' she whispered, with the momentary excitement which any little out-of-the-way occurrence produces in those who live a life void of surprises. And she glanced at Gilbert, who had heard what she said. He rose.

'I wonder whether it's Mr. Egremont! Thank you, Miss Trent; I'll go to the door.'

Lydia escaped up the stairs. Gilbert went out into the passage, and his surmise was confirmed. Egremont was there, sheltering himself under an umbrella from rain which was once more beginning to fall.

'Could I have a word with you?' he said, with

friendly freedom. 'I should have written, but I had
to pass so near——'

'I'm very glad. Will you come in?'

It was the first time that Egremont had been at
the house. Gilbert conducted him into the parlour,
and took from him his hat and umbrella.

'This is my mother,' he said. 'Mr. Egremont,
mother; you'll be glad to see him.'

The old lady regarded Walter with courteous
curiosity, and bowed to him. A few friendly words
were exchanged, then Egremont said to Grail:

'If you hadn't been in, I should have left a message, asking you to meet me to-morrow afternoon.'

Mrs. Grail was about to leave the room; Egremont
begged her to remain.

'It's only a piece of news concerning our library
scheme. I think I've found a building that will suit
us. Do you know a school in Brook Street, connected
with a Wesleyan Chapel somewhere about here?'

Gilbert said that he knew it; his mother also
murmured recognition.

'It'll be to let at the end of next quarter: they're
building themselves a larger place. I heard about it
this afternoon, and as I was told that evening classes
are held there, I thought I'd come and have a look at
the place to-night. At last it is something like what
we want. Could you meet me there, say at three,
to-morrow afternoon, so that we could see it together
in daylight—if daylight be granted us?'

Grail expressed his readiness.

'You were reading,' Walter went on, with a glance at the table. 'I mustn't waste your time.'

He rose, but Gilbert said:

'I should be glad if you could stay a few minutes. Perhaps you haven't time?'

'O yes. What are you busy with?'

Half an hour's talk followed, of course mainly of books. Egremont looked over the volumes on the shelves; those who love such topics will know how readily gossip spun itself from that centre. He was pleased with Grail's home; it was very much as he had liked to picture it since he had known that Gilbert lived with his mother. Mrs. Grail sat and listened to all that was said, a placid smile on her smooth face. At length Egremont declared that he was consuming his friend's evening.

'Perhaps you'll let me come some other night?' he said, as he took up his hat. 'I know very few people indeed who care to talk of these things in the way I like.'

Gilbert came back from the door with a look of pleasure.

'Now, isn't he a fine fellow, mother? I'm so glad you've seen him.'

'He seems a very pleasant young man indeed,' Mrs. Grail replied. 'He's not quite the picture I'd made of him, but his way of speaking makes you like him from the very first.'

' I never heard him say a word yet that didn't sound genuine,' Gilbert added. ' He speaks what he thinks, and you won't find many men who make you feel that. And he has a mind ; I wish you could hear one of his lectures ; he speaks in just the same easy running way, and constantly says things one would be glad to re-member. They don't understand him, Bower, and Bunce, and the others ; they don't *feel* his words as they ought to. I'm afraid he'll only have two or three when he begins again.'

' That's a pity, when he tries so hard to teach them.'

' What do you think Ackroyd said the other day ? " I can't see that it's much to talk of," he said. " Let him give back all the money he's got out of the men that work for him, and I'll think he means to be honest." That's Ackroyd's latest idea. I can't quite make out whether he believes what he says.'

' Well, I suppose the library will cost a good deal of money,' suggested the old lady.

' To be sure it will ; perhaps Ackroyd will see some-thing to be satisfied with at last. There'll be a heavy rent for the building, and there's no knowing how much he'll have to lay out in books. Then he'll have to engage a librarian—an educated man who no doubt 'll require a large salary ; assistants too, I dare say, as the library gets known. He is rich, no doubt, but how many rich men are willing to spend their money in that way ? '

'Mr. Ackroyd seems to have had a prejudice from the first, Gilbert.'

'I don't think it's a personal prejudice. The poor fellow has got into the wrong road ; he hears such a lot of nonsense at that club of his, and he makes it a point to see nothing good in any man who employs labour.'

Mrs. Grail turned presently to a different topic.

'Would you believe, Gilbert!' she murmured. 'Those two girls have saved up more than a pound to buy that poor old Mr. Boddy a top-coat for Christmas. When I went up with the jelly, Thyrza had the money out on the table ; she told me as a great secret what it was for. Kind-hearted things they are, both of them.'

Gilbert assented silently. His mother seldom elicited a word from him on the subject of the sisters.

On the following afternoon, Gilbert and Egremont met at the appointed place just as three was striking. Already night had begun to close in, a sad wind moaned about the streets, and the cold grey of the sky was patched about with dim shifting black clouds. Egremont was full of cheeriness as he shook hands.

'What a wonderful people we are,' he exclaimed, 'to have developed even so much civilisation in a climate such as this!'

The school building which they were about to inspect stood at the junction of two streets, which consisted chiefly of dwellings. In the nature of things it was ugly. Three steps led up to the narrow entrance,

N 2

which, as well as the windows on the ground floor, was surrounded with a wholly inappropriate pointed arch. Iron railings ran along the two sides which abutted upon pavements, and by the door was a tall iron support for a lamp; probably it had never been put to its use. There was only one upper storey, and the roof was crowned with a small stack of hideous metal chimneys.

'We must go round to the caretaker's house,' said Egremont, when they had cast their eyes over the face of the edifice.

The way was by a narrow passage between the school itself and the whitewashed side of an adjacent house; this led them into a small paved yard, upon which looked the windows of the caretaker's dwelling, which was the rear portion of the school building. A knock at the door brought a very dirty and very asthmatical old woman, who appeared to resent their visit. When Egremont expressed his desire to go over the school, she muttered querulously what was understood to be an invitation to enter. Followed by Gilbert, Egremont was conducted along a pitch-dark passage.

'Mind the steps!' snarled their guide.

Egremont had already stumbled over an ascent of two when the warning was given, but at the same moment a door was thrown open, giving a view of the main schoolroom.

''Tain't swep' out yet,' remarked the old woman. I couldn't tell as nobody was a-comin'. You can complain to them if you like; I'm used to it from all sorts, an' 'taint for much longer, praise goodness! Though there's nothink before me but the parish when the time does come.'

Egremont glanced at the strange creature in surprise, but it seemed better to say nothing. He began to speak of the aspects of the room with his companion.

The place was cheerless beyond description. In a large grate the last embers of a fire were darkening; the air was chill, and, looking up to the ceiling, one saw floating scraps of mist which had somehow come in from the street. The lower half of each window was guarded with lattice-work of thin wire; the windows themselves were grimy, and would have made it dusk within even on a clear day. The whitewash of the ceiling was dark and much cracked. Benches and desks covered half the floor. There were black-boards and other mechanical appliances for teaching, and on the walls hung maps and diagrams.

'The walls seem quite dry,' observed Walter, 'which is a great point.'

They laid their palms against the plaster. The old woman stood with one hand pressed against her bosom, the other behind her back; her head was bent; she seemed to pay no kind of attention to what was said.

'There's room here for some thousands of volumes,' Egremont said, moving to one of the windows. 'It will serve tolerably as a reading-room, too. Nothing like as large as it ought to be, of course, but we must be content to feel our way to better things.'

Gilbert nodded. In spite of his companion's resolute cheerfulness, he felt a distressing dejection creep upon him as he stood in the cold, darkening room. He could not feel the interest and hope which hitherto this project had inspired him with. The figure of the old caretaker impressed him painfully. For any movement she made she might have been asleep; the regular sound of her heavy breathing was quite audible, and vapour rose from her lips upon the air.

'What do you think?' Egremont asked, when Grail remained mute.

'I should think it will do very well. What is there upstairs?'

'Two class-rooms. We should use those for lectures. Let us go up.'

The old woman walked before them to a door opposite that by which they had entered. They found themselves in a small vestibule, out of which, on one hand, a door led into a cloak-room, while on the other ascended a flight of stone stairs. There was nothing noticeable in the rooms above; the windows here were also very dirty, and mist floated below the ceilings.

The caretaker had remained below, contenting herself with indicating the way.

'You seem disappointed,' Walter said. He himself had ceased to talk, he felt cold and uncomfortable.

'No, no, indeed I'm not,' Grail hastened to reply. 'I think it is as good a place as you could have found.'

'We don't see it under very inspiriting conditions.

Fire and light and comfortable furniture would make a wonderful difference, even on a day like this.'

Gilbert reproached himself for taking so coldly his friend's generous zeal.

'And books still more,' he replied. 'The room below will be a grand sight with shelves all round the walls.'

'Well, I must make further inquiries, but I think the place will suit us.'

They descended, their footsteps ringing on the stone and echoing up to the roof. The old woman still stood at the foot of the stairs, her head bent, the hand against her side.

'Will you go out here,' she asked, ' or do you want to see anythink else ? '

' I should like to see the back part again,' Egremont replied.

She led them across the schoolroom, through the dark passage, and into a small room which had the distant semblance of a parlour. Here she lit a lamp, then, without speaking, guided them over the house, of which she appeared to be the only inhabitant. There were seven rooms; only three of them contained any furniture. Then they all returned to the comfortless parlour.

' Your chest is bad,' Egremont remarked, looking curiously at the woman.

' Yes, I dessay it is,' was the ungracious reply.

' Well, I don't think we need trouble you any more

at present, but I shall probably have to come again in
a day or two.'

'I dessay you'll find me here.'

'And feeling better, I hope. The weather gives
you much trouble, no doubt.'

He held half a crown to her. She regarded it,
clasped it in the hand which was against her bosom,
and at length dropped a curtsey, though without
speaking.

'What a poor crabbed old creature!' Egremont
exclaimed, as they walked away. 'I should feel positively relieved if I knew that she went off at once to
the warmth of the public-house opposite.'

'Yes, she hasn't a very cheerful home.'

'Oh, but it can be made a very different house.
It has fallen into such neglect. Wait till spring sunshine and the paperhangers invade the place.'

They issued into a main street, and, after a little
further talk, shook hands and parted.

That night, and through the Sunday that followed,
Gilbert continued to suffer even more than his wont
from mental dreariness. The cold gloom of the future
library seemed to cling about him still; he had to
make constant demands upon reason to avoid thinking
despondently of the undertaking. On Sunday afternoon, Mr. Jarmey's concertina was more irritating and
depressing than ever. He could not fix his attention
upon a book, and Mrs. Grail was unable to draw him
into conversation.

About four o'clock she said :

' May I ask Lydia and Thyrza to come and have tea with us, Gilbert ? '

He looked up absently.

' But they were here last Sunday, mother.'

' Yes, my dear, but I think they like to come, and I'm sure I like to have them.'

' Let us leave it till next Sunday, mother. You don't mind ? I feel I must be alone to-night.'

It was a most unusual thing for Gilbert to offer opposition when his mother had expressed a desire for anything. Mrs. Grail at once said :

' I dare say you're right, my dear. Next Sunday 'll be better.'

The next morning he went to his work through a fog so dense that it was with difficulty he followed the familiar way. Lamps were mere lurid blotches in the foul air, perceptible only when close at hand ; the foot-fall of invisible men and women hurrying to factories made a muffled, ghastly sound ; harsh bells summoned through the darkness, the voice of pitiless taskmasters to whom all was indifferent save the hour of toil. Gilbert was racked with headache. Bodily suffering made him as void of intellectual desire as the meanest labourer then going forth to earn bread ; he longed for nothing more than to lie down and lose consciousness of the burden of life.

Then came Christmas Eve. The weather had changed ; to-night there was frost in the air, and the

light of stars made a shimmer upon the black vault.
Gilbert always gave this season to companionship with
his mother. About seven o'clock they were talking
quietly together of memories light and grave, of Gilbert's
boyhood, of his sister who was dead, of his father who
was dead. Then came a pause, whilst both were silently
busy with the irrecoverable past.

Mrs. Grail broke the silence to say :

' You're a lonely man, Gilbert.'

' Why no, not lonely, mother. I might be, but for
you.'

' Yes, you're lonely, my dear. It's poor company
that I can give you. I should like to see you with a
happier look on your face before I die.'

Gilbert had no reply ready.

' You think too poorly of yourself,' his mother resumed, ' and you always have done. But there's people
have a better judgment of you. Haven't you thought
that somebody looks always very pleased when you read
or talk, and sits very quiet when you've nothing to say,
and always says good-night to you so prettily ? '

' Mother, mother, don't speak like that ! I've thought
nothing of the kind. Put that out of your head ; never
speak of it again.'

His voice was not untender, but very grave. The
lines of his face hardened. Mrs. Grail glanced at him
timidly, and became mute.

A loud double knock told that the postman had
delivered a letter at the house. Whilst the two still

sat in silence Mrs. Jarmey tapped at their door and said :

'A letter for you, Mr. Grail.'

'From Mr. Egremont,' said Gilbert, as he resumed his seat and opened the envelope. 'More about the library, I expect.'

He read to himself.

'My dear Grail,—I have decided to take the school building on a lease of seven years, after again carefully examining it and finding it still to my mind. It will be free at the end of March. By that time I hope to have sketched out something of a rudimentary catalogue, and before summer the library should be open.

'I asked you to come and look over this place with me because I had a project in my mind with reference to the library which concerns yourself. I lay it before you in a letter, that you may think it over quietly and reply at your leisure. I wish to offer you the position of librarian : I am sure I could not find anyone better suited for the post, and certainly there is no man whom I should like so well to see occupying it. I propose that the salary be one hundred and fifty pounds a year, with free tenancy of the dwelling-house at present so dolorously occupied—I am sure it can be made a comfortable abode—and of course, gas and fuel. I should make arrangements for the necessary cleaning, &c., with some person of the neighbourhood ; your own duties would be solely those of librarian and reading-room superintendent.

'The library should be open, I think, from ten to ten, for I want to lose no possibility of usefulness. If one loafer be tempted to come in and read, the day's object is gained. These hours are of course too long for you alone ; I would provide you with an assistant, so that you could assure for yourself, let us say, four hours free out of the twelve. But details would be easily arranged between us. By-the-by, Sunday must *not* be a day of closing ; to make it so would be to deprive ourselves of the greatest opportunity. Your freedom for one entire day in the week should be guaranteed.

'I offer this because I should like to have you working with me, and because I believe that such work would be more to your taste than that in which you are now occupied. It would, moreover, leave you a good deal of time for study ; we are not likely to be overwhelmed with readers and borrowers during the daytime. But you will consider the proposal precisely as you would do if it came from a stranger, and will accept or reject it as you see fit.

'I leave town to-day for about a week. Will you write to me at the end of that time ?—Always yours, my dear Grail,

'WALTER EGREMONT.'

Mrs. Grail showed no curiosity about the letter ; the subject of the interrupted conversation held her musing. When Gilbert had folded the sheets, and, in the manner of one who receives few letters, returned it to its envelope, he said :

'Yes, it's about the library. He's taken the house for seven years.'

His mother murmured an expression of interest. For another minute the clock on the mantelpiece ticked loud; then Gilbert rose, and without saying anything, went out.

He entered his bedroom. The darkness was complete, but he moved with the certainty of habit to a chair by the head of the bed, and there seated himself. Presently he felt a painful surging in his throat, then a gush of warm tears forced its way to his eyes. It cost him a great effort to resist the tendency to sob aloud. He was hot and cold alternately, and trembled as though a fever were coming upon him.

In a quarter of an hour he lit the candle, and, after a glance at himself in the glass, bathed his face. Then he took down his overcoat from the door, and put it on. His hat too he took, and went to the parlour.

'I have to go out, mother,' he said, standing at the door. 'I'll be back by supper-time.'

'Very well, my dear,' was the quiet reply.

He walked out to the edge of the pavement, and stood a moment, as if in doubt as to his direction. Then he looked at the upper windows of the house, as we saw him do one night half a year ago. There was a light this time in the sisters' room.

He turned towards Lambeth Walk. The market of Christmas Eve was flaring and clamorous; the

odours of burning naphtha and fried fish were pungent
on the wind. He walked a short distance among the
crowd, then found the noise oppressive and turned into
a by-way. As he did so, a street organ began to play
in front of a public-house close by. Grail drew near;
there were children forming a dance, and he stood to
watch them.

Do you know that music of the obscure ways, to
which children dance? Not if you have only heard it
ground to your ears' affliction beneath your windows
in the square. To hear it aright you must stand in
the darkness of such a by-street as this, and for the
moment be at one with those who dwell around, in the
blear-eyed houses, in the dim burrows of poverty, in
the unmapped haunts of the semi-human. Then you
will know the significance of that vulgar clanging of
melody; a pathos of which you did not dream will
touch you, and therein the secret of hidden London
will be half revealed. The life of men who toil
without hope, yet with the hunger of an unshaped
desire; of women in whom the sweetness of their sex
is perishing under labour and misery; the laugh, the
song of the girl who strives to enjoy her year or two
of youthful vigour, knowing the darkness of the years
to come; the careless defiance of the youth who feels
his blood and revolts against the lot which would tame
it; all that is purely human in these darkened multi-
tudes speaks to you as you listen. It is the half-
conscious striving of a nature which knows not what

it would attain, which deforms a true thought by gross expression, which clutches at the beautiful and soils it with foul hands.

The children were dirty and ragged, several of them bare-footed, nearly all bare-headed, but they danced with noisy merriment. One there was, a little girl, on crutches; incapable of taking a partner, she stumped round and round, circling upon the pavement, till giddiness came upon her and she had to fall back and lean against the wall, laughing aloud at her weakness. Gilbert stepped up to her, and put a penny into her hand, then, before she had recovered from her surprise, passed onwards.

He came out at length by Lambeth parish church, which looks upon the river; the bells were ringing a harsh peal of four notes, unchangingly repeated. Thence he went forward on to Lambeth Bridge.

Unsightliest of all bridges crossing Thames, the red hue of its iron superstructure, which in daylight only enhances the meanness of its appearance, at night invests it with a certain grim severity; the archway, with its bolted metal plates, its wire-woven cables, over-glimmered with the yellowness of the gas-lamps which it supports, might be the entrance to some fastness of ignoble misery. The road is narrow, and after nightfall has but little traffic.

Gilbert walked as far as the middle of the bridge, then leaned upon the parapet and looked northwards. The tide was running out: it swept darkly onwards to

the span of Westminster Bridge, whose crescent of
lights it repeated in long unsteady rays. Along the
base of the Houses of Parliament the few sparse lamps
contrasted with the line of brightness on the Embankment opposite. The Houses themselves rose grandly
in obscure magnitude; the clock-tower beaconed with
two red circles against the black sky, the greater tower
stood night-clad, between them were the dim pinnacles,
multiplied in shadowy grace. Farther away Gilbert
could just discern a low, grey shape, that resting-place
of poets and of kings which to look upon filled his heart
with worship.

In front of the Embankment, a few yards out into
the stream, was moored a string of barges; between
them and the shore the reflected lamp-light made one
unbroken breadth of radiance, blackening the mid-
current. From that the eye rose to St. Thomas's
Hospital, spreading block after block, its windows
telling of the manifold woe within. Nearer was the
Archbishop's Palace, dark, lifeless; the roofs were
defined against a sky made lurid by the streets of
Lambeth. On the pier below signalled two crimson
lights.

The church bells kept up their clangorous discord,
softened at times by the wind. A steamboat came
fretting up the stream; when it had passed under the
bridge, its spreading track caught the reflected gleams
and flung them away to die on unsearchable depths.
Then issued from beneath a barge with set sail, making

way with wind and tide; in silence it moved onwards, its sail dark and ghastly, till the further bridge swallowed it.

The bells ceased. Gilbert bent his head and listened to the rush of the water, voiceful, mysterious, as though it whispered secrets. Sometimes he had stood there and wished that the dread tide could whelm him. His mood was far other now; some power he did not understand had brought him here as to the place where he could best realise this great joy that had befallen him.

But the wind blew piercingly, and when at length he moved from the parapet, he found that his arms were quite numb; doubtless he had stood longer than he thought. Instead of returning by the direct way, he walked along the Embankment. It was all but deserted; the tread of a policeman echoed from the distance. But in spite of the bitter sky, two people were sitting together on one of the benches, a young man and a work-girl; they were speaking scarcely above a whisper. Gilbert averted his face as he passed them, and for the moment his eyes had their pain-stricken look.

Issuing into Westminster Bridge Road, he found himself once more amid a throng. And before he had gone far he recognised a figure that walked just ahead of him. It was Ackroyd; he was accompanied by a girl of whom Gilbert had no knowledge—Miss Totty Nancarrow. They were talking in a merry, careless

way ; Ackroyd smoked a cigar, and Totty walked with
her usual independence, with that swaying of the
haunches and swing of the hands with palm turned
outwards which is characteristic of the London work-
girl.   Her laugh now and then rose to a high note ;
her companion threw back his head and joined in the
mirth.   Clearly Ackroyd was in a way to recover his
spirits.

At the junction of two ways they stopped.   Gilbert
stopped too, for he did not care to pass them and be
recognised.   He crossed the road, and from the other
side watched them as they stood talking.   Now they
were taking leave of each other.   Ackroyd appeared
to hold the girl's hand longer than she liked ; when she
struggled to get away, he suddenly bent forward and
snatched a kiss.   With a gesture of indignation she
escaped from him.

Gilbert had a desire to join Ackroyd, now that the
latter was alone.   But as he began to recross the
street, the young man moved on and turned into a
public-house.   Gilbert again stopped, and, disregarding
the crowds about him, lost himself in thought.   He
determined at length to go his way.

Mrs. Grail had supper ready, with some mince pies
of her own making.

'Each lot I make,' she said, as they sat down, 'I say
to myself they'll be the last.'

'No, no, mother ; we shall eat a good many together yet,' Gilbert replied, cheerily.   The wind had

brought a touch of colour to his cheeks and made his eyes glisten.

'Have you taken any upstairs?' he asked presently.

'No, my dear. Do you think I may?'

'Oh, I should think so.'

The old lady looked at him and grew thoughtful.

There was no work to rise to on the morrow. With a clear conscience Gilbert could sit on into the still hours which were so precious to him. And again, before going to rest, he stepped quietly from the house to look at the upper windows.

CHAPTER X.

TEMPTING FORTUNE.

THYRZA continued to be far from well. The day-long darkness encouraged her natural tendency to sad dreaming. When alone, in Lydia's absence at the work-room, she sometimes had fits of weeping; it was a relief to shed tears. She could have given no explanation of the sufferings which found this outlet; her heart lay under a cold weight, that was all she knew. Her being was repressed and struggled darkly with the forces which constrained it. With her sister she could often win an hour of cheerfulness, but it was paid for in headaches and dejection.

Lydia pursued her course with the usual method and contentment, yet, in these days just before Christmas, with a perceptible falling off in the animation which was the note of her character. Perhaps she too was affected by the weather; perhaps she was anxious about Thyrza; one would have said, however, that she had some trouble distinct from these. For Lydia to sit down with sewing and straightway forget it in an absence which cast shadow upon her face, was something so unlike her that Thyrza, observing it one evening, asked anxiously what was the matter. Lydia confessed a headache; but headaches did not affect her in that way.

On Christmas Eve she ran round to Paradise Street to make arrangements for the next day. Evidently it would not be wise for Thyrza to leave home; that being the case, it was decided that Mr. Boddy should come and have tea with the girls in their own room. Lydia talked over these things with Mary in the kitchen below the shop, where odours of Christmas fare were already rife. The parlour was full of noisy people, amid whom Mr. Bower was holding weighty discourse; the friends had gone below for privacy.

'So I shall keep the coat till he comes,' Lydia said. 'I know Thyrza would like to see his poor old face when he puts it on. And you might come round yourself, Mary, just for an hour.'

'I'll see if I can.'

'I suppose you'll have people at night?'

'I don't know, I'm sure. I'd much rather come and sit with you, but mother may want me.'

Lydia asked:

'Has Mr. Ackroyd been here lately?'

'I haven't seen him. I hope not.'

'Why do you say that, Mary?' asked Lydia, impatiently.

'I only say what I think, dear.'

Lydia for once succeeded in choosing wiser silence.

But that look which had no place upon her fair, open countenance came for a moment, a passing darkness which might be forecast of unhappy things.

At four o'clock on the following afternoon—this Christmas fell on a Friday—everything was ready in Walnut Tree Walk for Mr. Boddy's arrival. The overcoat, purchased by Lydia, after a vast amount of comparing and selecting, of deciding and rejecting and redeciding, was carefully hidden, to be produced at a suitable moment. The bitter coldness of the day gladdened the girls now that they knew the old man would go away well wrapped up. This coat had furnished a subject for many an hour of talk between them, and now as they waited they amused themselves with anticipation of what Mr. Boddy would say, what he would think, how joyfully he would throw aside that one overcoat he did possess, a garment really too far gone and with no pretence of warmth in it. Thyrza introduced a note of sadness by asking:

'What'll happen, Lyddy, if he gets that he can't earn anything?'

'I sometimes think of that,' Lydia replied gravely. 'We couldn't expect the Bowers to keep him there if he couldn't pay his rent. But I always hope that we shall be able to find what he needs. It isn't much, poor grandad! And you see we can always manage to save something, Thyrza.'

'But it wouldn't be enough—nothing like enough for a room and meals, Lyddy.'

'Oh, we shall find a way! Perhaps'—she laughed
—'we shall have more money some day.'

Two rings at the bell on the lower landing announced their visitor's arrival. Lydia ran downstairs
and returned with the old man, whose face was very red
from the raw air. He had a muffler wrapped about his
neck, but the veteran overcoat was left behind, for the
simple reason that Mr. Boddy felt he looked more
respectable without it. His threadbare black suit had
been subjected to vigorous brushing, with a little exercise of the needle here and there. A pair of woollen
gloves, long kept for occasions of ceremony, were the
most substantial article of clothing that he wore. A
baize bag, of which Lydia had relieved him, contained
his violin.

'I thought you'd maybe like a little music, my dear,'
he said as he kissed Thyrza. 'It's cheerin' when you don't
feel quite the thing. I doubt you can't sing though.'

'Oh, the cold's all gone,' replied Thyrza. 'We'll
see after tea.'

They made much of him, and it must have been
very sweet to the poor old fellow to be so affectionately
tended by these whom he loved as his own children.
When Lydia began to lay the table, she showed him a
plate of mince pies.

'Mrs. Grail brought us up these this morning,' she
said. 'There never was anything like her kindness
since Thyrza's been poorly. She wanted us to go and
have dinner with them.'

'And why didn't you?' asked Mr. Boddy. 'It would 'a been more like a Christmas to you.'

'We didn't like, grandad. If it had been Mrs. Grail alone, perhaps we might; but there's Mr. Grail, too, and we thought we might be in his way.'

'Why, what's he got to do, my dear?'

'Oh, I don't mean he's busy, but—well, we've thought he's been very quiet with us the last few times; haven't we, Thyrza?'

'I think it's only his way,' the younger sister remarked. 'He scarcely ever talks. He did one night to me, a long time ago: he told me all about Westminster Abbey; but he's always been quiet since then.'

'I don't know as I ever saw him,' said Mr. Boddy, 'but I've heard he's a worthy man.'

'Oh, we like him very much,' said Thyrza, anxious not to be misunderstood. 'It's natural enough if he doesn't want to be disturbed when he's at home. He told me that he was always troubling because he couldn't get enough time for reading. I feel a little sorry for him; he always looks unhappy. Doesn't he, Lyddy?'

Simple, cheerful chat sustained itself through teatime. Mary Bower was mentioned, and Lydia asked:

'Did she tell tales about me behaving badly in chapel last Sunday?'

'Not that I've heard, my dear,' replied Mr. Boddy.

'She must have noticed it, though she didn't say

anything. There was somebody just behind us, singing
—well, you can't think! I never heard such a squealy
voice in my life. I was in that terror lest I should
begin to laugh; I quite shook every now and then. I
know Mary saw me.'

'You oughtn't to go to chapel at all, Lyddy,' said
Thyrza, reprovingly.

'But I didn't mean any harm, dear. And it was
such a shocking squeal. I'm sure *you'd* have laughed!'

Mary herself came not long after tea, then Mr.
Boddy took out his violin from the bag and played all
the favourite old tunes, those which brought back their
childhood to the two girls. To please Mary, Lydia
asked for a hymn-tune, one she had grown fond of in
chapel. Mary began to sing it, so Lydia got her hymn-
book, and asked Thyrza to sing with them. The air
was a sweet one, and Thyrza's voice gave it touching
beauty as she sang soft and low. Other hymns followed;
Mary Bower fell into her gentler mood and showed how
pleasant she could be when nothing irritated her
susceptibilities. The hours passed quickly to nine
o'clock, then Mary said it was time for her to go.

'Do you want to stay a little longer, Mr. Boddy,'
she said, 'or will you go home with me?'

'I'd rather walk home in good company than alone,
Miss Mary,' he replied. 'I call it walking, but it's only
a stump-stump.'

'But it would be worse if you couldn't walk at all,'
Mary said.

'Right, my dear, as you always are. I've no call to grumble. It's a bad habit as grows on me, I fear. If Lyddy 'ud only tell me of it, both together you might do me good. But Lyddy treats me like a spoilt child. It's her old way.'

'Mary shall take us both in hand,' said Lydia. 'She shall cure me of my sharp temper and you of grumbling, grandad; and I know which 'll be the hardest job!'

Laughing with kindly mirth, the old man drew on his woollen gloves and took up his hat and the violin-bag. Then he offered to say good-bye.

'But you're forgetting your top-coat, grandad,' said Lydia.

'I didn't come in it, my dear.'

'What's that, then? I'm sure *we* don't wear such things.'

She pointed to a chair, on which Thyrza had just artfully spread the gift. Mr. Boddy looked in a puzzled way; had he really come in his coat and forgotten it? He drew nearer.

'That's no coat o' mine, Lyddy,' he said.

Thyrza broke into a laugh.

'Why, whose is it, then?' she exclaimed. 'Don't play tricks, grandad; put it on at once!'

'Now come, come; you're keeping Mary waiting,' said Lydia, catching up the coat and holding it ready.

Then Mr. Boddy understood. He looked from Lydia to Thyrza with dimmed eyes.

'I've a good mind never to speak to either of you again,' he said in a tremulous voice. 'As if you hadn't need enough of your money! Lyddy, Lyddy! And you're as bad, Thyrza; a grown up woman like you, you ought to teach your sister better. Why there; it's no good; I don't know what to say to you. Now what do you think of this, Mary?'

Lydia still held up the coat, and at length persuaded the old man to don it. The effect upon his appearance was remarkable; conscious of it, he held himself more upright and stumped to the little square of looking-glass to try and regard himself. Here he furtively brushed a hand over his eyes.

'I'm ready, Mary, my dear; I'm ready! It's no good saying anything to girls like these. Good-bye, Lyddy; good-bye, Thyrza. May you have a many happy Christmas, children! This isn't the first as you've made a happy one for me.'

Lydia went down to the door and watched the two till they were lost in darkness. Then she returned to her sister with a sigh of gladness. For the moment she had no trouble of her own.

Upon days of festival, kept in howsoever quiet and pure a spirit, there of necessity follows depression; all mirth is unnatural to the reflective mind, and even the unconscious suffer a mysterious penalty when they have wrested one whole day from fate. On the Saturday Lydia had no work to go to, and the hours dragged. In the course of the morning she went out to make

some purchases.　She was passing Mrs. Bower's without
intention of entering, when Mary appeared in the doorway and beckoned her.　Mrs. Bower was out; Mary
had been left in charge of the shop.

'You were asking me about Mr. Ackroyd,' she said,
when they had gone into the parlour.　'Would you
like to know something I heard about him last night?'

Lydia knew that it was something disagreeable;
Mary's air of discharging a duty sufficiently proved
that.

'What is it?' she asked, coldly.

'They were talking about him here when I came
back last night.　He's begun to go about with that
girl Totty Nancarrow.'

Lydia cast down her eyes.　Mary keeping silence,
she said:

'Well, what if he has?'

'I think it's right you should know, on Thyrza's
account.'

'Thyrza has nothing to do with Mr. Ackroyd; you
know that, Mary.'

'But there's something else.　He's begun to drink,
Lydia.　Mr. Raggles saw him in a public-house somewhere last night, and he was quite tipsy.'

Lydia said nothing.　She held a market bag before
her, and her white knuckles proved how tightly she
clutched the handles.

'You remember what I once said,' Mary continued.
There was absolutely no malice in her tone, but mere

satisfaction in proving that the premises whence her conclusions had been drawn were undeniably sound. She was actuated neither by personal dislike of Ackroyd nor by jealousy ; but she could not resist this temptation of illustrating her principles by such a noteworthy instance. ' Now wasn't I right, Lydia ? '

Lydia looked up with hot cheeks.

' I don't believe it ! ' she said vehemently. ' Who's Mr. Raggles ? How do you know he tells the truth ? —And what is it to me, whether it's true or not ? '

' You were so sure that it made no difference what any one believed, Lydia,' said the other with calm persistency.

' And I say the same still, and I always will say it ! You're *glad* when anybody speaks against Mr. Ackroyd, and you'd believe them, whatever they said. I'll never go to chapel again with you, Mary, as long as I live ! You're unkind, and it's your chapel-going that makes you so ! You'd no business to call me in to tell me things of this kind. After to-day, please don't mention Mr. Ackroyd's name ; you know nothing at all about him.'

Without waiting for a reply she left the parlour and went on her way. Mary was rather pale, but she felt convinced of the truth of what she had reported, and she had done her plain duty in drawing the lesson. Whether Lydia would acknowledge that seemed doubtful. The outburst of anger confirmed Mary in strange suspicions which had for some time lurked in her mind.

The sisters had perhaps never spent so dull a day together as this. Thyrza spoke but a few sentences all the afternoon; Lydia was sewing by the window or pretending to do so, also silent. Just after tea Thyrza said:

'Will you do something very kind for me, Lyddy?'

'What, dear?'

'Will you take a note to Totty Nancarrow's? I should like to see her, and she might come whilst you're at chapel to-morrow.'

'I don't like her to come here, Thyrza,' the sister said, with a sudden change of voice.

'I'm sure I don't see why she shouldn't, Lyddy.'

'You'll be able to go out soon. If you must see her, I'm sure you can wait till then.'

To Lydia's surprise, Thyrza answered nothing, and refrained from conversation for a long time. It was growing dusk, and Lydia even at the window could scarcely see to ply her needle. She bent her head lower, and a few tears fell upon her work.

On Sunday evening she dressed as if to go to chapel, and left the house at the usual hour. She had heard nothing from Mary Bower, and her resentment was yet warm. She did not like to tell Thyrza what had happened, but went out to spend the time as best she could.

Almost as soon as her sister was gone Thyrza paid a little attention to her dress and went downstairs. She

knocked at the Grails' parlour; it was Gilbert's voice
that answered.

'Isn't Mrs. Grail in?' she asked timidly, looking
about the room.

'Yes, she's in, Miss Trent, but she doesn't feel very
well. She went to lie down after tea.'

'Oh, I'm sorry.'

She hesitated, just within the door.

'Would you like to go to her room?' Gilbert
asked.

'Perhaps she's asleep; I mustn't disturb her.
Would you lend me another book, Mr. Grail?'

'Oh, yes! Will you come and choose one?'

She closed the door and went forward to the bookcase, on her way glancing at Gilbert's face, to see
whether he was annoyed at her disturbing him. It was
scarcely that, yet unmistakably his countenance was
troubled. This made Thyrza nervous; she did not
look at him again for a few moments, but carried her
eyes along the shelves. Poor little one, the titles
were no help to her. Gilbert knew that well enough,
but he was watching her by stealth and forgot to
speak.

'What do you think would do for me, Mr. Grail?'
she said at length. 'It mustn't be anything very hard,
you know.'

Saying that, she met his eyes. There was a smile
in them, and one so reassuring, so—she knew not what—
that she was tempted to add:

'You know best what I want. I shall trust you.'

Something shook the man from head to foot. The words which came from him were involuntary; he heard them as if another had spoken.

'You trust me? You believe that I would do my best to please you?'

Thyrza felt a strangeness in his words, but replied to them with a frank smile:

'I think so, Mr. Grail.'

He was holding his hand to her; mechanically she gave hers. But in the doing it she became frightened; his face had altered, it was as if he suffered a horrible pain. Then she heard:

'Will you trust your life to me, Thyrza?'

It was like a flash, dazzling her brain. Never in her idlest moment had she strayed into a thought of this. He had always seemed to her comparatively an old man, and his gravity would in itself have prevented her from viewing him as a possible suitor. He seemed so buried in his books; he was so unlike the men who had troubled her with attentions hitherto. Yet he held her hand, and surely his words could have but one meaning.

Gilbert saw how disconcerted, how almost shocked, she was.

'I didn't mean to say that at once,' he continued hurriedly, releasing her hand. 'I've been too hasty. You didn't expect that. It isn't fair to you. Will you sit down?

He still spoke without guidance of his tongue. He was impelled by a vast tenderness; the startled look on her face made him reproach himself; he sought to soothe her, and was incoherent, awkward. As if in implicit obedience, she moved to a chair. He stood gazing at her, and the love which had at length burst from the dark depths seized upon all his being.

'Mr. Grail——'

She began, but her voice failed. She looked at him, and he was smitten to the heart to see that there were tears in her eyes.

'If it gives you pain,' he said in a low voice, drawing near to her, 'forget that I said anything. I wouldn't for my life make you feel unhappy.'

Thyrza smiled through her tears. She saw how gentle his expression had become; his voice touched her. The reverence which she had always felt for him grew warmer under his gaze, till it was almost the affection of a child for a father.

'But should I be the right kind of wife for you, Mr. Grail?' she asked, with a strange simplicity and diffidence. 'I know so little.'

'Can you think of being my wife?' he said, in tones that shook with restrained emotion. 'I am so much older than you, but you are the first for whom I have ever felt love. And'—here he tried to smile—'it is very sure that I shall love you as long as I live.'

Her breast heaved; she held out both her hands to him and said quickly:

'Yes, I will marry you, Mr. Grail. I will try my best to be a good wife to you.'

He stood as if doubting. Both her hands were together in his; he searched her blue eyes, and their depths rendered to him a sweetness and purity before which his heart bowed in worship. Then he leaned forward and kissed her forehead.

Thyrza reddened and kept her eyes down.

'May I go now?' she said, when, after kissing her hands, he had released them at the first feeling that they were being drawn away.

'If you wish to, Thyrza.'

'I'll stay if you like, Mr. Grail, but—I think——'

She had risen. The warmth would not pass from her cheeks, and the sensation prevented her from looking up; she desired to escape and be alone.

'Will you come down and speak to mother in the morning?' Gilbert said, relieving her from the necessity of adding more. 'She will have something to tell you.'

'Yes, I'll come. Good-night, Mr. Grail.'

Both had forgotten the book that was to have been selected. Thyrza gave her hand as she always did when taking leave of him, save that she could not meet his eyes. He held it a little longer than usual, then saw her turn and leave the room hurriedly.

An hour later, Mrs. Grail came into the parlour. She did not wish to disturb her son, and took a seat by the fire. Gilbert, after turning a page, asked:

'Your head better, mother?'

'Yes, my dear. I've dozed a little.'

'Do you feel able to read a letter?'

She took her spectacles from the mantel-piece. Gilbert drew from its envelope and handed to her the letter he had received from Egremont on Christmas Eve. She read it, and turned round to him with astonishment.

'Why didn't you tell me this, child? Well now, if I didn't *think* there was something that night! Have you answered? Oh no, you're not to answer for a week.'

'What's your advice?'

'Eh, how that reminds me of your father!' the old lady exclaimed. 'I've heard him speak just with that voice and that look many a time. Well, well, my dear, it's only waiting, you see; something comes soon or late to those that deserve it. I'm glad I've lived to see this, Gilbert.'

He said, when they had talked of it for a few minutes:

'Will you show this to Thyrza to-morrow morning?'

She fixed her eyes on him, over the top of her spectacles, keenly.

'To be sure I will. Yes, yes, of course I will.'

'She's been here for a few minutes since tea. I told her if she'd come down in the morning you'd have something to tell her.'

'She's been here? But why didn't you call me? I must go up and speak.'

'Not to-night, mother. It was better that you weren't here. I had something to say to her—something I wanted to say before she heard of this. Now she has a right to know.'

Lydia returned shortly after eight o'clock. She had walked about aimlessly for an hour and a half, avoiding the places where she was likely to meet anyone she knew. She was chilled and wretched. Thyrza could not but observe this at the first glance.

'How cold you look, Lyddy!' she said, coming forward in a mood much changed from that in which her sister had left her. 'What's the matter with you? Have you come straight from chapel?'

'There's a bitter wind,' Lydia answered, moving away and kneeling before the fire.

'But your cheeks are like lumps of ice! Poor old Lyddy! Feel how warm mine are.'

She pressed her face against her sister's, kneeling by her, and her arms about her. Lydia turned with a little laugh.

'Why are you so fond of me all at once? You've scarcely spoken a word to me all day.'

'But you haven't spoken to me, neither. We've both of us been very sulky, haven't we? Won't you tell me what you've been thinking about?'

'There's nothing to tell, dear.'

'But I'm sure there is. Lyddy, I always tell you my secrets, but you won't tell me yours.'

Lydia continued to warm her hands; as the fire softened them, she kept putting first one, then the other, against her cheeks. She made no reply; Thyrza rose and stood looking down at her.

'That means you confess there *is* a secret, but you won't tell it.'

'Oh, Thyrza, what are you talking about secrets!' Lydia exclaimed impatiently. 'What nonsense!'

Thyrza said nothing more till her sister, having taken off her hat and jacket, had sat down in evident weariness. Then she knelt by her side again.

'When did you see Mr. Ackroyd last?' she inquired.

'I'm sure I don't know,' was the reply. 'I passed him in the Walk about a week ago.'

'But, I mean, when did you speak to him?'

'Oh, not for a long time,' said Lydia, smoothing the hair upon her forehead. 'Why?'

'He seems to have forgotten all about me, Lyddy.

The other looked down into the speaker's face with eyes that were almost startled.

'Why do you say that, dear?'

'Do you think he has?'

'He may have done,' replied Lydia, averting her eyes. 'I don't know. You said you wanted him to, Thyrza.'

'Yes, I did—in that way. But I asked him to be

friends with us. I don't see why he should keep away from us altogether.'

' But it's only what you had to expect,' said Lydia, rather coldly. In a moment, however, she had altered her voice to add: ' He couldn't be friends with us in the way you mean, dear. Have you been thinking about him ? '

She showed some anxiety.

' Yes,' said Thyrza, ' I often think about him—but not because I'm sorry for what I did. I shall never be sorry for that. Shall I tell you why? It's something you'd never guess if you tried all night. You could no more guess it than you could—I don't know what ! '

Lydia looked inquiringly.

' Put your arm round me and have a nice face. As soon as you'd gone to chapel, I thought I'd go down and ask Mr. Grail to lend me a book. I went and knocked at the door, and Mr. Grail was there alone. And he asked me to come and choose a book, and we began to talk, and—Lyddy, he asked me if I'd be his wife.'

Lydia's astonishment was for the instant little less than that which had fallen upon Thyrza when she felt her hand in Grail's. Her larger experience, however, speedily brought her to the right point of view; in less time than it would have taken her to express surprise, her wits had arranged a number of little incidents which remained in her memory, and had reviewed them all in the light of this disclosure. This was the

meaning of Mr. Grail's reticence, of his apparent coldness at times. Surely she was very dull never to have
surmised it. Yet he was so much older than Thyrza;
he was so confirmed a student; no, she had never sus-
pected this feeling.

All this in a flash of consciousness, whilst she pressed
her sister closer to her side. Then:

'And what did you say, dear?'

'I said I would, Lyddy.'

The elder sister became very grave. She bit first
her lower, then her upper lip.

'You said that at once, Thyrza?'

'Yes. I felt I must.'

'You felt you must?'

Thyrza could but inadequately explain what she
meant by this. The words involved a truth, but one of
which she had no conscious perception. Gilbert Grail
was a man of strong personality, and in no previous
moment of life had his being so uttered itself in look
and word as when involuntarily he revealed his love.
More, the vehemence of his feeling went forth in that
subtle influence with which forcible natures are able to
affect now an individual, now a crowd. Thyrza was
very susceptible of such impression; the love which
had become all-potent in Gilbert's heart sensibly moved
her own. Ackroyd had had no power to touch her so:
his ardour had never appealed to her imagination with
such constraining reality. Grail was the first to make
her conscious of the meaning of passion. It was not

passion which rose within her to reply to his, but the childlike security in which she had hitherto lived was at an end; love was henceforth to be the preoccupation of her soul.

She answered her sister:

'I couldn't refuse him. He said he should love me as long as he lived, and I felt that it was true. He didn't try to persuade me, Lyddy. When I showed how surprised I was, he spoke very kindly, and wanted me to have time to think.'

'But, dearest, you say you were surprised. You hadn't thought of such a thing—I'm sure I hadn't. How could you say "yes" at once?'

'But have I done wrong, Lyddy?'

Lydia was again busy with conjecture, in woman's way rapidly reading secrets by help of memory and intuition. She connected this event with what Mary Bower had reported to her of Ackroyd. If it were indeed true that Ackroyd no longer made pretence of loyalty to his old love, would not Grail's knowledge of that change account for his sudden abandonment of disguise? The two were friends; Grail might well have shrunk from entering into rivalry with the younger man. She felt a convincing clearness in this. Then it was true that Ackroyd had begun to show an interest in Totty Nancarrow; it was true, she added bitterly, connecting it closely with the other fact, that he haunted public-houses. Something of that habit she had heard formerly, but thought of it as long abandoned. How

would he hear of Thyrza's having pledged herself! For
he had not forgotten her, he had not forgotten her.
She knew him; he could not forget so lightly; it was
Thyrza's disregard that had driven him into folly.

Her sister was repeating the question.

'Oh, why couldn't you feel in the same way to—to
the other, Thyrza?' burst from Lydia. 'He loved you
and he still loves you. Why didn't you try to feel for
him? You don't love Mr. Grail.'

Thyrza drew a little apart, but kept her hands clasped
on her sister's lap.

'I feel I shall be glad to be his wife,' she said, firmly.
'I felt I must say "yes," and I don't think I shall ever be
sorry. I could *never* have said "yes" to Mr. Ackroyd,
Lyddy!' She sprang forward and held her sister
again. 'You know why I couldn't! You can't keep
secrets from me, though you could from anyone else.
You know why I could never have wished to marry
him!'

They held each other in that unity of perfect love
which had hallowed so many moments of their lives.
Lydia's face was hidden. But at length she raised it,
to ask solemnly:

'It was not because you thought this that you promised Mr. Grail?'

'No, no, no!'

'Blue-eyes, nobody'll ever love me but you. And I
don't think I shall ever have a sad minute if I see that
you're happy. I do hope you've done right.'

'I'm sure I have, Lyddy. You must tell Mary to-morrow. And grandad—think how surprised they'll be! Of course, everybody'll know soon. I shall go to work to-morrow, you know; I'm quite well again. And Lyddy, when I'm Mrs. Grail, of course, Mr. Ackroyd 'll come and see us.'

Lydia made no reply to this. She could not tell what had happened between herself and Mary Bower, and the mention of Ackroyd's name was now a distress to her. She moved from her seat, saying that it was long past supper-time.

Thyrza went down to see Mrs. Grail next morning just before setting out for work. The piece of news was communicated to her, and she hastened with it to her sister. But Gilbert had requested that they would as yet speak of it to no one; it was better to wait till Mr. Egremont had himself made the fact known among the members of his class. Lydia was much impressed with Gilbert's behaviour in keeping that good fortune a secret in the interview with Thyrza. It heightened her already high opinion of him, and encouraged her to look forward with hope. Yet hope would not come without much bidding; doubts and anxieties knocked only too freely at her heart.

For three days she did not see Mary Bower. When she went to tell Mr. Boddy what had come to pass, Mary was out. They met at length, by chance, between Walnut Tree Walk and Paradise Street. It was mid-day, and Lydia had little time to spare.

'They've told you about Thyrza?' she said, without meeting the other's look.

'Yes,' was the quiet answer.

'Will you come and see her to-night?'

'I can't to-night. Perhaps to-morrow.'

'I shall be glad if you can. Good-bye, Mary.'

'Good-bye, Lydia.'

Heavy-hearted both of them, but Lydia found it harder to bear. Her affectionate nature suffered deeply when wounded by someone she loved. Mary had the consolation of feeling that Lydia was being taught a truth.

The same night Lydia, returning from making a purchase for Mrs. Grail, met Ackroyd. It was at the Kennington Road end of Walnut Tree Walk. He seemed to be waiting. He raised his hat; Lydia bent her head and walked past; but a quick step sounded behind her.

'Miss Trent! Will you stop a minute?'

She turned. Luke held out his hand.

'It's a long time since we spoke a word,' he said, with friendliness. 'But we're not always going to pass each other like that, are we?'

Lydia smiled; it was all she could do. She did not know for certain that he had yet heard the news.

'I want you,' he continued, 'to give your sister my good wishes. Will you?'

'Yes, I will, Mr. Ackroyd.'

'Grail came and told me all about it. It wasn't

pleasant to hear, but he's a good fellow and I'm not surprised at his luck. I haven't felt I wanted to quarrel with him, and I think better of myself for that. And yet it means a good deal to me—more than you think, I dare say.'

' You'll soon forget it, Mr. Ackroyd,' Lydia said, in a clear, steady voice.

' Well, you'll see if I do. I'm one of the unlucky fellows that can never show what they feel. It all comes out in the wrong way. It doesn't matter much now.'

Lydia had a feeling that this was not wholly sincere. He seemed to take a pleasure in representing himself as luckless. Combined with what she had heard, it helped her to say :

' A man doesn't suffer much from these things. You'll soon be cheerful again. Good-bye, Mr. Ackroyd.'

She did not wait for anything more from him.

CHAPTER XI.

A MAN WITH A FUTURE.

MR. DALMAINE first turned his attention to politics at the time when the question of popular education was to the front in British politics. It was an excellent opportunity for would-be legislators conscious of rhetorical gifts and only waiting for some safe, simple subject whereon to exercise them. Both safe and simple was the topic which all and sundry were then called upon to discuss; it was impossible not to have views on education (have we not all been educated?), and delightfully easy to support them by prophecy. Never had the vaticinating style of oratory a greater vogue. Never was a richer occasion for the utterance of wisdom such as recommends itself to the British public.

Mr. Dalmaine understood the tastes and habits of that public as well as most men of his standing. After one abortive attempt to enter Parliament, he gained his seat for Vauxhall at the election of 1874, and from the day of his success he steadily applied himself to the political profession. He was then two-and-thirty; for twelve years he had been actively engaged in commerce,

and now held the position of senior partner in a firm
owning several factories in Lambeth.   Such a training
was valuable; politics he viewed as business on a larger
scale, and business, the larger its scale the better, was
his one enthusiasm.   His education had not been liberal;
he saw that that made no difference, and wisely pursued
the bent of his positive mind where another man might
have wasted his time in the attempt to gain culture.
He saw that his was the age of the practical.   Let who
would be an idealist, the practical man in the end got
all that was worth having.

He worked.   You might have seen him, for instance,
in his study one Sunday morning in the January which
the story has now reached; a glance at him showed
that he was no idler in the fields of art or erudition;
blue-books were heaped about him, books bound in law
calf lay open near his hand, newspapers monopolised
one table.   He is interested in all that concerns the
industrial population of Great Britain; he is making
that subject his speciality; he means to link his name
with factory Acts, with education Acts, with Acts for the
better housing of the work-folk, with what not of the
kind.   And the single working man for whom he veritably cares one jot is Mr. James Dalmaine.

He is rather a good-looking fellow, a well-built,
sound red-bearded Englishman.   His ears are not quite
so close against his head as they should be; his lips
might have a more urbane expression; his hand might
be a trifle less weighty; but when he stands up with his

back to the fire and looks musingly along the cornice of
the room, you admit that his appearance on a platform
will conciliate those right-thinking electors who desire
that Parliament should represent the comely, beef-fed
British breed. He is fairly well-to-do, though some
hold that he has speculated a little rashly of late ; he
feels very strongly, however, that his pedestal must be
yet more solid before he can claim the confidence of
his countrymen with the completeness that he desires.
Of late he has given thought to a particular scheme,
and not at all a disagreeable one, for enhancing his
social, and therefore political, credit. He is thinking
of her—the scheme, I would say—at present.

These chambers of his are in Westminster ; they are
spacious, convenient ; he has received deputations from
his constituents here. Lambeth is only just over the
water ; he likes to be near, for it is one of his hobbies,
one of the very few that he allows himself, to keep
thoroughly cognisant of the affairs of his borough—
which, as you are aware, includes the district of Lambeth
—even of its petty affairs. Some day, he says to himself,
he will in this way overlook Great Britain, will have
her statistics at his finger-ends, will change here, con-
firm there, guide everywhere. In the meantime he
satisfies himself with this section. He knows what is
going on in workmen's clubs, in places of amusement,
in the market streets. There is a pleasure in surveying
from a height the doing and driving of ordinary mortals ;
a member for Vauxhall studying his borough in this

spirit naturally comes to feel himself a sort of Grand Duke.

It was one o'clock. There came a knock at the door, followed by the appearance of a middle-aged man who silently proclaimed himself a secretary. This was Mr. Tasker; he had served Mr. Dalmaine thus for three years, prior to which he had been employed as a clerk at the works in Lambeth. Mr. Dalmaine first had his attention drawn to Tasker eight or nine years before, by an instance of singular shrewdness in the latter's discharge of his duties. From that day he kept his eye on him, took opportunities of advancing him. Tasker was born with a love of politics and with a genius for detail; Mr. Dalmaine discovered all this, and, when the due season came, raised him to the dignity of his private scribe. Tasker regarded his employer as his earthly Providence, was devoted to him, served him admirably. It was the one instance of Mr. Dalmaine's having interested himself in an individual; he had no thought of anything but his own profit in doing so, but none the less he had made a mortal happy. You observe the beneficence that lies in practicality.

Before going to luncheon on a Sunday it was Mr. Dalmaine's practice to talk of things in general with his secretary. To-day, among other questions, he asked, with a meaning smile:

'What of young Egremont's lectures? Has he re-commenced?'

'The first of the new course is to-night,' replied

Mr. Tasker, who sat bending a paper-cutter over his leg. Mr. Dalmaine, knowing his secretary, encouraged him to be on easy terms. In truth, he had a liking for Tasker. Partly it reciprocated the other's feeling, no doubt; and then one generally looks with indulgence on a man whom one has discovered and developed.

' Does he go on with his literature ? '

' No. The title is, " Thoughts for the Present." '

Mr. Dalmaine leaned back and laughed. It was a hearty laugh.

' I foresaw it, I foresaw it ! And how many hearers has he ? '

' Six only.'

' To be sure.'

' But there is something more. Mr. Egremont is going to present Lambeth with a free public library. He has taken a building.'

' A fact ? How do you know that, Tasker ? '

' I heard it at the club last night. He has informed the members of his class.'

' Ha ! He is really going to bleed himself to prove his sincerity ? '

They discussed the subject a little longer. Then Mr. Dalmaine dictated a letter or two that he wished to have off his mind, and after that bade Tasker good-day.

At half-past four in the afternoon he drove up to a house at Lancaster Gate, where he had recently been a not infrequent visitor. The servant preceded him with becoming stateliness to the drawing-room, and announced his name in the hearing of three ladies, who were pleasantly chatting in the aroma of tea. The eldest of them was Mrs. Tyrrell; her companions were Miss Tyrrell and a young married lady paying a call.

Mrs. Tyrrell was one of those excellently preserved matrons who testify to the wholesome placidity of woman's life in wealthy English homes. Her existence had taken for granted the perfection of the universe; probably she had never thought of a problem which did not solve itself for the pleasant trouble of stating it in refined terms, and certainly it had never occurred to her that social propriety was distinguishable from the Absolute Good. She was not a dull woman, and the opposite of an unfeeling one, but her wits and her heart had both been so subdued to the social code, that it was very difficult for her to entertain seriously any mode of thought or action for which she could not recall a respectable precedent. By nature she was indulgent, of mild disposition, of sunny intelligence; so endowed, circumstances had bidden her regard it as the end of her being to respect conventions, to check her native impulse if ever it went counter to the opinion of Society, to use her intellect for the sole purpose of discovering how far it was permitted to be used. And she was a happy woman, had always been a happy woman. She had known a little trouble in relation to her favourite sister's marriage with Mr. Newthorpe, for she foresaw that it could not turn out very well, and

she had been obliged to censure her sister for excessive
devotion to the pleasures of Society; it grieved her, on
the other hand, to think of her poor niece being brought
up in a way so utterly opposed to all the traditions.
But these were only little ripples on the smooth flowing
surface. You knew that she would never be smitten
down with a great sorrow : she was of those whom fate
must needs respect, so gracefully and sweetly do they
accept happiness as their right.

Mr. Dalmaine joined these ladies with the manner
of the sturdy Briton who would make himself agreeable
yet dreads the *petit maître*. His voice would have been
better if a little more subdued; he seated himself with
perhaps rather more of ease than of grace ; but on the
whole Society would have let him pass muster as a
well-bred man.

'You are interested in all that concerns your con-
stituency, Mr. Dalmaine,' said Mrs. Tyrrell; 'we were
speaking of Mr. Egremont's plan of founding a library
in Lambeth. You have heard of it ? '

' Oh yes.'

' Do you think it will be a good thing ? '

' I am very doubtful. One doesn't like to speak unkindly of such admirable intentions, but I really think
that in this he is working on a wrong principle. I so
strongly object to *giving* anything when it's in the
power of people to win it for themselves with a little
wholesome exertion. Now, there's the Free Library
Act ; if the people of Lambeth really want a library, let

them tax themselves and adopt the statutory scheme.
Sincerely, I believe that Mr. Egremont will do more
harm than good. We must avoid anything that tends
to pauperise the working classes.'

'How amusing!' exclaimed Paula. 'It's almost
word for word what mamma's just been saying.'

Paula was dressed in the prettiest of tea-gowns; she
looked the most exquisite of conservatory flowers. Her
smile to Mr. Dalmaine was very gracious.

'That really is how I felt,' said Mrs. Tyrrell. 'But
Mr. Egremont will never be persuaded of that. He
is so whole-hearted in his desire to help these poor
people, yet, I'm afraid, so very, very impractical.'

The young married lady observed:

'Oh, no one ought *ever* to interfere with philanthropy
unless they have a *very* practical scheme. Canon
Brougham was *so* emphatic on that point this morning.
So *much* harm may be done, when we mean everything
for the best.'

'Yes, I feel that very strongly,' said Dalmaine,
his masculine accent more masculine than ever after
the plaintive piping. 'I even fear that Mr. Egremont
is doing wrong in making his lectures free. We may
be sure they are well worth paying to hear, and it's
an axiom in all dealing with the working class that
they will never value anything that they don't pay for.'

'Oh, but Mr. Dalmaine,' protested Paula, 'you
couldn't ask Mr. Egremont to take money at the door!'

'It sounds shocking, Miss. Tyrrell, but if Mr.

Egremont stands before them as a teacher, he ought
to charge for his lessons. I assure you they would put
a far higher value on his lectures. I grieve to hear
that his class has fallen off. I could have foreseen that.
The basis is not sound. To put it in plain, even
coarse, language, all social reform must be undertaken
on strictly commercial principles.'

'How I should like to hear you say that to Mr.
Egremont!' remarked Paula. 'Oh, his face!'

'Mr. Egremont is an idealist,' said Mrs. Tyrrell,
smiling.

'Surely the very *last* kind of person to attempt
social reform!' exclaimed the young married lady.

The conversation drew off into other channels. Mr.
Dalmaine was supplied with the clearest opinions on
every topic, and he had a way of delivering them which
was most effective with persons of Mrs. Tyrrell's com-
position. In everything he affected sobriety. If he
had to express a severe judgment, it was done with
gentlemanly regret. If he commended anything, he
did so with a judicial air. In fact, it would not have
been easy to imagine Mr. Dalmaine speaking with an
outburst of natural fervour on any topic whatsoever.
His view was the view of common sense, and he
enunciated the barrenest convictions in a tone which
would have suited the profound originality.

A week later there was a dinner-party at the
Tyrrells', and Egremont was among the bidden.

He had persisted in his tendency to hold aloof from
general society, in spite of many warnings from Mrs.
Ormonde, but he could not, short of ingratitude, wholly
absent himself from his friends at Lancaster Gate.
Mrs. Tyrrell was no exception to the rule in her
attitude to Egremont; as did all matronly ladies,
she held him in very warm liking, and sincerely hoped
that a young man so admirably fitted for the refinements
of social life would in time get rid of his extravagant
idealism. A little of that was graceful; Society was
beginning to view it with favour when confined within
the proper bounds; but to carry it into act, and waste
one's life in wholly unpractical—nay, in positively
harmful — enterprise was a sad thing. She had
reasoned with him, but he showed himself so perverted
in his sense of the fitness of things that the task had
to be abandoned as hopeless. And yet the good lady
liked him. She had hoped, and not so long ago, that
he might some day desire to stand in a nearer relation
to her than that of a friend, but herein again she felt
that her wish was growing futile. Paula indulged in
hints with reference to her cousin Annabel, and Mrs.
Tyrrell began to fear that the strangely educated girl
might be the cause of Walter's extreme aberrations.

Egremont arrived early on the evening of the
dinner. Only one guest had preceded him. With
Mrs. Tyrrell and Paula were Mr. Tyrrell and the son
of the house, Mr. John, the Jack Tyrrell of sundry
convivial clubs in town. Mr. Tyrrell senior was a

high-coloured jovial gentleman of three score, great in
finance, practical to the backbone, yet with wit and
tact which put him at ease with all manner of men,
even with social reformers. These latter amused him
vastly ; he failed to see that the world needed any reforming whatever, at all events beyond that which is
constitutionally provided for in the proceedings of the
British Parliament. He had great wealth ; he fared
sumptuously every day ; things shone to him in a rosy
after-dinner light. Not a gross or a selfish man, for he
was as good-natured as he was contented, and gave very
freely of his substance ; it was simply his part in the
world to enjoy the product of other men's labour and
to set an example of glorious self-satisfaction. Egremont, in certain moods, had tried to despise Mr.
Tyrrell, but he never quite succeeded. Nor indeed
was the man contemptible. Had you told him with
frank conviction that you deemed him a poor sort of
phenomenon, he would have shaken the ceiling with
laughter and have admired you for your plain-speaking.
For there was a large and generous vigour about him,
and adverse criticism could only heighten his satisfaction in his own stability.

Something of the cold dignity in which she had
taken refuge at Ullswater was still to be remarked in
Paula's manner as she received Egremont. She held
her charming head very erect, and let her eyelids droop
a little, and the few words which she addressed to him
were rather absently spoken. With others, as they

arrived, she was sportively intimate. Her bearing had
gained a little in maturity during the past half year,
but it was still with a blending of *naïveté* and capricious
affectation that she wrought her spell. Her dress was
a miracle, and inseparably a part of her ; it was impossible to picture her in any serious situation, so entirely
was she a child of luxury and frivolous concern. Exquisite as an artistic product of Society, she affected
the imagination not so much by her personal charm as
through the perfume of luxury which breathed about
her. Egremont, with his radical tendencies of thought,
found himself marvelling as he regarded her ; what a life
was hers ! Compare it with that of some little work-
girl in Lambeth, such as he saw in the street—what
spaces between those two worlds ! Was it possible that
this dainty creation, this thing of material omnipotence,
would suffer decay of her sweetness and in the end die ?
The reason took her side and revolted against law ; it
would be an outrage if time or mischance laid hold
upon her.

Yet there was something in Paula which he did not
recognise. Since she could formulate desires, few had
found impression on her lips which were not at once
gratified ; an exception caused her at first rather
astonishment than impatience. Such astonishment
fell upon her when she understood that Egremont's
coming to Ullswater was not on her account. In truth,
she wished it had been, and from that moment the
fates were kind enough to notice Paula's poor little

existence, and bid her remember she was mortal. She
took the admonition ill, and certainly it was impertinent
from her point of view. She had slight philosophy,
but out of that disappointment Paula by degrees drew
an understanding that she had had a glimpse of a
strange world, that something of moment had been at
stake.

Egremont, standing in the rear of a chatting group,
had all but dreamed himself into oblivion of the present when he heard loud announcement of 'Mr. Dalmaine.' It was some time since he had met the Member
for Vauxhall. Looking upon the politician's well-knit
frame, his well-coloured face with its expression of
shrewd earnestness, he for a moment seemed to himself
to shrink into insignificance. After sitting opposite
Dalmaine for an hour at the dinner-table, he was able
to regard the man again in what he deemed a true
light. But the impression made upon one by an object
suddenly presented when the thought is busy with far
other things will as a rule embody much essential truth.
As a force, Egremont would not have weighed in the
scale against Dalmaine. Putting himself in conscious
opposition to such a man, he had but his due in a
sense of nullity.

Mr. Tyrrell was kind to him in the assignment of
a partner. A pretty, gentle, receptive maiden, anxious
to show interest in things of the mind—with such a
one Walter was at his best, because his simplest and
happiest. He put away thought of Lambeth—which

in truth was beginning to trouble his mind like a fixed
idea—and talked much as he would have done a couple
of years ago, with bright intelligence, with natural enjoyment of the hour.   It was greatly his charm in such
conversation that had made him a favourite with pleasant people of the world.   In withdrawing himself
from the sphere of these amenities he was opposing the
free growth of his character, which in consequence
suffered.   He was cognisant of that ; he knew that he
was more himself to-night than he had been for some
months.   But the fixed idea waited in the background.

When the ladies were gone, he saw Dalmaine rise
and come round the table towards him.

' I'm glad to see you again,' Dalmaine began, de-
positing his wine-glass and refilling it.   ' Pray tell me
something about your lectures.   You have resumed
since Christmas, I think ? '

Egremont had no mind to speak of these things.
It cost him an effort to find an answer.

' Yes, I still have a few hearers.'

And at once he was angry with himself for falling
into this confession of failure.   Dalmaine was the last
man before whom he would affect humility.

' I am sure,' observed the politician, ' everyone who
has the good of the working classes at heart must feel
indebted to you.   It's so very seldom that men of culture
care to address audiences of that kind.   Yet it must
be the most effectual way of reaching the people.
You address them on English Literature, I think ? '

Egremont did not care to explain that he had now a broader subject. He murmured an affirmative. Dalmaine had hoped to elicit some of the 'Thoughts for the Present,' and felt disappointment.

'An excellent choice, it seems to me,' he continued, making his glass revolve on the table-cloth. 'They are much too ignorant of the best wealth of their country. They have so few inducements to read the great historians, for instance. If you can bring them to do so, you make them more capable citizens, abler to form a judgment on the questions of the day.'

Egremont smiled.

'My one aim,' he remarked, 'is to persuade them to forget that there are such things as questions of the day.'

Dalmaine also smiled, and with a slight involuntary curling of the lip.

'Ah, I remember our discussions on the Atlantic. I scarcely thought you would apply those ideas in their —their fulness, when you began practical work. You surely will admit that, in a time when their interests are engaging so much attention, working men should— for instance—go to the polls with intelligent preparation.'

'I'd rather they didn't go to the polls at all,' Walter replied. He knew that this was exaggeration, but it pleased him to exaggerate. He enjoyed the effect on the honourable member's broad countenance.

'Come, come!' said Dalmaine, laughing with appearance of entering into the joke. 'At that rate, English freedom would soon be at an end. One might as well abolish newspapers.'

'In my opinion, the one greatest boon that could be granted the working class. I do my best to dissuade them from the reading of newspapers.'

Dalmaine turned the whole matter into a jest. Secretly he believed that Egremont was poking contemptuous fun at him, but it was his principle to receive everything with good humour. They drew apart again, each feeling more strongly than ever the instinctive opposition between their elements. It amounted to a reciprocal dislike, an irritation provoked by each other's presence. Dalmaine was beginning to suspect Egremont of some scheme too deep for his fathoming; it was easier for him to believe anything, than that idealism pure and simple was at the bottom of such behaviour. Walter, on the other hand, viewed the politician's personality with something more than contempt. Dalmaine embodied those forces of philistinism, that essence of the vulgar creed, which Egremont had undertaken to attack, and which, as he already felt, were likely to yield as little before his efforts as a stone wall under the blow of a naked hand. Two such would do well to keep apart.

On returning to the drawing-room, Egremont kept watch for a vacant place by Paula. Presently he was able to move to her side. She spread her fan upon her lap, and, ruffling its edge of white fur, said negligently:

'So you decided to waste an evening, Mr. Egremont'

'I decided to have an evening of rest and enjoyment.'

'I suppose you are working dreadfully hard. When do you open your library?'

'Scarcely in less than four or five months.'

'And will you stand at the counter and give out books, like the young men at Mudie's?'

'Sometimes, I dare say. But I have found a librarian.'

'Who is he?'

'A working man in Lambeth. One of the most sympathetic natures I have ever met; a man who might have gone on all his life making candles—that is how things are arranged.'

'Making candles? What a funny change of occupation! And you really think you are doing good in that disagreeable place?'

'I can only hope.'

'You are quite sure you are not doing harm?'

'Does it seem to you that I am?'

Paula assumed an air of wisdom.

'Of course I have no right to speak of such things, but it is my opinion that you are destroying their sense of self-respect. I don't think they ought to have things *given* them; they should be encouraged to help themselves.'

He examined her face. It was obvious that this profound sentiment had not taken birth in Paula's charming little head, and he guessed from whom she had derived it.

'I have no doubt Mr. Dalmaine would agree with you,' he said, smiling. 'I believe I have heard him say something of the kind.'

'I'm glad to hear it. Mr. Dalmaine is an authority in such matters.'

'And I, the very reverse of one?'

'Well, I really do think, Mr. Egremont, that you are taking up things for which you are not—not exactly suited, you know.'

She said it with the prettiest air of patronage, looking at him for a moment, then as usual, letting her eyes wander about the room.

'Miss Tyrrell,' he replied with gravity that was half genuine, 'tell me for what I *am* exactly suited, and you will do me a vast kindness.'

She reflected.

'Oh, there are lots of things you do very nicely indeed. I've seen you play croquet beautifully. But I've always thought it a pity you weren't a clergyman.'

Walter laughed.

'Well, a local preacher is next to it.'

Both were at once carried back to the evening at Ullswater. Paula kept silence; her eyes were directed towards Dalmaine, who almost at the same moment looked towards her. She played with her fan.

' You know that my uncle has been ill ? ' she said.

' No, I have heard nothing of that.'

Paula looked surprised

' Don't you hear from—from them ? '

' I have a letter from Mr. Newthorpe very occasionally. But surely the illness has not been serious ? '

' Mamma heard this morning about it. I don't know what's been the matter. I shouldn't wonder if they come to London before long.'

Egremont shortly changed his place, and saw that Dalmaine took the vacant seat by Paula. The two seemed to get on very well together. Paula was evidently exerting herself to be charming ; Dalmaine was doing his best to trifle.

He sought more information from Mrs. Tyrrell regarding Mr. Newthorpe. She seemed to fear that her brother-in-law might have been in more danger than Annabel in her letter admitted.

' They certainly must come south,' she said. ' They are having a terrible winter, and it has evidently tried Mr. Newthorpe beyond his strength. You have influence with him, I believe, Mr. Egremont. Pray join me in my efforts to bring them both back to civilisation.'

' I fear my influence will effect nothing if yours fails,' said Walter. ' But Mr. Newthorpe should certainly not risk his health.'

He next had a chat with Mr. John Tyrrell junior. Paula's brother was two-and-twenty, a frankly sensual youth, of admirable temper, great in turf matters, with

a genius for conviviality. Jack's health was perfect, for
he had his father's habit of enjoying life without excess,
and his stamina allowed a wide limit to the term
moderation. Like the rest of his family, he had the
secret of conciliating good-will; there was no humbug
in him, and one respected him as a fine specimen of
the young male developed at enormous expense. For
Egremont he had a certain reverence; a man who
habitually thought was clearly, he admitted, of a higher
grade than himself, and he had no objection whatever
to proclaim his own inferiority. Egremont, talking
with him, was half disposed to envy Jack Tyrrell.
What a simple thing life was with limitless cash, a
perfect digestion, and good humour in the place of
brains!

His room seemed very cold and lonely when he got
back to it shortly before midnight. The fire had been
let out; the books round the walls had a musty appearance; there was stale tobacco in the air. He paced
the floor, thinking of Annabel, wondering whether she
would soon be in London, longing to see her. And
before he went to bed, he wrote a letter to Mr. Newthorpe, expressing the anxiety with which he had heard
of his illness. Of himself he said little; the few words
that came to his pen concerning the Lambeth crusade
were rather lifeless.

He was being talked of meanwhile in the Tyrrells'
drawing-room. The last guest being gone, there was

chat for a few minutes between the members of the family.

'Egremont isn't looking quite up to the mark,' said Mr. Tyrrell, as he stood before the fire, hands in pockets.

'I thought the same,' said his wife. 'He seems worried. What a deplorable thing it is, to think that he will spend large sums of money on this library scheme!'

Mr. Tyrrell made inarticulate noises, and at length laughed.

'He must amuse himself in his own way.'

'But after all, papa,' said Paula, whose advocacy went much by the rule of contraries, 'it must be a good thing to give people books to read. I dare say it prevents them from going to the public-house.'

'Shouldn't wonder if it does, Paula,' he replied, with a benevolent gaze.

'Then what's your objection?'

'I don't object to the library in particular. It's only that Egremont isn't the man to do these kind of things. It is to be hoped that he'll get tired of it, and find something more in his line.'

'What *is* his line?'

'Ah, that's the question! Very likely he hasn't one at all. It seems to me there's a good many young fellows in that case nowadays. They have education, they have money, and they don't know what the deuce to do with either one or the other. They're a cut above you, Mr. Jack; it isn't enough for them to live

and enjoy themselves. So they get it into their heads
that they're called upon to reform the world—a nice
handy little job, that'll keep them going. The girls,
I notice, are beginning to have the same craze. I
shouldn't wonder if Paula gets an idea that she'll be a
hospital-nurse, or go district-visiting in Bethnal Green.'

'I certainly should if I thought it would amuse me,'
said Paula. 'But why shouldn't Mr. Egremont do
work of this kind? He's in earnest; he doesn't only
do it for fun.'

'Of course he's in earnest, and there's the absurdity
of it. Social reform, pooh! Why, who are the real
social reformers? The men who don't care a scrap for
the people, but take up ideas because they can make
capital out of them. It isn't idealists who do the work
of the world, but the hard-headed, practical, selfish men.
A big employer of labour 'll do more good in a day, just
because he sees profit 'll come of it, than all the moon-
ing philanthropists in a hundred years. Nothing solid
has ever been gained in this world that wasn't pursued
out of self-interest. Look at Dalmaine. How much
do you think he cares for the factory-hands he's always
talking about? But he'll do them many a good turn;
he'll make many a life easier; and just because it's his
business to do so, because it's the way of advancing
himself. He aims at being Home Secretary one of
these days, and I shouldn't wonder if he is. There's
your real social reformer. Egremont's an amateur,
a dilettante. In many ways he's worth a hundred of

Dalmaine, but Dalmaine will benefit the world, and it's well if Egremont doesn't do harm.'

In all which it is not impossible that Mr. John Tyrrell hit the nail on the head. Much satisfied with his little oration, he went off to don a jacket and enjoy a cigar by his smoking-room fire.

A couple of days later, Mr. Dalmaine called at the house before luncheon. After speaking with Mrs. Tyrrell, he had a private interview with Paula. The event was referred to in a letter Paula addressed to her cousin Annabel in the course of the ensuing week.

'Dear Bell,—We are much relieved by your letter. It is of course impossible to stay among these mountains for the rest of the winter; I hope uncle will very soon be well enough to come south. The plan of living at Eastbourne for a time is no doubt a good one. You'll have Mrs. Ormonde to talk to. She is very nice, though I've generally found her a little serious; but then she's like you in that. I think it's a pity people trouble themselves about things that only make them gloomy.

'I have a little piece of news for you. It really looks as if I was going to be married. In fact, I've said I would be, and I think it likely I shall keep my word. My name will be Mrs. Dalmaine. Don't you remember Mr. Egremont speaking of Mr. Dalmaine and calling him names? From that moment I made up my mind that he must be a very nice man, and when we made his acquaintance I found that I wasn't so far wrong. You see, poor Mr. Egremont so hates everything and everybody that's practical. Now I'm practical, as you know, so it's right I should marry a practical man. Papa has the highest opinion of Mr. Dalmaine's abilities; he thinks he has a great future in politics. Wouldn't it be delightful if one's husband really became Prime Minister or something of the kind! And, to tell you a secret, Mr. Dalmaine is firmly convinced that I'm the cleverest girl he's ever known; of course he likes me for other things as well that we needn't talk about, but he's made up his mind that I'm just the wife for a man who has social and political ambitions. You know I didn't really think that I was clever at all. Of course it isn't in *your* way, but I shouldn't wonder if I surprise myself and everybody else when I have a *salon* and receive people of importance.

'We shall be married, I dare say, before the beginning of the season. You will probably be at Eastbourne then. I'm awfully afraid to hint at such a thing, but you know one must have bridesmaids, and there's a certain cousin of mine who would look very sweet and distinguished on such an occasion. But she might shudder at such frivolities.

'Do you know, *Bella mia*, it really *is* a pity that Mr. Egremont is going on in this way! He's going to spend enormous sums of money in establishing a library in Lambeth. It's very good of him, of course, but we are all so sure it's a mistake. Shall I tell you *my own* view? Mr. Egremont is an idealist, and idealists are *not* the people to do serious work of this kind. The real social reformers are the hard-headed, practical men, who at heart care only for their own advancement. If you think, I'm sure you'll find this is true. You see that I am beginning to occupy myself with serious questions. It will be necessary in the wife of an active politician. But if you *could* hint to Mr. Egremont that he is going shockingly astray. He dined with us the other night, and doesn't look at all well. I am so afraid lest he is doing all this just because you tell him to. Is it so?

'But I have fifty other letters to write. My best love to uncle; tell him to get well as quickly as possible. I wonder that dreadful lonely place hasn't killed you both. I shall be *so* glad to see you again, for I do really like you, Bell, and I know you are awfully wise and good. Think of me sometimes and hope that I shall be happy.—Yours affectionately,

'PAULA TYRRELL.'

CHAPTER XII.

LIGHTS AND SHADOWS.

EGREMONT's face, it was true, showed that things were not altogether well with him. It was not ill-health, but mental restlessness, which expressed itself in the lines of his forehead and the diminished brightness of his eyes. During the last two months of the year he had felt a constant need of help, and help such as would alone stead him he could not find.

It was no mere failing of purpose. He prepared his lectures as thoroughly as ever, and delivered them with no less zeal than in the first weeks ; indeed, if anything, his energy grew, for, since his nearer acquaintance with Gilbert Grail, the latter's face before him was always an incentive. There was much to discourage him. More than half his class fell from lukewarmness to patent indifference ; they would probably present themselves until the end of the course, but it was little likely that they would recommence with him after Christmas. He was obliged to recognise the utter absence of idealism from all save Grail—unless Bunce might be credited with glimmerings of the true light.

Yet intellectually he held himself on firm ground. To have discovered one man such as Grail was compensation for failure with many others, and the project of the library was at all times a vista of hope. But Egremont was not of those who can live on altruism. His life of loneliness irked him, irked him as never yet. The dawn was a recurrence of weariness; the long nights were cold and blank.

The old unrest, which he had believed at an end when once ' the task of his life ' was discovered, troubled him through many a cloud-enveloped day. Had he been free, it would have driven him on new travels. Yet that was no longer a real resource. He did not desire to see other lands, but to make a home in his own. And no home was promised him. The longer he kept apart from Annabel, the dimmer did the vision of her become; he held it a sign that he himself was seldom if ever in her mind. Did he still love her? Rather he would have said that there lay in him great faculty of love, which Annabel, if she willed it, could at a moment bring into life ; she, he believed, in preference to any woman he had known. It was not passion, and the consciousness that it was not often depressed him. One of his ideals was that of a passion nurtured to be the crowning glory of life. He did not love Annabel in that way; would that he could have done!

This purely personal distress could not but affect his work. A month before the end of the year he came to the resolve to choose a new subject for the succeeding course of lectures. Forgetting all the sound arguments by which he had been led to prefer the simple teaching of a straightforward subject to any more ambitious prophecy, he was now impelled to think out a series of discourses on—well, on things in general. He got hold of the title, 'Thoughts for the Present,' and the temptation to make use of it proved too great. English literature did not hold the average proletarian mind. It had served him to make an aquaintance with a little group of men ; now he must address them in a bolder way, reveal to them his personality. Had he not always contemplated such revelation in the end ? Yes, when he found his class fit for it. But he was growing impatient with this slow progress—if indeed it could be called progress at all. He would strike a more significant note.

Walter was in danger, as you very well understand. There is no need at this time of day to remind ourselves of teachers who have fallen into the fatal springe of apostolicism. Men would so fain be prophets, when once they have a fellow mortal by the ear. Egremont could have exposed this risk to you as well as any, yet he deliberately ignored it in his own case—no great novelty that. 'Have I not something veritably to say ? Are not thoughts of and for the present surging in my mind ? Whereto have we language if not for the purpose of uttering the soul within us ? ' So he fell to work on his introductory lecture, and for a few days had peace—nay, lived in enthusiasm once more.

His week of absence at Christmas, of which we have heard, was spent again in Jersey. To the roaring music of the channel breakers he built up his towers and battlements of prophecy. More, he wrote a poem, and for a day wondered whether it might be well to read it to his audience as preface. A friendly sprite whispered in his ear, and saved him from too utter folly. The sprite had not yet forsaken him ; woe to him if ever it should ! He wrapped the poem in a letter to Mr. New-thorpe, and had a very pleasant reply, written, as he afterwards heard, only a day or two before Mr. Newthorpe fell ill. Annabel sent her message ; ' the verses were noble, and pure as the sea-foam.'

On returning to town, he sent a note to Grail, asking him to come in the evening to Great Russell Street, or, if that were inconvenient, to appoint a time for a meeting in Walnut Tree Walk. Gilbert accepted the invitation, and came for the first time to Egremont's rooms.

Things were not ill with him, Gilbert Grail. You saw in the man's visage that he had put off ten years of haggard life. His dark, deep eyes spoke their meanings with the ardour of soul's joy ; his cheeks seemed to have filled out, his brows to have smoothed. It was joy of the purest and manliest. His life had sailed like some battered, dun-coloured vessel into a fair harbour of sunlight and blue, and hands were busy giving to it a brave new aspect. He could scarce think of all his happiness at once ; the coming release from a hateful

drudgery, and the coming day which would put
Thyrza's hand in his, would not go into one perspective.
Sometimes he would all but forget the one in thinking
of the other. Now let the early mornings be dark and
chill as they would, let the sky lower in its muddy
gloom, let weariness of the flesh do its worst—those two
days were approaching. Why, was he not yet young?
What are five-and-thirty years behind one, when bliss
unutterable beckons forward? It should all be forgotten, that grimy past poisoned through and through
with the stench of candles. Books, books, and time
to use them, and a hearth about which love is busy—
what more can you offer son of man than these?

He had written his acceptance, had endeavoured
to write his thanks. The words were ineffectual.

Egremont received him in his study with gladness. This man had impressed him powerfully, was
winning an ever larger place in his affection. He
welcomed him as he would have done an old friend,
for whose coming he had looked with impatience.

'Do you smoke?' he asked.

No, Gilbert did not smoke. The money he formerly
spent on this had long been saved for the purchase of
books. Egremont's after-dinner coffee had to suffice to
make cheer. It was a little time before Grail could
speak freely. He had suffered from nervousness in
undertaking this visit, and his relief at the simplicity
of Egremont's rooms, by allowing him to think of what
he wished to say, caused him to seem absent.

'I've already begun to jot down lists of obvious books,' Egremont said. 'I have a good general catalogue here, and I mean to go through it carefully.'

Gilbert was at length able to speak his thought.

'I ought to have said far more than I did in my letter, Mr. Egremont. I tried to thank you, but I felt I might as well have left it alone. I don't know whether you have any idea what this change will mean to me. It's more than saving my life, it's giving me a new one such as I never dared to hope for.'

'I'm right glad to hear it!' Walter replied, with his kindest look. 'It comes to make up to me for some little disappointment in other things. I'm afraid the lectures have been of very slight use.'

'I don't think that. I don't think any of the class 'll forget them. It's likely they'll have their best effect in a little time; the men'll think back upon them. Now Bunce has got much out of them, I believe.'

'Ah, Bunce! Yes, I hoped something from him. By-the-by, he is rather a violent enemy of Christianity, I think?'

'I've heard so. I don't know him myself, except for meeting him at the lectures. Yes, I've heard he's sometimes almost mad about religious subjects.'

Egremont told the story about Bunce's child, which he had had from Mrs. Ormonde. And this led him on to speak of his purpose in this new course of lectures. After describing his plan:

'And that matter of religion is one I wish to speak

of most earnestly. I think I can put forward a few ideas which will help a man like Bunce. He wants to be made to see the attitude of a man who retains no dogma, and yet is far more a friend than an enemy of Christianity. I think that lecture shall come first.'

He had not yet made ready his syllabus. As before, he meant to send it to those whose names were upon his list. His first evening would be at the beginning of February.

' I shall try with Ackroyd again,' he said. ' Perhaps the subject this time will seem more attractive to him.'

Gilbert looked grave.

' I'm anxious about Ackroyd,' he replied. ' He's had private trouble lately, and I begin to be afraid it's driving him into the wrong road. He isn't one that can easily be persuaded. I wish you might succeed in bringing him to the lectures.'

Egremont tried to speak hopefully, but in secret he felt that his power over men was not that which draws them from the way of evil and turns them to light. For that is needed more than love of the beautiful. For a moment he mused in misgiving over his ' Thoughts for the Present.'

They began to talk of those details in the library scheme which Egremont had left for subsequent discussion.

' As soon as the premises are in my hands,' he said, ' I shall have the house thoroughly repaired. I should like you to see then if any alteration 'can be made which would add to your comfort. As soon as the place can be made ready, it will be yours to take possession of. That should be certainly by the end of April. Shall you be free to leave your present occupation then ? '

'I can at any time. But I am glad to have a date fixed. I'm going to be married then.'

It was said with a curious diffidence which brought a smile to the hearer's face. Egremont was surprised at the intelligence, glad at the same time.

'That is good news,' he said. 'Of course I had thought of you living with your mother. This will be better still. Your future wife must, of course, examine the house ; no doubt she'll be a far better judge than you of what needs doing. Why, I am delighted to hear this, Grail! I tell you what we'll do. Let us wait till the end of February, then we'll persuade that extraordinary old woman to let you have an afternoon of inspection. But I should think you may safely fix the beginning of April. By that time I hope to have the shelves up in the library, and when you are back from your honeymoon we shall go to work together on arranging books. That'll be a rare time! We shall throw up our arms, like Dominie Sampson, and cry "Prodigious!"'

He grew mirthful, indulging the boyish humour which, as a reaction from his accustomed lonely silence, came upon him when he had a sympathetic companion. To Gilbert this was a new phase of Egremont's character :

he, sober in happiness, answered the young man's merriment with an expressive smile.

Gilbert could not stay beyond ten o'clock, for he had to walk home. Egremont offered to go some part of the way with him, and they set out together. In continuous talk they threaded the by-ways between Tottenham Court Road and Charing Cross. There was a frosty air; the stones rang pleasantly beneath the tread. Egremont was tempted to go on as far as Westminster. Under the clock-tower they shook hands like men who mean something by the grip, and each went his way homewards.

Grail had merely mentioned the fact of his intended marriage. As he tramped along the broad desert of Whitehall, Egremont wondered much within himself what kind of woman such a man might have chosen to share his life. Had he contemplated marriage for some time, and been prevented from it by stress of circumstances? It was not easy to picture the suitable partner for Grail. Clearly she must be another than the thriftless, shiftless creature too common in working-class homes. Yet it was not likely that he had met with anyone who could share his inner life. Had he, following the example of many a prudent man, chosen a good, quiet, modest woman, whose first and last anxiety would be to keep his home in order and see that he lacked no comfort within her province to bestow? It was probable. She would no doubt be past youth; suppose her thirty. She would have a face which pleased by its homely goodness ; she would speak in a gentle voice, waiting upon superior wisdom.

'Come, come!' Walter exclaimed to himself. 'I am getting too patronising. After all, Grail is a fellow who might well please a young and pretty woman, provided she had common sense. Why should he not choose his wife as I myself should ? '

The conclusion was that he felt really curious to know the future Mrs. Grail.

A few days before that appointed for the first lecture of this new course, Egremont received a letter of which the address surprised him. It bore the Penrith post-mark ; the writing must be Annabel's. He had very recently written to Mr. Newthorpe, who was not yet well enough to attempt the journey southwards ; this reply by another hand might signify ill news. And that proved to be the case. Annabel wrote :

'Dear Mr. Egremont,—Father desires me to answer your very kind letter of a week ago. He has delayed, hoping from day to day to be able to write himself. I grieve to say that he is suffering more than at any time in the last month. I am very anxious, full of trouble. Mrs. Tyrrell wishes to come to me, and I am writing by this post to say that I shall be very glad of her presence. Our doctors say there is absolutely no ground for fear, and gladly I give them my faith ; but it tortures me to see my dear father so overcome with pain. The world seems to me very dark, and life a dreadful penalty.

'We read with the greatest interest of what you are doing and hoping. I cannot tell you how we rejoiced in the happiness of Mr. Grail. That is a glorious thing that you have done. I trust his marriage may be a very happy one. When we are at Eastbourne and father is well again, we must come to see your library and no less your librarian. Do not be discouraged if your lectures seem to fail of immediate results. Surely good work will have fruit, and very likely in ways of which you will never know.

'The Tyrrells will have constant news of father, and I am sure will gladly send it on to you.—I am, dear Mr. Egremont, yours sincerely,

'ANNABEL NEWTHORPE.'

It was the first letter he had received from Annabel. For some days he kept it close at hand, and looked over it frequently; then it was laid away with care, not again to be read until the passing of years had given it both a sadder and a dearer significance.

CHAPTER XIII.

THYRZA SINGS AGAIN.

EGREMONT had a fear that he might seem ungrateful to the man Bower. It was Bower to whom he had gone for help when he first sought to gather an audience, and on the whole the help had been effectual. Yet Bower had not borne the test of nearer acquaintance: Egremont soon knew the vulgarity of his nature, and had much difficulty in sustaining the show of friendly intercourse with him. One evening in mid-February, he called the portly man to speak with him after lecture, and, with what geniality he could, explained to him the details of his library project and told whom he had chosen for librarian. Bower professed himself highly satisfied with everything, and, as usual, affected Egremont disagreeably with his subservience. The latter was not surprised to find that Grail had kept silence on the subject; but it was time now for the arrangements to be made public.

From the lecture-room, Mr. Bower went to a club where he was wont to relax himself of evenings; here he discussed the library question with such acquaint-

ances as were at hand. He reached home just after
the closing of the shop. Mary was gone to bed. Mrs.
Bower had just finished her supper, and was musing
over the second half of her accustomed pint of ale.
Her husband threw himself into a chair, with an exclamation of scornful disgust.

'What's wrong now?' asked Mrs. Bower.

'Well, I don't know what *you'll* call it, but *I* call
it the damnedest bit of sneaking behaviour as I ever
knew! He's given the librarianship to that fellow
Grail. There's the 'ouse at the back for him to live
in, and rent free, no doubt; and there's a good lumping
salary, *that* you may go bail. Now what do you think
o' that job?'

'And him not as much as offering it to you!'

'Not so much as offerin' it! How many 'ud he
have got to hear his lectures without me, I'd like to
know! I shouldn't have taken it; no, of course I
shouldn't; it wouldn't a' suited me to take a librarianship.
But it was his bounden duty to give me the first offer.
I never thought he'd make one of *us* librarian; if it
had been some stranger, I shouldn't have made so much
of it. But to give it to Grail in that sneaking, under-
handed way! Why, I'd be ashamed o' myself. I've a
rare good mind never to go near his lectures again.'

'You'd better go,' said Mrs. Bower, prudently.
'He might pay you out at the works. It 'ud be a
trick just like him. after this.'

'I'll think about it,' returned the other, with

dignity, sitting very upright, and gathering his broad beard into his hand.

'Why, there now!' cried his wife, struck with a sudden thought. 'If that doesn't explain something! Depend upon it—*depend* upon it—that's how Grail got Thyrza Trent to engage herself to him! He'll a' known it for some time, Grail will a' done. He's a mean fellow, or he'd never a' gone and set her against Mr. Ackroyd, as it's easy to see he did. He'll a' told her about the 'ouse and the salary, of course he will! If I didn't think there was something queer in that job!'

Mr. Bower saw at once how highly probable this was.

'And that is why they've put on such hairs, her an' Lydia,' Mrs. Bower pursued. 'It's all very well for Mary to pretend as there's nothing altered. It's my belief Mary's got to know more than she'll tell, and Lydia's quarrelled with her about it. It's easy enough to see as they *have* fell out. Lydia ain't been to chapel since Christmas, an' you know yourself it was just before Christmas as Egremont went to the 'ouse to see Mr. Grail. If she'd been a bit sharper, she'd never a' told Mary that. I ain't surprised at Thyrza doin' of under-handed things; I've never liked her over-much. But I thought better of Lydia.'

'I've not quarrelled with *them*,' said Mr. Bower, magnanimously. 'And girls must look out for themselves, and do the best for themselves they can. But that soft-spoken, sneaking Hegremont! You should

a' seen him when he had the cheek to tell me about
it; you'd a' thought he was going to give me a five-
pound note.'

'Now, you'll see,' said Mrs. Bower, 'they'll take off
old Boddy to live with them.'

'So much the better.   He can't earn his living much
longer, and who was to pay us for his lodging and keep,
I'd like to know?'

Thus did the worthy pair link together conjectural
cause and effect, on principles which their habit of mind
dictated.

On one point Mrs. Bower was right.   Mary and
Lydia had not come together since the former's triumph
over her friend.   Lydia still visited the shop to see Mr.
Boddy, but generally at the times when Mary was away
at prayer-meetings.   Mary never went to Walnut Tree
Walk.   Though she would gladly have put an end to
the coldness, obstinacy of conviction held her aloof in
the hope that Lydia would come and acknowledge her
error.   Lydia, on the other hand, contrary to her habit
of repentance after an indulgence of temper, could not
take the first step in this case; she was wounded too
deeply, and every day that passed without a sign of con-
trition on Mary's part increased her resentment.   Moreover, she knew only too well that in matter of fact
Mary was being daily justified; other people had stories
to tell her of Ackroyd.   Human nature, and perhaps
woman's nature in particular, was thus strongly arrayed
against a reconcilement.   Under the circumstances, one

likes Lydia Trent none the worse for being so human
and so womanly.

She gave no explanation to Thyrza. Though there
had come that moment of confession between them,
Lydia could not speak of Ackroyd to her sister. On a
subject such as this she kept reserve even with herself.
A natural pride, a kind of shame, forbade her even to
think her thoughts to the end : when they besieged her
she found refuge in hard work. There was no sign that
she suffered at all, the good Lyddy ; the trouble of those
days before Christmas was lost in the anticipation of the
great change that was soon to come upon her sister's
life. To that she had resolved to look forward cheerfully, especially after something that befell between
her and Gilbert a day or two after the engagement.
She went down to the parlour in the evening and found
Gilbert alone. He rose and came to her with hand held
out.

' So you'll be my sister ? ' he said, in the voice which
could be so gentle.

It brought a sudden rush of tears to the girl's eyes.
She said, choking :

' I shall feel I'm giving you more than half my life,
Mr. Grail.'

' But you won't have any fear in giving it, Lydia ? '

' No—no, indeed I shan't. I know you'll be very
kind to her.'

He said that which made her smile and strengthened
her in confidence. And the better she came to know

Gilbert, the warmer grew her affection for him. They were made to be friends; in both were the same absolute honesty of character, the same silent depths of tenderness, the same stern self-respect. Brother and sister henceforth, with the bond of a common love which time, whether it brought joy or sorrow, could but knit closer.

From the first there was, of course, an understanding that the marriage should take place as soon as the house was ready for Gilbert's tenancy. Thyrza went secretly and examined the dwelling from the outside, more than once. That Lydia would come and live there went without saying. She pretended to oppose this plan at first; said she must be independent.

'Very well,' said Thyrza, crossing her hands on her lap, 'then I shan't be married at all, Lyddy, and Mr. Grail had better be told at once.'

There was laughing, and there were kind words.

'I don't think you ought still to call him Mr. Grail,' said Lydia.

'Gilbert? I shall have to say it to myself for a few days. Still, it's a nice name, isn't it?'

Yes, that point needed no discussion; where Thyrza abode, there abode Lydia, until—but sadness lay that way. Mrs. Grail was equally clear as to the arrangements concerning herself; she would keep two rooms and continue to live in Walnut Tree Walk. Thyrza thought this would be unkindness to the old lady, but Mrs. Grail had a store of wisdom and was resolute. In practice, she said, she would not at all feel the loneli-

ness ; she could often be at the house, and it had occurred
to her that her son in the Midlands would be glad to
send one of his two girls to live with her for, say, half
a year at a time. Gilbert understood the good sense of
this disposition.

The weather continued doleful, until at length, in
the last week of February, there came a sudden change.
A rioting east wind fell upon the murky vapours of the
lower sky, broke up the leaguer of rain and darkness,
and through one spring-heralding day drove silver fleece
over deeps of clear, cold blue. The streets were swept
of mire ; eaves ceased to distil their sooty rheum :
even in the back-ways of Lambeth there was a sunny
gleam on windows and a clear ring in all the sounds of
life.

It was Saturday. Between Egremont and Grail it
had been decided that the latter should to-day take
Thyrza to inspect the house. Egremont had gained the
surly compliance of the caretaker—the most liberal
treatment made no difference in the strange old woman's
moroseness—and Grail, promising himself pleasure from
Thyrza's surprise, said nothing more than that he wished
to see her at three in the afternoon.

The sisters did not come home together from their
work. Lydia had an engagement with Mrs. Isaacs, of
whom we have heard, and went to snatch a pretence of
a dinner in a little shop to which she resorted when
there was need. Thyrza, leaving the work-room at
half-past one, did not take the direct way to Walnut

Tree Walk; the sun and the keen air filled her with a spirit of glad life, and a thought that it would be nice to see how her future home looked under the bright sky came to her temptingly. The distance was not great; she soon came to Brook Street and, with some timidity, turned up the narrow passage, meaning to get a glimpse of the house and run away again. But just as she reached the entrance to the rear-yard, she found herself face to face with someone whom she at once knew for the caretaker whom Gilbert had described to her. The old woman's eye held her. She was half frightened, yet in a moment found words.

'Please,' she said —it seemed to her the only way of explaining her intrusion—'is there anyone in the school now?'

The old woman examined her, coldly, searchingly.

'No, there ain't,' she replied. 'Is it you as is a-goin' to live here?'

This was something like witchcraft to Thyrza.

'Yes, I am,' fell from her lips.

'All right. You can go in and look about. I ain't nothink to hide away.'

Thyrza was in astonishment, and a little afraid. Yet she dearly wished to see the interior of the house. The old woman turned, and she followed her.

'There ain't no need for me to go draggin' about with you,' said the caretaker, when they were within the door. 'I've plenty o' work o' my own to see to.'

'May I look into the rooms, then?'

' Didn't I say as you could ?   What need o' so many words ? '

Thyrza hesitated ; but, the old creature having begun to beat a door-mat, she resolved to go forward boldly.   She peeped into all the cheerless chambers, then returned to the door.

' Don't you want to see the school-rooms ? ' the old woman asked.   ' Go along that passage, and mind the step at the end.

Thyrza was bolder now.   The aspect of the house had not depressed her, for she knew that it was to be thoroughly repaired and furnished, and she was pre-disposed to like everything she saw.   It would be her home, hers and Lyddy's ; the dignity of occupying a whole house would have compensated for many little discomforts.   Thanking the old woman for her direction she went along the dark passage, and came into the large school-room.   And this was to be filled with books ! She looked at the maps and diagrams for a few moments : though it was so bright a day, the place still kept much of its chill and gloom.   Gilbert had told her of the rooms up above, and she thought she might as well complete her knowledge of the building by seeing them. At the first landing on the staircase she came to a window by which the sun streamed in brilliantly ; the rays gladdened her.   It was nice that the old woman had remained behind ; the sense of being quite alone, together with the sudden radiance, affected her with a desire to utter her happiness, and as she went on she sang in a sweet undertone, sang without words, pure music of her heart.

In one of the two rooms above, Egremont happened to be taking certain measurements. Impatient to get his plans completed in detail, he had resolved to come for half an hour on this same day which had been appointed for Grail's visit. Curious as he was to see the woman whom Grail was about to marry—as yet he knew nothing more of her than her casually learnt name—delicacy prevented him from using the opportunity this afternoon would give; the two were to arrive at three o'clock, and long before that time he would have finished his measuring and be gone. And now he was making his last notes, when the sound of as sweet a voice as he had ever heard made him pause and listen. The singer was approaching; her voice grew a little louder, though still in the undertone of one who sings but half consciously. He caught a light footstep, then the door was pushed open.

His hand fell. Even such a face as this would he have desired for her whose voice had such a charm. Her dress told him her position; the greater was his wonder at the features, which seemed to him of faultless delicacy—more than that, of beauty which appealed to him as never beauty had yet. Thyrza stood in alarm; the murmur had died instantly upon her lips, and for a moment she met his gaze with directness. Then her eyes fell; her cheeks recovered with interest the blood which they had lost. She turned to retreat.

But Egremont stepped rapidly forward, saying the first words that came to him.

'Pray don't let me be in your way! I'm this moment going—this moment.'

From her singing, he concluded that she was accustomed to be here. Thyrza again met his look. She guessed who this must be. The kindness of his face as he stood before her caused her to speak the words she was thinking:

'Are you Mr. Egremont, sir?'

Then she was shocked at her boldness; she did not see the smile with which he replied:

'Yes, that is my name.'

'I am Miss Trent. Perhaps you have—perhaps Mr. Grail has told you——'

This, Miss Trent? This, Gilbert Grail's wife? His astonishment scarcely allowed him to relieve her promptly.

'Oh then, we already know each other, by name at least. You have come to look at the building. Mr. Grail is downstairs?'

'No, sir. I came in alone. I thought I should like to see——'

'Of course. You have been over the house?'

He wondered rather at her coming alone, but supposed that Grail was withheld by some business.

'Yes, sir,' she answered.

'I'm afraid you think it doesn't look very promising. But I'm sure we can do a great deal to improve it.'

'I think it's very nice,' Thyrza said, not at all out of politeness, but because she did indeed think so.

'I will do my best to make it so, as soon as it is vacant. These two rooms,' he added, loth to take leave at once, 'we shall use for lectures. Have you been into the other one?'

He led the way, taking up his hat from the desk. Thyrza was overcoming her timidity. All she had ever heard of Egremont prepared her to find him full of gentleness and courtesy and good humour; already she thought that far too little had been said in his praise. His singular smile occupied her imagination; she wished to keep her eyes on his face, for the pleasure of following its changes. Indeed, like her own, his features were very mobile, and the various emotions now stirring within him animated his look. She kept at a little distance from him and listened with the keenest interest to all he said. When he paused, after telling her the number of books he had decided to begin with, she said:

'Mr. Grail does so look forward to it. I'm sure nothing could have made him so happy.'

Egremont was pleased with a note of sincerity, of self-forgetfulness in these words. He replied:

'I am very glad. I know he'll be at home among books. Are you fond of reading?'

'Yes, sir. Mr. Grail lends me books, and explains what I don't understand. I shall be glad when I know more.'

'No doubt you will find plenty of time.'

'Yes, sir. I shan't go to work then. But of course there'll be the house to look after.'

Egremont glanced towards the windows and murmured an assent. Thyrza moved a little nearer the door.

'I think I'll go, now I've seen everything.'

'I am going myself.'

She preceded him down the stairs. He watched her ungloved hand touch place after place on the railing, watched her slightly bent head with its long braid of gold and the knot of blue ribbon. At the turning to the lower flight, he caught a glimpse of her profile, and felt that he would not readily forget its perfectness. At the foot he asked:

'Do you wish to pass through the house? If not, this door is open.'

'I'll go this way, sir.'

She just raised her face.

'Good-bye, Miss Trent,' he said, offering his hand.

'Good-bye, sir.'

Then he opened the door for her. After standing for a few moments in the vestibule, he went to speak a word to the caretaker.

Thyrza walked home, looking neither to right nor to left. There was a little spot of colour on each cheek which would not melt away. Reaching the room upstairs, she sat down without taking off her things. She ought to have prepared her dinner, but did not think of it, and at length she was startled by hearing a clock strike three.

She ran down to the Grails' room. Gilbert and his mother had just finished their meal. The latter gossiped for a moment, then went out.

'I want you to go somewhere with me,' Gilbert said.

'Yes, I'm quite ready; but——'

'But——'

'I have something to tell you, Gilbert   I wonder whether you'll be cross.'

'When was I cross last, Thyrza?'

'No, but I'm not sure whether I ought to have done something. As I was coming home, I thought I'd walk past the house. When I got there, I thought I'd just go up the passage and look. And that old woman met me, and asked me if it was me that was going to live there. How *did* she know?'

Gilbert laughed.

'That's more than I can tell.'

'But that isn't all. She said I might go in and look about if I liked. And I thought I would—did I do wrong?'

She saw a shade of disappointment on his face. But he said:

'Not at all. Did you go over all the rooms?'

'Yes. But there's something else. I went into those school-rooms upstairs, never thinking there was

anyone there, because the old woman told me there
wasn't. But there *was*—and it was Mr. Egremont.'

' Really ? Did he know who you were ? '

' I told him, Gilbert.'

He laughed again, and there was a look of pride in
his eyes.

' Well, there's nothing very dreadful yet. And did
he speak nicely ? '

' Yes, very nicely. And when I went away, he shook
hands.'

' It's a very queer thing that you happened to go
just to-day. That's exactly where I meant to take you
this afternoon. I'm rather disappointed.'

' I'm very sorry. But couldn't I go with you again ?
We shall be alone this time : Mr. Egremont said he was
just going.'

' It won't tire you ? '

' Oh, but I should like to go ! I made up my mind
which'll be Lyddy's room. I wonder whether you'll
guess the same.'

' Come along, then ! '

CHAPTER XIV.

MISTS.

PAULA TYRRELL was married at Easter. Convenience dictated this speed—in other words, Paula resolved to commence the season as Mrs. Dalmaine and in a house of her own. Mr. Dalmaine had pointed out the advantage of using the Easter recess. As there was scarcely time to select and make ready an abode for permanence. it was decided to take a house in Kensington, which friends of the Tyrrells desired to let for the year.

Annabel was not present at the wedding. It was the second week in March before Mr. Newthorpe felt able to leave Ullswater, and Annabel had little mind to leave him for such a purpose immediately after their establishment at Eastbourne. Indeed, she would rather not have attended the wedding under any circumstances.

Her father had been gravely ill. There was organic disease, and there was what is vaguely called nervous breakdown ; it was too clear that Mr. Newthorpe must count upon very moderate activity either of mind or body henceforth. He himself was not quite unprepared for this collapse ; he accepted it with genial pessimism. Fate had said that his life was to result in nothing—nothing, that is, from the point of view of his early aspirations. Yet there was Annabel, and in her the memory of his life's passion. As he lay in silence through the days when spring combated with winter, he learned acquiescence ; after all he was among the happier of men, for he could look back upon a few days of great joy, and forward without ignoble anxiety.

He felt that the abandonment of Ullswater was final, yet would not say so to Annabel. Mrs. Ormonde had made ready a house at a short distance from her own, and here the two would live at all events into the summer ; beyond that, all must hinge on circumstances. They broke the journey for a couple of days in London, staying with their relatives. During those days Paula behaved very prettily. A certain affection had grown up between her and her uncle whilst she was at Ullswater, and the meeting under these dolefully changed conditions touched her best feelings. Yet with her cousin she was reserved ; her behaviour did not bear out the evidence of latent tenderness and admiration contained in that letter of hers which we saw. Annabel had looked for something more. Just now she was longing for affection and sympathy, and Paula was the only girl friend she had. But Paula would only speak of Mr. Dalmaine and, absurdest thing, of politics. Annabel retired into herself. She was glad to reach at length the quiet house by the sea, glad to be near Mrs. Ormonde.

The circumstances of Annabel's early life had worked happily with her inherited disposition. Her father, had he been free to choose, would have planned her training differently, but in all likelihood with less advantage than she derived from the compromise between her parents. Though at the time of her mother's death she still waited for formal recognition as a member of Society, being but sixteen, she was of riper growth than the majority of young ladies who in that season were being led forth for review and to perfect themselves in arts of civilisation. From her mother she had learnt, directly or indirectly, much of that little world which deems the greater world its satellite ; from her father she received love of knowledge and reverence for the nobler modes of life. She was marked by a happy balance of character; all that came to her from without she seemed naturally to assimilate in due proportions ; her tastes were those of an imaginative temper, tending to joyousness but susceptible of grave impressions. She relished books, yet never allowed them to hold her from bodily exercise ; she knew the happiness of solitude, yet could render welcomest companionship ; at one time she conversed earnestly with those older and wiser than herself, at another she was the willing playmate of laughing girls. She was loved by those who could by no possibility have loved one another, and in turn she seemed to discover with sure insight what there was of strength and beauty in the most diverse characters. With this breadth of sympathy she developed a self-consciousness of the kind to which most women never attain; habitually studying herself, and making comparison of herself with other, she cultivated her understanding and her emotions simultaneously.

Her time of serious study only began when she exchanged London for the mountain solitude. Henceforth her father's influence exerted itself freely, and Annabel had just reached the age for profiting most by it. Her bringing up between a brilliant drawing-room and a well-stocked library had preserved her from the two dangers to which English girls of the free-born class are mainly exposed : she escaped Puritanism, yet was equally withheld from frivolous worldliness. But it was well that this balance, admirably maintained thus far, should not be submitted to the risks of such a life as awaited her, if there had come no change of conditions. She would be a beautiful woman, and was not unaware of it ; her social instincts, which Society would straightway do its best to abuse, might outweigh her spiritual tendencies. But a year of life by Ullswater consolidated her womanhood. She bent herself to books with eagerness. The shock of sorrow compelled her to muse on problems which as yet she had either not realised, or had solved in the light of tradition, childwise. Her mind was ripe for those modern processes of thought which hitherto had only been implicit in her education.

To her father Annabel's companionship was invaluable. She repaid richly out of the abundance of her youthful life that anxious guidance which he gave to her thoughts. Her loving tact sweetened for him many an hour which would else have been spent in profitless brooding; when the signs of which she had become aware warned her that he needed to be drawn from himself, she was always ready with her bright converse, her priceless sympathy. Without her he would seldom have exerted himself to wander far from the house, but Annabel could at any time lead him over hill and valley by pretending that she had need of a holiday. Their communion was of a kind not frequently existing between father and daughter; fellowship in study made them mental comrades, and respect for each other's intellectual powers was added to their natural love. What did they not discuss? From classical archæology to the fire-new theories of the day in a and science, something of all passed at one time or another under their scrutiny.

Yet there was the limit imposed by fine feeling. Mr. Newthorpe never tried to pass the sacred bound which parts a father's province from that of a mother. There was much in the girl's heart that he would gladly have read, yet could not until she should of herself reveal it to him. For instance, they did not very often speak of Egremont. When a letter arrived from him,

Mr. Newthorpe always gave it to Annabel to read; at
other times that was a subject on which he spoke only
when she introduced it. After Walter's departure
there had been one conversation between them in which
Annabel told what had come to pass; she went so
far as to speak of a certain trouble she had on Paula's
account.

'I think you must use your philosophy with regard
to Paula,' her father replied. 'Of course I know nothing of the circumstances, but,' he smiled not unkindly,
'the child I think I know pretty well. Don't be
troubled. I have confidence in Egremont.'

'I have the same feeling in truth, father,' Annabel
said, 'and—I feel nothing more than that.'

'Then let it rest, dear. I certainly have no desire
to lose you.'

So much between them. Thereafter, both spoke
of Egremont, when at all, in an unconstrained way.
Annabel showed frank interest in all that concerned
him, but as far as Mr. Newthorpe could discern, nothing more than the interest of friendliness. As the
months went on, he discerned no change. Her life
was as cheerful and as steadily industrious as ever;
nothing betrayed unsettlement of the thought. If her
father by chance entered the room where she studied,
he found her bent over books, her face beautiful in
calm zeal.

The first grave symptoms of illness in her father
opened a new chapter of Annabel's life. It was time

to lay aside books for a little; the fated scheme of her existence required at this point new experiences. The student's habit does not readily reconcile itself to demands for practical energy and endurance, and it is no shame to tell of Annabel that when the first strain of fear-stricken love was relaxed, she fell for a few days into grievous weakness of despondency. It is pleasant to imagine woman as the ever-ready, all-enduring angel of household help; if the truth must be told, that quality is for the most part assured at the expense of intellectual development. Annabel's exercise in the virtues deemed by pre-eminence womanly was of the slightest; summoned from her study to all the miseries of a sick-room, it was mere nervous force that failed her. At the end of a week she was herself all but needing care. She would not fail utterly; there was too much of nobleness in her character. When her father had his relapse, she was able to face the demand upon her more sternly. But the trial through which she was passing was a severe one. With the invalid she could keep a bright face, and make her presence, as ever, a blessing to him. Alone, she cared no longer for her books, nor for the beauty that was about her home. You remember that passage in her letter to Egremont: 'The world seems to me very dark, and life a dreadful penalty.' She could have uttered much on that text to one from whom she had had no secret.

It was the time of Annabel's revolt.

One day, when Mr. Newthorpe was again recovering

strength, there came a letter from Mrs. Tyrrell which
announced the date of Paula's marriage. Annabel
received the letter to read. As she was sitting with her
father a little later, he said, with a return of his humorous mood :

'I wonder on what footing Egremont will be in the
new household?'

'I suppose,' Annabel replied, 'his acquaintance
with Mr. Dalmaine will continue to be of the slightest.'

He paused a little, then, quietly :

'I am glad of this marriage.'

Annabel said nothing.

'It proves,' he continued, 'that we did well in not
thinking too gravely of a certain incident.'

Annabel led the conversation away. She had
singular thoughts on this subject. Paula's letter, first
announcing the engagement, made mention of Egremont in a curious way; and it was at least a strange
hap that Paula should be about to marry the man
against whom Egremont had expressed such an antipathy.

Her father said no more, but Annabel had a new
care for her dark mood to feed upon. She felt that
the words 'I am glad of this marriage' concerned herself. They meant that her father was glad of the
removal of what was perchance one barrier between
Egremont and herself. And in these long weeks in
which she was anguished by the spectacle of suffering,
it had become her first desire to be of comfort to the
sufferer. Her ideal of a placid life was shattered ; the

things which availed her formerly now seemed weak to rely upon. In so dark a world, what guidance was there save by the hand of love ?

Her childhood was behind her. When she thought of marriage, it was not as an untrained girl thinks. Asceticism and the world's ignoble motives were equally far from her; from books and from nature she had learnt to deal honestly with her heart. Mr. Newthorpe could see no good in the moral prejudice which desires that a young woman should go forth into the world with a bandage about her eyes and ears, and will make believe that she does so, even though the contrary should be flagrantly evident. The education he had favoured was not that of the convent. Annabel stood on an intellectual equality with the man who sought to win her, and there was so much the less danger that her life would fall into frustration. When Egremont bade farewell to Ullswater that rainy day of summer, she had asked herself: Should I have felt that all the joy of my being was gone from me, if he had left without speaking those words ? And for answer she could only shake her head and smile. Replying to him, she had spoken what she believed to be the very truth.

Those letters of his to her father she read with deep attention. It was a very lovable nature that they unconsciously revealed; she recognised that, and her kindness for the writer grew, her respect for him grew; but she did not love him.

She was in full intellectual sympathy with him, and

the thought of becoming his wife had no painful associations; but could she bring herself to abandon that
ideal of love which had developed with her own development? Must she relinquish the hope of a great passion,
and take the hand of a man whom she merely liked
and respected. It was a question she must decide, for
Egremont, when they again met, might again seek to
win her. The idealism which she derived from her
father would not allow her yet to regard life as a compromise, which women are so skilled in doing practically, though the better part in them to the end revolts.
Yet who was she, that life should bestow its highest
blessing upon her? What arrogance was this, that
made conscience of the desire for happiness? And
then—how could she tell?—was she capable of con-
ceiving that passionate love which had exalted others
to the heaven of heavens? It might well be that
intellect was too predominant in her.

When at the Tyrrells' house in London, she feared
lest Egremont should come. Mrs. Tyrrell spoke much
of him the first evening, lamenting that he had so withdrawn himself from his friends. But he did not come.

At Eastbourne, Mr. Newthorpe's health began to
improve. Even in a week the change was very marked.
He seemed to have taken a resolve to restore the old
order of things by force of will. Doubtless his conversations with Mrs. Ormonde about Annabel were an
incentive to effort; relieved from the weight of suffering, he could see that the girl was not herself. On

Paula's marriage day, he said, in the course of conversation with Annabel :

'Your aunt desires very much to have you with her for a part of the season. What do you think of it? Would you care to go up in May?'

Annabel did not at once reject the idea.

'It is my opinion that you need some such change,' her father continued. 'The last quarter of a year has done you harm. In a month I hope to be sound enough.'

'I will think of it,' she said. And there the subject rested.

The town was secretly attracting her. The odour of the Tyrrells' house had exercised a certain seduction. Though she saw but one or two old acquaintances there, the dining-room, the drawing-room, brought the past vividly back to her. She was not so wholly alien to her mother's blood that the stage-life of the world was without appeal to her, and circumstances were favourable to a revival of that element in her character which I touched upon when speaking of her growth out of childhood. It is a common piece of observation that studious gravity in youth is succeeded by a desire for action and enjoyment. Annabel's disposition to study did not return, though quietness was once more restored to her surroundings. And thus, though the settlement at Eastbourne seemed a relief, she soon found that it did not effect all she hoped. Her father began to take up his books again, though in a desultory, half-hearted way. Annabel could not do even that. A portion of each day she spent with Mrs. Ormonde; often she walked by herself on the shore; a book was seldom in her hand.

Two or three days before the end of March, Mr. Newthorpe spoke of Egremont.

'I should like to see him. May I ask him to come and spend a day with us, Annabel?'

'Do by all means, father,' she answered. 'Mrs. Ormonde heard from him yesterday. He came into possession of his library-building the other day.'

'I will write, then.'

This was Monday; on Wednesday morning Egremont came. The nine months or so which had passed since these three met had made an appreciable change in all of them. When Egremont entered the room where father and daughter were expecting him, he was first of all shocked at the wasting and ageing of Mr. Newthorpe's face, then surprised at the difference he found in Annabel—this too of a kind that troubled him. He thought her less beautiful than she had been. With no picture of her to aid him, he had for long periods been unable to make her face really present to his mind's eye—one of the sources of his painful debates with himself. When it came, as faces do, at unanticipated moments, he saw her as she looked in walking back with him from the lake-side, when she declared that the taste of the rain was sweet. Is it not the best of life, that involuntary flash of memory upon instants of the eager past? better than present joy, in which there is ever a core of disappointment; better, far better, than hope, which cannot warm without burning. Annabel was surpassingly beautiful as he knew her in that brief vision. Beautiful she still was, but it was as if a new type of loveliness had come between her and his admiration; he could regard her without emotion. The journey from London had been one incessant anticipation, tormented with doubt. Would her presence conquer him royally, assure her dominion, convert his intellectual fealty to passionate desire? He regarded her without emotion.

Yet Annabel was not so calm as she wished to be. Only by force of will could she transact the greetings without evidence of more than friendly pleasure. This irritated her, for up to an hour ago she had said that his coming would in no way disturb her. When, after an hour's talk, she left her father and the guest together, and went up to her room, the first feeling she acknowledged to herself was one of disappointment. Egremont had changed, and not, she thought, for the better. He had lost something—perchance that freshness of purpose which had become him so well. He seemed to talk of his undertakings less spontaneously, and in a tone—she could not quite say what it was, but his tone perhaps suggested the least little lack of sincerity. And her agitation when he entered the room? It had meant nothing, nothing. Her nerves were weak, that was all.

She wished she could shed tears. There was no cause for it, surely none, save a physical need Such a feeling was very strange to her.

They had luncheon; then, as his custom was, Mr. Newthorpe went apart to rest for a couple of hours. Mrs. Ormonde was coming to dine; the hour of the meal would be early, to allow of Egremont's return to town. In the meantime the latter obtained Annabel's consent to a walk. They took the road ascending to Beachy Head.

'You still have opportunity of climbing,' Egremont said.

'On a modest scale. But I am not regretting the mountains. The sea, I think, is more to me at present.'

They were not quite at ease together. Conversation turned about small things, and was frequently broken. The day was not very bright, and mist spoiled the view landwards. The sea was at ebb, and sluggish

Annabel of her own accord reverted to Lambeth.

'You must have had many pleasures arising from your work,' she said, ' but one above all I envy you. I mean that of helping poor Mr. Grail so well.'

'Yes, that is a real happiness,' he answered, thoughtfully. 'The idea of making him librarian came to me almost at the same moment as that of establishing the library. I didn't know then all that it would mean to him. I was fortunate in meeting that man, one out of thousands.'

'He must be deeply grateful to you.'

'We are good friends. I respect him more than I can tell you. I don't think you could find a man, in whatever position, of more sterling character. His love of knowledge touches me as something ideal. It is monstrous to think that he might have spent all his life in that candle factory.'

Annabel reflected for a moment. Then a look of pleasure lighted her face, and she spoke with a revival of the animation which had used to appeal so strongly to his sympathies.

'See what one can do! You become a sort of providence to a man. Indeed, you change his fate; you give him a new commencement of life. What a strange thought that is? Do you feel it as I do?'

'Quite, I think. And can you understand that it has sometimes shamed me? Just because I happen to have money I can do this! Isn't it a poor sordid world? Not one man, but perhaps a hundred, could be raised into a new existence by what in my hands is mere superfluity of means. Doesn't such a thought make life a great foolish game? Suppose me saying, "Here is a thousand pounds; shall I buy a yacht to play with, or—shall I lift a living man's soul out of darkness into light?"'

He broke off and laughed bitterly. Annabel glanced at him. She noticed that thoughts of this cast were now frequent in his mind, though formerly they had been strange to him. He used to face problems with simple directness, in the positive spirit or with an idealist's enthusiasm; now he leaned to scepticism, though it was his endeavour to conceal the tendency. She was struck with the likeness of this change in him to that which she herself was suffering; yet it did not touch her sympathies, and she was anxious forthwith to avoid coincidence with him.

'You yourself offer the answer to that,' she replied. 'The very fact that you have exerted such power, never mind by what means, puts you in a relation to that man which is anything but idle or foolish. Isn't it rather a great and moving thing that one can be a source of such vast blessing to another? Money is only the accident. It is the kindness, the human feeling, that has to be considered. You show what the world might be, if all men were human. If I could do one act like that, Mr. Egremont, I should cry with gratitude!'

He looked at her, and found the Annabel of his memory. With the exception of Mrs. Ormonde, he knew no woman who spoke thus from heart and intellect at once. The fervour of his admiration was rekindled.

'It is to you one should come for strength,' he said, 'when the world weighs too heavily.'

Annabel was sober again.

'Do you often go and see him at his house?' she asked, speaking of Grail.

'I am going on Friday night. I have not been since that one occasion which I mentioned in a letter to Mr. Newthorpe. I had to write to him yesterday about the repair of the house he is going to live in, and in his reply this morning he asked me to come for an hour's talk.'

'You were curious, father told me, about the wife he had chosen. Have you seen her yet?'

'Yes. She is quite a young girl.'

He was looking at a far-off sail, and as he replied his eyes kept the same direction. Annabel asked no further question. Egremont laughed before he spoke again.

'How absurdly one conjectures about unknown people! I suppose it was natural to think of Grail marrying someone not quite young and very grave.'

'But I hope she is grave enough to be his fitting companion?'

He opened his lips, but altered the words he was about to speak.

'I only saw her for a few minutes—a chance meeting. She impressed me favourably.'

They walked in a leisurely way for about half an hour, then turned. Mists were creeping westward over Pevensey, and the afternoon air was growing chill. There was no sound from the sea, which was divided lengthwise into two tracts of different hue, that near the land a pale green, that which spread to the horizon a cold grey.

Nothing passed between them which could recall their last day together, nothing beyond that one exclamation of Egremont's, which Annabel hardly appeared to notice. Neither desired to prolong the conversation. Yet neither had ever more desired heart-sympathy than now.

Annabel said to herself: 'It is over.' She was spared anxious self-searching. The currents of their lives were slowly but surely carrying them apart from each other. When she came into the drawing-room to offer tea, her face was brighter, as if she had experienced some relief.

Mrs. Ormonde had not seen Egremont for some six weeks. The tone of the one or two letters she had received from him did not reassure her against misgivings excited at his latest visit. To her he wrote far more truly than to Mr. Newthorpe, and she knew, what the others did not, that he was anything but satisfied with the course he had taken since Christmas in his lecturing. 'After Easter,' was her advice, 'return to your plain instruction. It is more fruitful of profit both to your hearers and to yourself.' But Egremont had begun to doubt whether after Easter he should lecture at all.

'Mr. Bunce's little girl is coming to me again,' she said, in the talk before dinner. 'You know the poor little thing has been in hospital for three weeks?'

'I haven't heard of it,' Egremont replied. 'I'm sorry that I haven't really come to know Bunce. I had a short talk with him a month ago, and he told me then that his children were well. But he is so reticent that I have feared to try further to get his confidence.'

'Why, Bunce is the aggressive atheist, isn't he?' said Mr. Newthorpe.

Mrs. Ormonde smiled and nodded.

'I fear he is a man of misfortunes,' she said. 'My friend at the hospital tells me that his wife was small comfort to him whilst she lived. She left him three young children to look after, and the eldest of them—she is about nine—is always ill. There seems to be no one to tend them whilst their father is at work.'

'Who will bring the child here?' Egremont asked.

'She came by herself last time. But I hear she is still very weak; perhaps someone will have to be sent from the hospital.'

During dinner, the library was discussed. Egremont reported that workmen were already busy in the school-rooms and in Grail's house.

'I'm in correspondence,' he said, 'with a man I knew some years ago, a scientific fellow, who has heard some-how of my undertakings, and wrote asking if he might help by means of natural science. Perhaps it might be well to begin a course of that kind in one of the rooms. It would appeal far more to the Lambeth men than what I am able to offer.'

This project passed under review, then Egremont himself led the talk to widely different things, and thereafter resisted any tendency it showed to return upon his special affairs. Annabel was rather silent.

An hour after dinner, Egremont had to depart to catch his train. He took leave of his friends very quietly.

'We shall come and see the library as soon as it is open,' said Mr. Newthorpe.

Egremont smiled merely.

Mr. Newthorpe remarked that Egremont seemed disappointed with the results of his work.

'I should uncommonly like to hear one of these new lectures,' he said. 'I expect there's plenty of sound matter in them. My fear is lest they are over the heads of his audience.'

'I fear,' said Mrs. Ormonde, 'it is waste both of his time and that of the men. But the library will cheer him; there is something solid, at all events.'

'Yes, that can scarcely fail of results.'

'I think most of Mr. Grail,' put in Annabel.

'A true woman,' said Mrs. Ormonde, with a smile. 'Certainly, let the individual come before the crowd.'

And all agreed that in Gilbert Grail was the best result hitherto of Egremont's work.

END OF THE FIRST VOLUME

PRINTED BY
SPOTTISWOODE AND CO., NEW-STREET SQUARE
LONDON